T ▬ D'ANGELO

VT

VARSITY
Tiebreaker

GINGER SCOTT

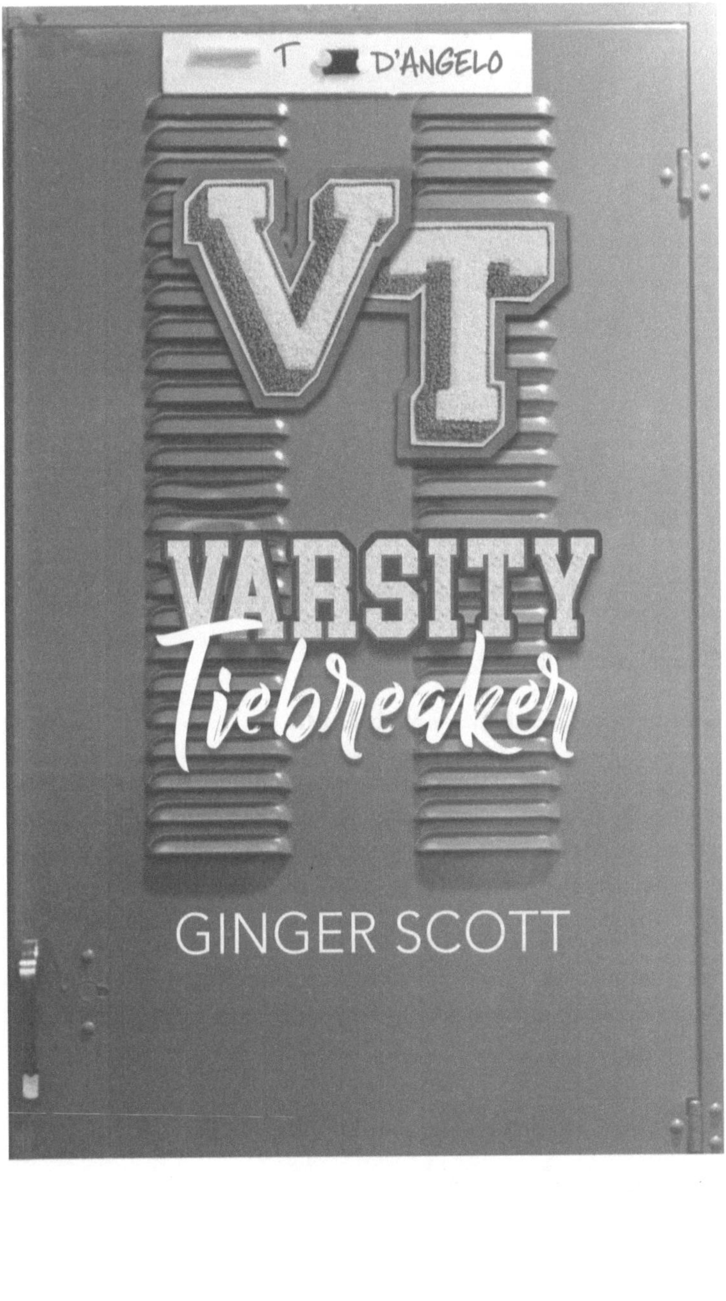

For Tory's biggest fans.
Y'all are gonna have to fight Ana for him.

TORY D'ANGELO

I've never really gotten the appeal of flowers. I mean, one, they're super fleeting. Every time my mom's gotten flowers, I swear they're dead within three days. Feels like a major waste of money. Of course, my mom's flowers probably came from the man she was having an affair with, so it's entirely possible my perspective is tainted. Even so, what do flowers say about a person's feelings for someone else?

I like you enough to pop into the grocery store and pick up this pre-arranged bundle of plant clippings wrapped in plastic.

I mean, yeah. Flowers are pretty and shit, but there are a lot of things that are pretty. Cakes are pretty, and you can eat those. A perfect three-pointer drained within seconds, nothing but net . . . that's a thing of beauty. Art, a really hot red dress, or hell, a puppy! All of that is as aesthetically pleasing as a bundle of flowers. Yet here I am, clipping the stems off some weedy-smelling plant shit over my kitchen trash while my best friend June tells me what a good idea this is.

"She's going to love them," June assures me while she reaches toward my bundle, tugging on the stem of something. She pulls it free and dumps it into the trash with the stems I chopped off at an angle because "angles take in the water better" or whatever.

"She won't love that one?" I cock a brow and laugh. I'm still not sold on any of this.

"That one's dead."

I form an O with my mouth and drop my chin to stare at the drooping flower where it lies in the trash.

"Huh." I nod.

June giggles then wraps her hands around the bouquet, holding it steady so I can slip the giant band around the stems again. I never thought my best friend would be a girl, let alone June Mabee. I've pretty much picked on her since she got boobs, probably before that if I'm being honest. I still call her Maybe Mabee. June and I collided in epic fashion a couple of months ago. We kicked off our senior year on a strange note, going through some really awful shit together. We're kinda honeymooning at the whole best friend thing, I guess, but she's not sick of me yet and turns out Maybe Mabee doles out some pretty solid advice. Though, I'm not totally sold on the whole flowers thing.

"You sure this isn't stupid? I feel really stupid." I'm sweating, and I've already showered from basketball practice, changed my shirt twice and put on a whole lot of deodorant. This is strange territory for me. To put it succinctly, I have a fucking crush. It's bizarre because hooking up with any girl at Public High—or in our whole town of Allensville, really—has never been an issue for me. June says it's because I'm used to being chased, and maybe that's true. But I also think it's because the girl I'm trying to impress has never, not once, shown an ounce of interest in my presence. In fact, if I had to make a guess, I would bet on her hating me.

"Abby is going to die . . . in a good way!" June's said that a lot, that little add-on of *in a good way*. Feels like a hedged bet to me.

Abby Cortez is June's *other* best friend.

Fine.

She's her *real* best friend, and I'm the new guy June hangs out with sometimes while she waits on her boyfriend, Lucas. *My* real best friend. Along with my twin brother, Hayden, we've become our own clique. Except for the little part about me being pretty sure Abby hates me. Oh, and me wanting to kiss her candy lips and wrap her legs around my waist just before I lay her back on the hood of my car.

This is complicated. But flowers is the key. June swears by it.

"You look amazing," June says, stepping into me and brushing something from the shoulder of my shirt. I went with a button down, mostly because this shirt is snug on my arms and chest, making me look a little bit beast-mode. I don't need June to tell me how much Abby likes man candy. She was digging on the new guy, Cannon, for a while, and she noted his arms and chest a few times. Apparently, though, he's moody as fuck. Thank God!

"Where's your brother?" June asks.

"Job interview," I answer, bending down to catch my

reflection in the glass front of the oven. I actually have product in my hair. *Who am I?*

"Wow. D'Angelo boys are going to work?" June mocks.

I shrug as I stand and face her.

"It's hard to be around here, and Hayden's had a harder time than I have. I think he wants something to fill the free time." June's eyes soften, but she's careful not to let them dip into pity. We don't do that around here.

My dad moved out a month ago. It's still pretty fresh for all of us. My mom was having an affair with Lucas's dad, and when it all came out, it basically blew up both of our families.

"Have you guys talked to your dad lately?" June asks. Our pops said we could go to Indianapolis with him if we wanted to, but this is our senior year. We're primed to win state this basketball season, and we both decided we couldn't give up on that. Staying here means sticking out the next few months in a house with a parent we pretty much have lost all respect for.

"Our first family therapy session is next week, with *both* of them. It promises fireworks," I say. June grimaces in response.

"You sure it's not weird, me forcing some double-date with you and Luc?" I squint through my question, and a small part of me wants her to let me off the hook. I've never been afraid of rejection, but with Abby, I put it at a solid fifty-fifty that she kicks me in the nuts when I ask her out.

"Stop," June protests, laughing at my nervous behavior. "It's sweet. And it will make you both more comfortable. Plus, it's Eight Lanes. Bowling is the easiest first date ever."

"Says the Eight Lanes employee who bowls a two-hunny," I say, one brow arched.

June's laughter ticks up but stops when we're interrupted by the familiar rumble of Lucas's truck in the driveway. I start to jump in place because he is supposed to bring Abby to the house with him and suddenly I'm full of enough energy to power a lightning bolt.

"It's go time," I say under my breath. June squeezes my arm and offers me a reassuring smile.

Lucas busts through the door first, and I puff out my cheeks to indicate how stressed I am. But something about the look in his eyes freezes me to the floor. My jumping stops, and my heart does too.

"Abort. Mission," Lucas says, pointing at me then staring intently into his girlfriend's eyes.

"What the—" My protest is cut short when Abby follows Lucas through the door in a rush, her hand gripped firmly in my brother's. My eyes see nothing else. I'm blatantly staring at the place where my crush and my twin are fused together.

What the actual fuck?

"I got the job, yo!" my brother says. At least, it sounds like his voice. I couldn't testify he said the words because I'm not looking at his mouth. I'm looking at the way Abby is holding his elbow with her other hand, bouncing with excitement. That's two hands she has on him now. Two. Hands.

"Did you hear me, bro? I got the job!"

I shake my head—*literally* shake my head—and force my gaze to meet Hayden's. We are nearly physically identical, but our personalities are vastly different. Where I'm loud, he's quiet. My confidence is offset by his reservation. I believe I can make any girl fall in love with me. And Hayden . . . he's never had a girlfriend. Ever.

Until—

"You're looking at the new host at Two-fers," my brother says, holding up his new work shirt. It's bright red with two weenies embroidered on the pocket. It's ridiculous, and my natural instinct is to make fun of it, but I can't seem to find a single funny thing to say.

"Wow," I say, over-exaggerating this terribly small word.

"Right?" He pushes at my shoulder, pressing the shirt into me to take. I unfold it and stare at it while I fake laugh. I toss it on the counter and hold my hand up for him to slap, and we grip each other and pull in for a hug. My eyes catch June's over my brother's shoulder, and they are full of pity. *Motherfucking pity!*

"I hope it's cool that I invited Hayden to come with us?" Abby asks from somewhere behind me. I can't bear the thought of turning around and looking at her.

"Of course. Yeah, totally," I croak out. I cough to cover my weak-ass voice.

"I just gotta change, and we can go. What's with the flowers, dude?" my brother asks, pointing to my fisted palm that's nearly choking the bouquet to death with my grip.

"Oh," I say, lifting them and feeling suddenly numb. "I—"

"He lost a bet," June says, coming to my rescue.

Hayden nods, accepting her answer, then dashes up the stairs, leaving the rest of us here in this instantly shrinking space.

"That a new thing there?" June says to her friend in a half-whisper I wish I didn't hear.

"We've been talking a lot, with everything they're going through, and I don't know, it just sorta . . ." Abby's head waggles side-to-side, but it's the blush that colors her cheeks that has me defeated.

Just sorta.

The sudden need to rush from the room hits me, and I march across the kitchen toward June. "Here you go, a bet's a bet," I say, shoving the flowers I knew were a bad idea into her chest. She hugs them and lets out an "*oof.*"

I keep walking, making eyes at Lucas on my way out, knowing he'll follow me to his truck so I can scream obscenities and feel like a fool with only him as my witness.

"Wow, someone's a sore loser," Abby teases from over my shoulder.

I huff out a laugh, not even able to lob one of my normal comebacks because she's so dead-on. I *am* a sore loser. I'm also done catching feelings for some girl.

2

ABBY CORTEZ

It's not that June was quiet on the way to the bowling alley. It's that she's *still* quiet now that we're inside. Things between my best friend and Lucas mended quickly, and very dramatically. I mean, yeah, they've been meant for each other since grade school, but a whirlwind romance like they had, right on the tail of the unraveling of so many lies—I just hope their honeymoon period hasn't hit a brick wall so soon.

I've been searching for the right time to tell her my big news, but ever since we left the twins' house, June's been oddly busy. Quiet, yes, but also busy. Like now, for instance. While the rest of us are sitting on the table at lane eight waiting for June to bring us our bowling shoes, she's standing at the counter shining them. They're ugly bowling shoes! Why would we care if they glisten under the neon glow of this dump?

I'm dying to talk to my friend. I almost wish we hadn't

planned this bowling thing. I'd *so* rather be curled up across from her on her bed, jammies and all, while I spill my guts of the things I'm anxious about. This is my moment. It's the one thing an actor hopes for, the big payoff after thousands of auditions. This deal means I might not be back for graduation, and prom is probably, definitely a no-go, but it's a *movie*. Totally worth it . . . *I think.*

It also probably means my dad's legal pursuits will get even nastier, if that's possible, but *damn it!* I've been wishing for this break since I was six years old and singing my ass off on the community center stage as Indiana's first Latina Annie. I got a perm for that shit, so if all this movie role requires is that I miss the last three months of my senior year, well, fuck it, man. Prom dresses are ugly anyway.

"Are we gonna bowl or open up a shoe store?" Tory shouts across the lanes toward June, who is still running a rag over the tops of the shoes on the counter. I knew I could count on Tory's impatience to break the ice. As sweet as his brother is, he's not a boat rocker. Tory D'Angelo, however, is the Ozzy Osborn of boats. He rocks things to the point of fire.

"I know how important your footwear is to you!" June shouts back to him. I laugh, but Tory only grumbles and sinks into the chair attached to the scoring computer.

"He's just mad because I'm a better bowler than he is," Hayden says, his voice crawling over my shoulder as he bends over the seat behind me. He lightly kisses my neck, then squeezes my shoulders. I exhale heavily, feeling my tension fall away with the pressure of his hands.

Never in a million years would I imagine a world where I am dating Hayden D'Angelo. The only thing less likely is a universe where me and Tory are a thing. But Hayden is just . . . so easy. He called me out of the blue weeks ago, and we've talked every night. He needs someone who understands what a messy divorce feels like; someone who isn't his brother, and isn't his friend who's going through the same thing with his own family. I'm that person. *Kid of a messy divorce* should be a bullet point on my resume. Nothing new to Hollywood, I suppose.

"Nines, right?" June holds a pair of shoes out for me, letting them dangle from the tethered laces hooked on her finger.

"Yep," I say, followed by a tight smile. She hits me with a matching expression. Something is definitely off. Besides, she knows I wear nines. She wears nines. I wear her shoes all the time!

Hayden's body falls into the seat attached to mine, his large frame making me instantly feel crowded. I slip my foot into my shoe and glance to the left at his, noting the size before he puts his foot inside.

Twelves.

I finish tying my laces, then slide my other shoes underneath my seat. Tory has typed in our names, and he put me at the end. I'm glad about that because me and sports of any kind are not on the same page. I'm not even sure how this ball comes off my fingers when the time is right. June has worked here for more than a year, and in that time, all I've ever done is drink sodas and roll pool balls back and forth in the bar area while waiting for her to get off.

Hayden leaves the space next to me and I glance up at him in time to catch his wink and smile. He's adorable, the way his hair squiggles down over his forehead and one eye is always squinting just a little more than the other. I've often heard that twins try to differentiate themselves from each other as they get older, sort of a way to stand out and break away from their carbon copy. I see the evidence of that when I stare at the D'Angelo boys. Hayden is a little sloppy sometimes, but in a cute way. He wears a lot of T-shirts, always half tucked under slightly wrinkled button downs, and his jeans are sometimes, maybe, just a little tiny bit too short. Again . . . in a cute way. He wears the beach boy look, if that's a thing in Indiana. As good as he is at basketball, I wouldn't flinch seeing him run by with a long board under his arm and board shorts slung low on his hips. I'm probably the only one who thinks that since basketball is religion in this state. The brothers share the same hazel eye color, the same light brown hair that's sometimes amber, sometimes gold, depending on the season, and the same body type that *oh-my-God!* The twins have always been hot. And they are identical. But through their own efforts, they're also very much not. Tory is polished. His hair is somehow always in the perfect place, even after a two-hour basketball practice or after pulling off a football helmet. His wardrobe looks like the ones I see on the commercial shoots I do. Things match, like the kind of match you see on department store mannequins or in catalogues. And he must time his shaving just right because where Hayden is always baby-face fresh, Tory is frat-boy stubble.

He's also frat-boy brash. In all the years we've known each other, Tory D'Angelo is the one person I can count on to always have something snarky to say, his own little flair for turning me off. Lately, though, he's been tempered. Not quiet, but just not . . . *Tory.* I've spent a lot of time talking with Hayden about his parents' fallout, and there's no way Tory isn't feeling it too. In his own way.

"Look at you, throwing an eleven-pounder, Mabee," Tory teases as June walks up with a bright green ball cupped in her hands. She curls one arm to form a bicep and Tory laughs.

"Can I use yours?" I ask her, standing and walking over to the ball return where she's just sat the green ball down. June twists her mouth up on one side and Tory snickers before turning his body away from me in his seat. I stare at the top of his head, doing my best to burn laser beam holes through his skull.

"What's so funny?" I object, shifting my stare from his head to June's face.

"It's just, eleven is kinda heavy," my friend says, tapping her finger on the 11 etched into the ball.

"It's fucking eleven pounds. That's like a cat!" I reach for the ball as she laughs at my comparison.

"You're not throwing a cat down the lane, Abby."

I glare at her while I poke my fingers awkwardly in the holes. They're enormous, and too far apart.

"I know I'm not throwing a fucking cat at pins, June. That would be cruel."

Her eyes widen as she glares at my hand along the smooth surface. Her mouth pops open, but before she can talk me out of it, I drop the ball on the return with a *clunk* and brush my hands off on one another, determined to throw the eleven-pounder.

"I'm using yours. Thanks," I say, taking the seat next to Tory. He gets up the second I sit.

"Are you seriously that appalled by my ball selection?" I shoot my question at him, but he keeps walking toward the balls to pick his own.

This vibe is strange, as if I've walked in mid-fight, or to an intervention that's not quite fully started. *What the f—?*

June slips into the seat Tory just vacated and types on the keyboard, changing Lucas's name to Princess. I smirk and puff out a laugh.

"Funny, right?" she says, pushing enter just before the boys come back with their balls.

Tory goes first, stepping up on the smooth wooden floor and positioning his feet with this super serious stance. He holds the ball in front of his body, lining it up, then takes three quick steps toward the pins, launching the ball down the lane dead center. Pins explode at the other end, leaving one standing on either side.

"Nice!" I say as he walks back toward us.

"It's a seven-ten split. Nothing nice about that," he huffs.

I shrug and glance to June, not knowing what the hell is so wrong with what I just said.

"It's really hard to knock both of those down now at once," June explains in a whisper.

I look back up to Tory as he stands with his hand hovering over the stream of air blowing from a vent on the ball return.

"Don't choke," I say just before his ball appears on the rack. He only offers me a sideways glance.

"I love when you two give each other shit," Hayden says, stepping up behind me and running his palms along my shoulders, then squeezing gently.

"Yeah, don't choke, bro!" Hayden tacks on. Tory's feet stop short of the arrows on the floor and his hand holding the ball lowers to his hip as he turns and looks at his brother, his head leaning to the side. Hayden bends down and rests his chin on my head, wrapping his arms around my neck and shoulders completely. Tory's body quakes with a short laugh.

"Fifty bucks says I nail it," Tory says. Even though he's talking to his brother, his eyes are on me, almost as if he wants me to take the bet. Hayden's arms relax and unwind from around me as he stands tall and pulls out his wallet.

"I've got twenty," he says to his brother.

Tory's mouth ticks up on one side. "So, you'll owe me thirty."

The pregnant pause as they dare each other is filled with the pumping beat of the pop music on the Eight Lanes' sound system.

"Deal," Hayden says.

Tory nods in agreement, and their little rivalry is sealed.

"He's going to blow it." Hayden's voice carries over my shoulder.

I lean in, resting my elbows and palms on the small counter in front of me, suddenly not sure whether I'm rooting for Tory to succeed or fail. He rolls his shoulders and positions the ball in front of him, just as he did before, only his body is lined up on the far right side of the lane. My gut knots as he begins his approach, and all I can envision is his ball roaring angrily down the right gutter.

I hold my breath with his release, a mixture of hexes and hopes coming from everyone else.

"Do it, Dude! Do it!" Lucas shouts as Tory's ball teeters along the very edge of the lane, practically skating without spin as it heads toward the single pin on the right.

"No way it kicks around. Not enough juice, bro. Not enough—" Hayden's curse is cut off by the flinging pin that strikes into and takes out its twin on the far side of the lane.

"Yes!" June and I both say together. I guess I was rooting for Tory to make it. I feel as though maybe he needs a win.

Tory saunters back to us and his brother steps out from behind me with his hand outstretched to congratulate his brother. After they shake, Tory comes in close and pats Hayden's chest with a heavy palm.

"Better hope you get tips at Two-fers," he says, his eyebrows lifting just before his gaze sinks down to where I'm sitting. "Unless you wanna make another deal? Double or nothing?"

The smile on my face flattens under the heat of his eyes. I don't get the sense he's bargaining with dollars anymore, and the insinuation pisses me off.

"I'm not on the table," I interject, turning to the side and crossing my legs. My bare knee pops through the ragged hole in my jeans and my green sweater falls down on one shoulder as I cross my arms over my chest.

A slow laugh brews in Tory's chest, soundless at first until it comes out loud as he holds his stomach.

"I don't know what your obsession is with me having you on a table, but that's not appropriate now, Cortez. You went and picked the wrong brother." It's a typical barb from him, the kind I'm used to mostly, but there's also an extra bite to it, and I can tell it's made everyone uncomfortable. Hayden shoves his brother, pushing into his shoulder and knocking Tory off balance.

"Not cool, Dude. Knock that shit off," he says, throwing the twenty dollars at his brother's chest. Tory catches it against his sweatshirt, crinkling it up in his palm. "I owe you thirty."

Hayden moves toward the balls to take his turn, brushing into his brother's shoulder, clearly on purpose. Tory's body twists from the force and his half smile lingers on his lips as he looks down at the money in his palm. His mouth finally shuts into a tepid straight line and he pushes the money into the back pocket of his jeans, the prize apparently no longer worth bragging about.

"Glad this isn't awkward or anything," Lucas says from behind me.

"He's just going through things," June adds, her eyes softening on mine. She's trying to communicate to me without words, using our *friend* code, hoping I understand. I do. Hayden is a talker, and he's opened up to me about how hard his parents' split and the ugly way it all came to a head has affected him. Tory locks it all inside. I identify with him more than he thinks.

Hayden takes his turn, only knocking down nine. When June vacates the seat next to me to get her ball, Hayden slides in, a tight look on his face from the reaction from his brother. I can tell by the way he avoids his brother completely that it bothers him, but I'm not sure I'm the person who should step in to ease the situation. I tend to inflame things with Tory.

"Of course she bowled a double," Hayden mutters as June spins on her heels and holds both hands up in the air to gloat.

"I mean, she does kinda work here," I say, leaning into him. He leans back, meshing our shoulders together.

"Gotta love it when your girl kicks your ass in a sport," Lucas grumbles teasingly, cradling his ball in both hands and bending forward to dust a kiss on June's lips.

"That was sexist, but the kiss was sweet, so I'll forgive you," my friend says. Hayden and I both laugh, but stop at the sound of Tory's feet slapping against the floor in his slick bowling shoes. I glance over my shoulder, expecting to see his goofy grin or his hand up to high-five June for putting Lucas in his place; but instead, my gaze locks with his and there isn't a smile to be found. His mouth is pure nothingness, a lifeless line. He's in a dark place.

I wait for him to wander down the row of balls and out of earshot before I mention my thoughts to Hayden while Lucas takes his turn.

"Do you think you should go talk to him?" I spare another glance as I lean in closer to Hayden. His hand flattens along my thigh, his fingers curling to scratch at the frayed threads of one of the holes in my jeans. It tickles, and I let out a little giggle that catches Tory's attention.

"Nah, he's just moody. Probably stressed about therapy next week." Hayden's words conflict with my gut and the look on Tory's face, but I don't need to poke my nose into more drama. I have enough of my own.

"You're up!" Hayden brings me back to the action on the lanes, and I stand, wiping my hands along my hips. I have no clue what I'm doing.

"Green ball, I'm gonna make you my bitch," I say, wrapping my hands around the ball June used. I bring it toward my stomach, masking the strain I feel because this shit is way heavier than I thought it was.

"Just remember, your goal is straight," June encourages, clasping her hands together like she's praying. She's probably hoping I don't launch this sucker at her feet.

"Need help?" Hayden gets up from his seat, and I can imagine how this whole scene plays out, with him standing behind me, holding my arms and helping me push the ball forward from between my knees like a child. It's a cliché romantic scenario but I'm having none of it. Hayden is sweet, and comforting. But we are not doing the romance thing. And I won't be handled like a baby.

"I got it!" The words come out forcefully, and his slight flinch tells me I might have offended him.

I work to soften it.

"If you help me, nobody is going to believe I got this strike all on my own."

Hayden's mouth curves on one side and he sits back down with a nod and a chuckle, knowing that I'm talking shit I can't back up. This is my way.

My focus returns to the line of pins sixty feet or so away from me. This ball in my hands feels twice as heavy as it did before, when I tested it. No matter. It's just a rock. And I just need to push this rock on the floor with enough umph to knock over one of those things at the end. Easy.

Doing my best to mimic the approach everyone made

before me, I hold the ball in front of me and stretch my palm as wide as it will go, inserting my fingers in the damn holes that I can barely reach. After I line up my ball with what I estimate to be about the middle, I slide my slick bowling shoe-clad feet along the floor toward the line where the lane officially begins. My arm drops to my side, swinging as my hand clenches with every bit of strength I have not to drop this heavy fucker on my feet. The ball rocks back then swings forward across my hip and I let go when my body is lined up with the pins as good as it's going to.

"*Ohhh, shit!*"

Lucas's exclamation registers in my mind a fraction before I realize what I've done. My arm did not swing straight at all. Far from straight, actually. More of a veering extremely to the right. And the ball slipped out maybe a little later than I planned, causing it to fling rather than roll. Not that it matters, because it bounced two full lanes over, careening into the gutter of lane six, then swishing its way toward the dark pins still guarded by that thingamabob that lines them up.

I want to repeat what Lucas just shouted, but all I can seem to do is stare at my results with my mouth gaping open. The ball is slowing, and by the time the slow drawled "fuuuuck" leaves my lips, the green sphere that I was so sure I could handle is stalled in the middle of lane six's gutter.

"Here." Tory's tone isn't his usual tongue-in-cheek, and I'm sure my expression shows how surprised I am by it when I turn to face him. He's holding an orange ball, an eight stamped in its surface. His eyes dip and see what I'm noticing, so he shifts his hand and covers the number completely.

"It's just a ball. That one isn't made for you. This one is, though." He isn't laughing, and that's odd. No jokes about how I can't even handle throwing a ball straight. Tory D'Angelo must truly be broken because he's not even picking on the low hanging fruit to tease me. His low-key demeanor is unsettling.

"Ohhh-kayyyy." I cock my head slightly in trained suspicion. Tory breathes out a short laugh through is nose.

"Fingers go in the holes," he finally says through a crooked grin.

"Double entendre in that statement?" I plunge my fingers in and hook my thumb in the final hole, lifting the ball from Tory's palm in a brisk, confident movement. It's lighter, and the right fit.

"Just helping a girl out," he says, again avoiding the shot I teed up for him.

I turn my attention back to the still complete set of pins waiting for me, and shuffle my feet forward, pushing my shoes together and squinting as I align the ball with the center. Tory's still in my periphery, and I catch him walk away but do a full turn and come back, stopping a couple feet to my right.

"Can I?" he asks.

I turn my head to face him, finding his open palms waiting tentatively, slightly reaching toward me. I nod quickly.

"Go on," I say, twisting my lips.

"Oh, sure, you'll take his help," Hayden hollers. He's joking, but there's a hint of jealousy in the tone. *I think.*

"She wants help from winners," Tory says back, glancing to his brother briefly before meeting my gaze and winking at me. There's a sudden lightness to his face and his smile reaches his eyes.

Tory places one palm along my back and holds my shoulder with the other, pushing lightly as I scoot to my left with his guidance.

"You're lining your body up, but the ball is to your right, in your hand. You have to sort of correct for that. Make sense?"

It does. I nod.

He taps his foot into the side of my shoe a few times.

"Relax your legs, soldier. This isn't marching band."

A breathy laugh falls from my lips as I realize how tense I am. I do as he says, even adding a few inches of space between my feet, and bending my knees.

"Okay, so now . . . instead of the pins," he says, timidly moving closer to my shoulder until he's so near I can smell the spearmint of the gum he spit out in the parking lot on our way in. I don't flinch but I can't help but react to his closeness, turning my head to face him just as he does the same. When our eyes meet, he swallows hard. I can't help but see it. Hayden is watching, and I'm sure Tory doesn't want this to seem weird. It's not weird. Only, it *feels* weird.

"The arrows," he finally mutters, clearing his throat. His eyes shift out toward the lane, and I follow the direction of his gaze.

"What arrows?" I ask, scanning the pins. Tory leans in

more and points toward the middle of the floor, where the small arrows are painted on the lane.

"Those aren't for decoration?" I ask.

His body shakes with a short laugh at my side. "No, Abby. Those aren't decoration."

I glance at him briefly, catching the smirk. I shrug in response, partly to signal that he should make some space. He seems to get my hint, and drops his hands down to the pockets of his jeans, shuffling backward.

"Well, go on, then," he says, nodding his head toward the pins.

Using Tory's technique, I take a deep breath and line my arm up with the center of the lane, using the arrows to guide me. With nothing to lose, I pace forward and let my arm swing the surprisingly light ball, letting it go in just the right spot. I leave my hand in the air and walk back as it rolls forward, aiming for dead center.

"Go, baby! Go, baby!" Hayden's voice echoes behind me, and soon his hands are on my hips. My ball makes contact and knocks over seven pins, and Hayden lifts me up, spinning me in his arms and swinging me around in a giant bear hug as if I just achieved world peace . . . at the Olympics.

I smile because I'm proud, even as Lucas reminds us all that it's only a seven.

I catch Tory's eyes over his brother's shoulder and he holds up his hands and gives me a golf clap with a nod.

"Thank you," I mouth.

My God, that is the first time I have ever said those words to this boy.

The strange undertone of competitiveness between the

twins carries us through the next nine frames, but by the time we start the second one they seem to have settled whatever silent pissing match they had going on. June kicks all of our asses anyhow, breaking two-ten for the first time, which I guess is a really big deal in bowling.

When Tory gathers our shoes to return to the counter and Hayden and Lucas drift over to the pool tables, I pounce on the free moment with June so I can finally tell her my news. I sit in a seat opposite her and fold my legs under me.

"You know Jordan Shotcraft?" I know she does. She has seen every single one of his movies. He's *dad* hot, and married to one of our favorite singers, Lillian Ash.

"Oh, my God, did you get to meet him?" June is literally sitting on her hands and swinging her legs. She's gonna die when I tell her.

"Better," I say, letting my sly grin sit there to hold the moment. Her eyes widen slowly.

"No!" She grabs my arms and pulls them toward her, causing me to laugh and lose my balance. I unfurl my legs, but not in time to stop my fall. Before I hit the ground, though, Tory wraps his arm around my body from the empty seat next to me.

"I have that effect on women," he says, giving me his classic wink as he rights me in my seat. The mint scent from his gum is now replaced by the faint aroma of his cologne. It's different than Hayden's—maybe richer, woodsier, if that's a thing.

I'm trying to form a clever response when June kicks her feet forward and touches my knees with the toes of her shoes. I shift my focus to her and her eyes are still wide.

"Abby Cortez, you better tell me now. And if it's what I think it is, you better take me with you." Her head shakes on its own just to show me how firm she is about this.

"You're looking at Jordan Shotcraft's surprise teenaged daughter in his next rom com." June's screaming before I get the last word out, and within a blink, she's wrapped her arms around me, practically sitting in my lap.

My eyes tear with happiness. I squealed when I got the news, but seeing my friend's reaction just makes things so incredibly real.

June's reaction draws Lucas and Hayden back to our seats, so once everyone gathers around and June leaves my lap, I feed them the details.

"It was down to me and another unknown actress, and I guess they liked my attitude."

Tory snorts a laugh, so I shoot him a glare.

"You're hardly unknown," June says. "You're the face of Allensville Yogurt!"

"This stuff is *great!*" Lucas pipes in, pumping his arm just like I do in my biggest commercial deal to date. The yogurt company ad paid me the most of any job I've ever landed, even more than the modeling spreads that have been in major magazines. This movie deal, though . . . it's a game changer.

"Filming starts in early March," I say, leading to a noticeable hush from everyone.

"Wow," June says, shaking her head while keeping the smile plastered on her face. I knew this would be the hard part. We had plans, she and I.

"I know. Prom . . . and maybe graduation, but—"

My best friend grabs my hands and gives them a little shake.

"No buts. This is huge. *Massive!* We'll have our own celebrations, and you deserve this." Her boost to my doubts does the trick, and for the first time since I was offered the contract, I feel one-hundred percent ready to take this leap.

"I'm going to need to run a lot of lines over the next couple months," I say through nervous laughter.

"Okay." My friend nods, tears forming at the sides of her eyes from what I can tell is genuine pride. "No kissing scenes for me, though."

"Damn," Lucas adds, drawing a laugh from all of us.

"That's what Hayden's for," I say, turning my attention to the guy who probably deserved to get this news from me one-on-one. He doesn't seem upset, though. In fact, he stands and holds one hand to his chest, his other out in front of him.

"Romeo, Oh Romeo . . ." he starts, clearly showcasing his insincere acting skills.

I kick at him and he grabs my hand, pulling me to my feet and hugging me.

"I'm actually really bad at that stuff, but I'll do whatever I can," he assures.

"You sure you don't mind me taking over your weekends for a while?" I ask, already knowing my mom will be too busy working. When I feel the sway of his embrace pause, I peel back to look him in the eyes.

"Weekends, huh?" His mouth falls into a regretful grimace.

"Your new job," I respond, piecing it together. I guess I

knew he'd have to work weekends a lot. Basketball practice and the season are pretty intense, so weekends are really his only chance to pick up hours.

"Hey, but Tory can fill in. Actually, of the two of us, he's the actor." Hayden moves to my side, his arm slung over my shoulder, and a sudden tightness grips my chest at his suggestion. Tory seems equally surprised by the suggestion, popping his head up fast and flitting his attention between me and his brother.

"Me?" He points to himself. "I mean, nah, I'm not the best to practice with."

"He's being modest. Yo, check it." Hayden drops his arm from around me and pulls his phone from his pocket, scrolling through his videos and pictures while I awkwardly smile at Tory and he awkwardly smiles back. "Yeah, here it is. Look."

Hayden holds his phone out for me to watch his screen, and a tall, skinny near-exact version of his younger self is standing at the center of a stage under a spotlight.

"If music be the food of love, play on." Tory is probably in seventh or eighth grade in this video, and the fact it's on his brother's phone still baffles me almost as much as that I'm watching him recite a monologue from Shakespeare's Twelfth Knight.

"Okay, okay, that's enough," Tory says, swiping the phone from his brother's hand and closing the video.

"Dude, you were good. He was good," Hayden says, glancing around at all of us. I wonder if the dent between my brows is as deep as the ones on Lucas and June's foreheads.

"You did theater?" I ask.

"Yeah, I mean nah. Not really." Tory leans against the bar top near our seating area and exhales heavily. "I auditioned for a bunch of things one summer. I thought maybe I'd try acting, but ya know . . ."

He holds out two open palms.

I tilt my head to the side.

"He always got in trouble for being a smart ass," Hayden blurts out, slapping his brother's chest. He takes his phone back and points at his brother. "Doesn't mean you weren't good, though."

Tory shrugs.

"So, will you?" I ask. I already regret it, but the panic of not being ready with my lines down by the time filming starts overrides the epic bad idea this is.

Tory's face wrinkles in hesitation as he takes a long breath.

"I don't know. I mean . . ." He glances to his brother first, then to June, almost as if he's taking a vote or eliciting permission. He doesn't bother to look to Lucas, making his own mind up instead.

"Fine, yeah. We can run lines. But don't make fun of me when I'm not that good." He stands straight and dives his hands into his pockets while he rigidly scrunches his shoulders.

"Don't worry. I'm sure there are plenty of other things I can make fun of you for," I say, falling into my more familiar role with this D'Angelo. A sharp laugh leaves his chest.

"No doubt," he says. He smiles at me with tightly closed lips, then pivots, pausing when June stands up in front of him. "No doubt," he repeats, for some reason speaking directly to her.

What a fucking weird day. I bowled a forty-one. I have a boyfriend. Tory D'Angelo has acting chops. And I just made plans to spend every free weekend in the books with him. Lord help me if I get a call to star in the reboot of the Twilight Zone.

3

TORY

It's amazing how many different ways June found to tell me that agreeing to read lines with Abby is a bad idea.

"It's sort of your fault I'm in this predicament, you know," I say, tossing her the ball at the end of my driveway. Hayden left to take Abby home and Lucas fell asleep on our couch while playing video games.

"How is this my fault?" She bounces the ball at her feet then lifts it overhead, jumping and pushing it toward the hoop on our garage. It falls several feet short, and I catch it, bouncing it to her to try again.

"You could have agreed to do the kissing scenes with her," I say, letting my imagination toy with the idea of those two making out in front of me. Can't lie; I've visualized it a few times since June made the joke.

She holds the ball against her hip and sneers at me.

"There probably aren't even any kissing scenes," she says, holding her glare on me for a beat before palming the ball with both hands and throwing it hard at the ground. It bounces toward me in a high arc, but I step back and catch it with one hand. I dribble out toward her, then spin and take a short jump shot, sinking it without touching the rim.

"I have to work a lot too. You know that. I'm saving for college, and as good as business is going for my mom, it's not booming so much that I can slack off."

June is trying to save enough that she's able to swing state school instead of junior college. With Lucas going to MIT after we graduate, I think she's a little worried about the long distance relationship thing. Even though she's focused on going somewhere affordable in Indiana, I wouldn't be surprised if she eventually ended up in Boston.

If I'm being honest with myself, I actually wanted to get trapped into helping Abby. I know it deep down. Even now, as I try to convince myself that it's not really about spending time with her. It is. It's *all* about spending time with her. I sure as hell won't say that out loud to anyone, though. Not even June.

"You know, you really don't have anything to worry about. I'm over it," I lie. I'm an excellent liar. I do it for my brother all the time, pretending I'm handling this divorce situation and public embarrassment over our mom's affair with my best friend's dad. It's easier for Hayden if I have my shit together. He's always been the worrier and the fixer, and he's got his head and hands full right now fixing our family. He doesn't need to add me to his list. As far as he knows, I'm handling it all just fine.

"Really?" June grabs the ball from my hands while I'm lost in thought.

"Really, what?" I take the ball back from her and toss it

from one hand to the other. When she lunges for it again, I grip it hard and step back.

"You're over it," she says. She levels me with a stare that threatens to call me on my bullshit. I play it off with a cocky smile, dribbling the ball through my legs a few times before driving it toward our hoop, palming it with my right hand, and dunking it with enough force that the entire backboard rattles where it's bolted to the eave of our house.

"That's right," I say when my feet land on the ground. I brush my hands off and reach for June with an open palm to shake on it. She takes my hand in hers and squeezes tight. *Holy decent grip, Batman!*

"Bullshit," she says.

"*Pfft*, whatever. I shook on it," I say, letting go of her hand and turning around as I stretch my fingers wide. Yeah, it's bullshit, but what am I going to do? Tell Abby no? Tell her I'm not comfortable spending time with her because all I do is think about kissing her, which is super sketch since she's my brother's girl now? Yeah, I'm not saying all that. I'm tucking that shit deep into the pit of my soul and pretending it's all a dream.

June walks out to the street where the ball has rolled and stops it with her foot.

"Hayden's back!" she shouts, seconds before the Subaru I share with my brother roars into the driveway. June picks up the ball and bounces it near the sidewalk, clearly giving me and my brother space. She's anticipating Hayden to ask me questions about my behavior all day, but she doesn't know Hayden like I do. He's all about avoidance and pretending.

My brother pulls the car into our garage, into the

gaping space left from the spot where our dad's SUV is usually parked.

"You wanna get in some one-on-one?" Hayden asks me, leaving the car door open so the stereo can blast Drake's latest drop into our garage. Mom hates it when we do this. Her bedroom is above the garage, and she's been sleeping a lot more than she's been working as a substitute at the nearby grade school. She doesn't dare yell at us about it, though. She kinda lost her authority, what with the daily hookups and all.

"Sure," I say, holding my hands open toward June, signaling for the ball. I glance at her in time to catch the warning look on her face. I roll my eyes and eventually she tosses me the ball.

"First to eleven cuz I'm hungry, yo," I say as I dribble out to the center of our vacant driveway.

June lingers inside our garage for a while, but she gives up after the first few possessions result in off-the-rim shots by both Hayden and myself. I think she was sticking around to make sure I didn't let my edge slip again. I got a little alpha in our bowling match.

"Dude, you talk to Coach yet about Thursday?" Hayden always talks through our games. It's fuckin' annoying.

"Yeah, I did Friday. He said to keep him posted when we have therapy. I mean, what's he gonna do, bench us?" I tip the ball out of Hayden's hands when he lets his guard down, and laugh.

"Damn it!" He's on me fast, trying to right his wrong. He's not nearly as aggressive as I am, but he's agile. Swift.

He's always been faster, and his shots are prettier. Mine are a lot more effective, though.

"You figure out what you're gonna say?" he asks. His hands are stretched out and his footwork matches mine. I lower my shoulder and fake a drive, pulling back instead for a jump shot. Finally, one of us sinks something.

"One-oh, key it up," Hayden says.

I jog to the ball and bring it back to the top of our imaginary three-point line.

"I figure this lady, she'll ask us a bunch of questions. I'll just answer whatever I'm feeling at the time," I say.

I send a deep three up spontaneously since Hayden's distracted. It bangs off the rim. He hates that I don't have a plan. I'd bet he has a notebook full of bullet points he'll memorize before our session so he knows exactly what to say. I'm not sure that's the best way for therapy to go, though . . . planned out and shit.

"You think Dad really wants to go to these?" Hayden asks, dribbling out and faking a drive only to pull back and hit a fade-away shot. It's pretty, floating through the air without rotation and landing in the hoop with the grace of a butterfly.

Quiet. Agile. Pretty.

I lunge for the ball and push it into his chest, my competitive beast awakening.

"Simmer down, now," he teases, loving the fact that he knows how to push my buttons on the court.

"Shut up and set up," I grumble, only making him laugh harder.

We play the next few points without serious talk, climbing

the score to five to six, his lead. Hayden can't stand leaving questions unanswered though, so when he calls for a water break and tosses the ball into the dry grass alongside our driveway, he brings up his question about our dad again. I chew on it while he heads toward the old fridge that keeps the water, beer and soda cold. He tosses me a water, but I waggle my finger to throw me a beer instead. He does, but takes a water for himself, making me look like the failing youth. Whatever. I want a beer.

"I think Dad's probably pretty hurt, so . . . no. I don't think he wants anything to do with Mom or therapy or talking about his feelings right now. Fuck, I don't want any of this. Do you?" I pop the cap off my beer and take a swig. The cool touch of the liquid on my tongue makes me go in for more. This is why people shouldn't drink beer when they're thirsty; half is gone before Hayden answers my question.

"I just want it all to go back to how it was. I wish we were all still oblivious, ya know?" He tips his water back and eyes me for my response. My face sours.

"Hayd . . . we ain't ever going back to what it was. Our old holiday card, picturesque fake-ass family? That was a lie. There's no putting the shit that came out back in the bottle, and I don't need a therapist to tell me I need to come to terms with that." My harsh words dent his fragile ego, and I feel a touch of guilt. I quickly drown that with more beer.

"Let's go," I say, setting my two-thirds empty bottle on a ledge in the garage before jogging out to the ball.

I turn back to the garage, expecting to see Hayden walking toward me, ready to ball, but he hasn't budged. He's caught in his feelings. I'm in insensitive dick mode.

This isn't going to work. I sigh and prop the ball on my hip, no longer in the mood to play. I just want to drain our hot water in the shower and turn my skin lobster pink. I'm starting to feel the chill in the air.

"Look, man. This sucks for all of us. Probably sucks for Mom, too. And maybe things were broken that we didn't see. Either way, you and I are going to have to stick through this raw end of the deal. It's our senior year, Hayd. Senior fucking year. I'm not going to let them ruin that for me."

I move back into the garage and drop the ball at my feet, stopping its bounce with my foot and nudging it into the corner. I pick up my beer and hold it out to my brother on my way inside the house.

"You shouldn't let any of this ruin your happiness either, man." I take one more drink to toast my worthless wise words. Hayden's eyes stay on me the entire time, full of skepticism. I turn my back and head toward the garage door into our mudroom. When I pull the door wide, Hayden hits me with one more of the thoughts he just can't stop processing in his head. This one is super fucking unexpected.

"You're cool with me and Abby, right?"

I grip the door knob hard enough that my veins define in my forearm and grind my back teeth together.

"Yeah. I mean, if you're into her. Whatever, dude. Good for you, *pff*." I speak over my shoulder so I only have to pretend with half my face.

He doesn't respond, but I'm looking his way enough to catch the smile and nod. I leave it at that, letting the door fall shut behind me. I give June and Lucas a quick nod good-bye as they get ready to leave, and I keep my truth contained all the way upstairs, not letting it go until I step into the shower and practically drown myself in the spray of water falling from the nozzle. I let it fill my mouth over and over again, and I growl through it a few times while I know Hayden's still outside. Eventually, his music kicks on in his room on the other side of our shared bathroom, so I keep my show of frustration to the quiet kind, resting my palms flat on the wall and bending my head down low enough that the water cascades around my neck and face, blurring away any expression that remotely resembles jealousy. It takes me forty minutes to wash my feelings down the drain, about how long as it takes to run this house out of hot water.

4

ABBY

There are a lot of reasons why December is my least favorite month.

One: It's my birthday month. The fifteenth. Right smack in the middle of the Christmas countdown, and usually in the middle of Hanukkah, which means I've never really had a birthday party with friends, and my presents from my relatives have become lump sums of cash that encompass both Christmas and birthday gifts in one.

Two: I hate being cold, and December in Indiana is gross. It's also often wet. My hair takes work to turn haphazard corkscrews into soft waves. December makes it all a moot point. December is for ponytails and buns.

Three: December is when my dad left. He left my mom with a mountain of debt. He left like a coward in the middle of the night. He left without warning, after a lot of years of ugly fighting. He took off before I got my first big commercial deal and modeling contract. When I did, two years after being off the radar, minus divorce papers and a virtual court appearance, he showed up with flowers and balloons for my birthday. More like he showed up with bribes, thinking he could win me over and become my manager. It's been one messy custody battle ever since. I've only had to visit him once in Miami, two years ago. In December.

Today marks the first day of the worst month on the calendar. December can suck a dick.

"Thanks for driving." June picked me up for school today in her mom's van. My car needs tires and my mom won't let me drive until I get new ones. Dad won't pay for them, which is part of their agreement, even though I have plenty of cash saved in my accounts.

"That's not the point," my mom keeps saying.

I don't know, though. Kinda feels like the point is I need tires and have found a way to be self-sustaining. I'm almost eighteen, and I plan on calling my own financial shots soon.

"It's nice getting to drive. I miss my car, though. The minivan doesn't really scream *cool*," June says as we pull into our usual spot at the front of the school.

"I don't know. I mean, you're cool enough to always get this prime real estate in the student lot without having to fight for it," I say, tipping the mirror to check the smoothness of today's twisty up-do. Strands are already falling away and framing my face like wispy baby doll hairs.

"I get this spot because it's right in front of the principal's office, and almost everyone else hides vape or pot in their car so nobody *wants* to park here." June kills the engine and gives me a sideways look.

"It's cool not to be the pot-smoking vaper," I say,

folding my arms over my chest to hold my position. Laughter breaks free from June's lips almost immediately as she reaches over her seat to grab her backpack.

"Okay, Nancy Reagan." She gets out, thinking she proved a point.

I step out on my side and shut the door just as she locks it with the key fob.

"Joke's on you. I have no idea who Nancy Reagan is." I'm lying. I totally get her joke, but it's going to piss her off more that I don't, and then she'll forget all about not driving a cool car.

"Just say no?"

I glance up and purse my lips in feigned consideration, then shake my head when my gaze falls back to her.

"Ronald Reagan's wife? He was president in the eighties? And she was the First Lady? Just . . . say . . . no?" She's getting worked up. I live for this. My hand grips my phone in my pocket.

"No," I say, just as she requested.

She groans with frustration, and I pull my phone out to snap a photo of her at the perfect moment. My cherry on top.

"Damn it!" June chides.

I can't help but laugh hard.

"You were fucking with me, weren't you?" my friend demands. She'll get over it in seconds. She always does.

"Bitch, I totally know who Nancy Reagan is. Do you think I'm stupid?" I snap one more photo, this time with her mouth open wide, ready to argue. She snaps it shut and grumbles, which only makes me laugh more.

"I'm making that one my lock-screen photo," I tease.

She rolls her eyes, and I set the photo to save. I'll change it with a new one tomorrow, but today this photo gives me joy. More importantly, though, now June couldn't care less about driving a minivan and parking it front and center. That's old news.

On instinct, I duck and roll when an arm slinks over my shoulder. It takes me three full seconds to realize it's Hayden's arm doing the act. He's wearing his Allensville Public hoodie, number fourteen on the back. Tory's wearing his, too, only he's two. Must be a team thing.

"Sorry, didn't mean to scare you," Hayden says, cautiously opening his arm for me to tuck myself next to him on my own terms. I do, but the weight of his arm on my shoulders feels heavy—suffocating.

"What's with the twin matchy-matchy?" I ask, tugging on the cord from his hood. He shoves his free hand into the front pocket and puffs the sweatshirt out to look down at our school's logo. It's a cartoonish drawing of a massive eagle carrying away a bloody piece of prey. There's a constant debate among students whether it's a rabbit or another bird of some sort. Whatever it is, it's gross. There was a petition to change the mascot logo my freshman year, but apparently the guy who drew it is some famous local artist, so we're stuck with these gory sweatshirts and stuff.

"Did you forget? Game day!" Hayden steps to the side and pulls his arms free of his hoodie one at a time.

"Today is the first game?" I'm a bad girlfriend because saying I forgot wouldn't even be close to the truth. I never paid attention enough in the first place to even know it was game day.

"Yeah. You're coming, right?" He pulls the hoodie over his head, messing up his wavy hair. It's cute.

"Of course. June?" I turn to my friend who is already making out with Lucas against the back of his truck. They have a lot of time to make up for, but I swear they're always locked mouth-to-mouth.

I'm about to turn back to Hayden and tell him I'll be there, with or without June, when the tight fit of his dark gray hoodie swallows up my head and chokes at my neck.

"Uh, no. I don't . . ." I struggle to find air under the enormous fleece-lined sweater. My eyes finally find Hayden's smile, and I instantly feel guilty for wanting to rip this thing off of me. The messy bun that was already falling apart is also unraveling.

"I like seeing you in my number," Hayden says. I catch Tory's snicker just over his brother's shoulder, and when our eyes meet he covers his laugh with a fist to his mouth and a lame-ass cough.

"It's a little big on me," I say, following through and poking my arms into the sleeves after dropping my bag to my feet. Hayden reaches toward the top of my head and I strain to stare straight upward as he tugs free the band I was using to hold my hair in place.

"It's cute that it's big," he says, handing me my hair tie. I put it around my wrist, once I *find* my wrist.

"Okay, well, I'll get it back to you after first hour, I guess."

"Keep it. Wear it to the game," he interjects before I can conjure an excuse.

"Oh, uh, okay," I stammer.

June has snapped out of her love fest by Lucas's truck

and steps up on the curb to stand behind me and comb out my wild hair with her fingers.

"Look who's got spirit," she says, sarcasm tainting every word. It was only a few months ago that I gave her shit for just sitting at the football games. I never forced a giant sweatshirt on her with a wild bloodbath pictorial painted on the chest, though.

"Haha, yeah, look at me. Woo!" I raise both of my hands and waggle them with pretend pompoms before bending down to pick up my bag and work the straps up over the massive thickness of the material I'm wearing. I can actually *feel* my hair growing out in all directions. I'm going to look like a palm tree by lunch hour.

"Okay, well, I'll see you at lunch, and after the game." Hayden flattens both of my cheeks with his palms, puckering my lips out as he bends down and kisses me. His kisses are sweet, and he sprinkles them often. Being with him feels a lot like dating a boy from the 1950's. He made a big deal about holding hands, and we've never really full-on made out. We kiss, but it's got this weird unwritten time limit on how long it goes on.

Hayden holds out a fist and pounds it against his brother's and Lucas's, and everyone heads their separate ways, leaving me and June alone to walk through the main hallway together. She's in independent study just down the hallway from my bio class. Lately, I feel as if this two-minute walk through throngs of students is the only time she and I have to catch up.

"So, are you going to tell me how all of this"—she pauses to tug at the sleeve of Hayden's hoodie —"happened?"

"He's nice," I say, which makes me immediately cringe because God, that sounds lame. Our story is a lot more complicated than *nice,* but I'm not totally sure I have a full handle on it so nice is the best I've got.

"Yeah, he always has been. Since when has that been your thing? I thought you were hooking up with that new—"

"Cannon?" I answer for her. "Cannon is hot. And I tried to get on his radar, but that boy has major shit going on, and he's so focused on baseball and the new coach at school. It was literally all he ever talked about."

"Yeah, okay, but then how did you get to Hayden?" June asks.

I sigh and roll up one of the sleeves at my wrist.

"We have a lot in common, and I'm sure you've had to help Lucas navigate a lot of this. Us fucked-up family kids have to guide each other, ya know?" I give her a sideways smile and she nods.

"Yeah, I get that. I've been sort of preoccupied with Lucas lately and we haven't talked much, but I thought surely Miss Love Sucks would have filled me in on settling down with a guy like Hayden D'Angelo," June says.

"That's my nickname? Miss Love Sucks?" I say it in a joking way, but there's a tender pang at my side. *Am I truly that jaded?*

"Well, it is now. I just made it up, but you know what I mean. You've never had a *boyfriend,* per se. You have had guys you're talking to, and then guys you are *seriously* talking to. You just jumped right into a label with this one." She laughs through her assessment of my love life, and I guess on most points, she's right.

"Huh," I respond, letting the hurt show a little.

"Hey, no, I didn't mean it like that," June says. We've reached the independent study room, but before she leaves me to step inside she softly touches my elbow and moves us to the other side of the walkway, away from the students rushing to beat the bell.

"I know, yeah. I guess I didn't realize all of that. I mean, Hayden and I *were* talking, and maybe that's what it was. We *talked.* We talked about the way my dad left, all of the shit I'm going through now, how he's filing all of this crap to get his name on my company even though I'm about to be eighteen."

I stop short of telling her the worst of it. I'm not ready to relive some things. Not until I absolutely have to.

"Abs, I'm so sorry. I didn't realize how bad things have gotten with your dad," June says, hugging me with one arm. I let her, because she's June and she is a kind soul, but I'd rather not be a thing people have to say *sorry* about.

"It is what it is," I say. That's such a dumb, meaningless phrase, yet it's the only thing that fits my situation. The only way my problems could go away would be with a time machine. I'd go back to being Annie and whisper in my ear: *"Don't dream big, little girl. That house of cards is mighty fragile."*

"It wasn't all about me, though," I continue, shaking away my own thoughts. "Hayden is having a hard time with his parents too. He feels angry, but he has no idea what to do with those feelings because he's not really the angry type."

I don't go into the guilt he feels because that's his dragon to battle. When he wants others to know everything, they will. And if he never wants that, then that's his choice. Our relationship is built on confiding in each other, creating a space to dump our baggage and move on. It's what gives us both peace—we are each what we need.

"No, he's not an angry kind of guy," June agrees. "I still remember in fourth grade when Hayden rescued the kittens underneath our grade school portable art room. His mom helped him nurse those things until they could get them adopted."

"I remember that! I totally wanted one, but my parents said our household wasn't the kind of place for kittens. No truer words than that!" I'm old enough now to realize a kitten would only have been one more thing for my parents to fight over.

"I'm glad you're happy," June slips in, bringing me back to the subject we're *actually* talking about—me and Hayden.

"Thanks," I say, the words basically an act of autopilot. I'm not sure I'm smiling right now, but the commotion of the last warning bell gets me off the hook. June rushes in, shouting something about missing lunch for an SAT meeting or something.

I ratchet up the sleeves of Hayden's sweatshirt and make my way to my classroom, squeezing in just before the teacher shuts the door, and like a heatwave, I'm pummeled with stares. Okay, maybe I'm not really pummeled, but there are a few people near the back of the class who are definitely eyeing me in this hoodie. There's going to be talk about it, like me dating someone is major TMZ news, but whatever.

I'm happy. *Right?*

5

TORY

Hayden forgot about the SAT meeting. I remembered the moment he told Abby he'd meet her for lunch. I probably should have said something then, but I didn't. I didn't because I've got a super selfish streak, and I was planning on skipping the SAT meeting. I'm fine with the score I have. A solid nine-eighty works for the places I want to go. Besides, state schools are lenient on test scores when you drain threes like I do. I also knew Abby would skip it. She took her first test the same day I did, and she bragged about being two hundred points higher than me when our results came in. She also said she'd never take that test again.

I feel like a dick now that I'm in the moment, though. I'm clearly taking advantage of the fact my brother and all of our friends won't be here so I can have Abby all to myself. I didn't account for the fact Abby and I don't really hang on our own, though. It's always been in groups. When June and Lucas were going through their shit, Abby and I were the co-pilots, steering those two together. That's when my feelings got all fuckin' weird, too.

I pay the cart guy four bucks for the same chicken burrito, chips and drink I've been buying at this school for four years, then pull my phone from my pocket when it buzzes. I balance the cardboard food box in my other hand.

It's a text from Hayden.

Hey, totally forgot about this SAT thing. Tell Abby for me?

I was prepared for this. I type back my nonchalant response.

Got it.

Abby is sitting in her usual spot, the one in the far corner of the cafeteria where the windows meet and the sun peeks through the trees. She's pulled her knees up on the bench and keeps glancing over her shoulder, out the window, probably wondering where Hayden is. She's usually surrounded by people—Lola, Naomi, June, Lucas . . . me and my brother. She's become the top of the pyramid in our social structure, the one who isn't afraid to speak her mind and who would speak up for her friends in a heartbeat. I'm not sure where I fall in that hierarchy. I can't say she'd get in someone's face to defend me, but then again, I don't need her to. I'm pretty quick to handle my own defense.

"Seat taken?" It's not even clever, and she calls me on it with a look that says I'm a fucking dumbass. I straddle the bench on the other end from her, leaving a solid six feet of distance between us, and plop my wrapped burrito down between my knees.

"They're all in that SAT meeting," I say.

"Yeah, I know." She shrugs and pops one of the chips from her bag in her mouth.

I nod, suddenly kicked off the map of what I should say next.

"Cool." That's what comes out.

"You really sticking with that nine-eighty?"

I glance up at her with one raised brow and breathe out a laugh. I wonder how this became our way with each other—little digs, barbs and insults until enough of them add up to equal a conversation.

"Well, I mean, it's no eleven-eighty." I hold my palms up, arms out, beating her to her punchline.

"It sure the fuck isn't." Her eyes do that little righteous flutter with her words. I laugh it off and turn my focus to my burrito.

She continues to take nibbles at her chips, pushing the bread around from her sandwich. Meanwhile, I bear down and chomp about half of my burrito in three bites. A worry line seems to be permanently pressed into her forehead, and I stare at it for several seconds until she glances up and meets my glare.

"What's up with you?" I say through a full mouth.

She glowers.

"Nothing." Her short clipped answer is irritable, and it's also a lie.

"Come on. I'm good at listening," I say. I actually am. I rarely say shit that matters to people because sharing my thoughts and feelings is uncomfortable. It's turned me into a really good free therapist. Lucas unloads on me constantly.

Abby chews through a few more bites while she studies

me with her bullshit meter running full blast. She finally gives in and disposes of her half-eaten meal in the crumpled-up paper it came in and slides a few feet closer to me on the bench. We're facing each other, her feet flat on the wood in front of me. I note the red heart doodled on the side of her right Van and the broken version drawn on the left. I feel like there's a story there.

"I turn eighteen in two weeks. I've had that date circled on my calendar for years because it's supposed to mean that the bullshit back-and-forth stuff between my parents, which has really only been about money, stops. It's supposed to mean *I* decide where I go, with whom, when and what my business amounts to. But—"

Abby's mouth pulls tight as she shrugs. My stomach sinks with sympathy.

"Eighteen means you're an adult though, right?" I shift in my seat, moving my foot up to the table so I can scoot a little closer. I'm not doing it for predatory reasons, which I think Abby might suspect given the way she just tucked her knees tighter into her chest. I'm doing it to make our bubble smaller, so she can talk and share without the nosy-ass ears floating around the lunchroom. There are a lot of those around this place, especially when it comes to Abby. She's considered "famous" around our parts.

"I'm more like a *half* adult," she says, laughing at her definition.

"How so?"

Her long lashes flit against her cheeks, golden brown like her hair, which she's tied into this messy knot at the base of her neck. She has the faintest dusting of freckles on her round cheeks, partly covered with makeup but never so thick that the real her doesn't shine through. She mashes her lips together, the satin red on her lips glimmering as she forms a wry smile.

"I guess my parents are considered *investors* in the start-up of my career. All the modeling classes, acting classes, photo sessions for headshots, clothes and makeup." She waggles her head side to side as she twirls her finger around her face with a giggle. It pulls a breathy smile from me in response.

"Okay, yeah. But that's also parenting, right? I mean, my mom and dad put Hayden and me in youth basketball for years, then club, and there were shoes—*oh how there have been shoes.*" I make the same head waggling motion and finger twirl she did, only this time at my feet, which are in loosely laced Jordan Ones that I literally shined up with a baby wipe this morning.

Abby is amused at my comparison, and she lets her legs fall loose from her hold, her feet landing on the ground as she straddles the bench in front of me, leaning forward and bracing her palms on the wood as if she's a gymnast about to lift herself into some sort of hand stand. She stares at the carved-out G+T for long seconds while her laughter fades.

"It wouldn't be a big deal if this was all just my mom. She's my manager, and I have never once felt like one of those abused child stars. I know what my savings account looks like, and I know she doesn't pull shady shit you see in the tabloids. It's always been me and her, and then the world. But the fact that my dad is like, I don't know, forcing his way on the team? It feels more like the custody hearings have turned into employment ones. I mean, the last time he actually came in with all these receipts from when I was six and seven."

I'm not sure she realizes she's trembling, but she is, so to stop her from digging any deeper in a place so public and so filled with the fumes of microwave pizza and Coke machines, I reach forward and rest my hand on top of hers. We both freeze, and I'm pretty sure my palm is already sweating. Her gaze lifts to meet mine, but I don't let go of her hand just yet. I don't make this touch a big deal, even though it sort of is. That's not why I did it, and I don't want to cheapen it. With our eyes locked on one another, I let the air fill with silence just long enough for a ragged, emotional breath to fall from her lips.

"You have every right to feel the way you do," I say.

"And how's that?" she fires back. Her hand shifts under mine, but she doesn't pull it away.

"You feel like your dad sees a business opportunity where he should see his daughter."

She swallows and keeps her gaze on mine for a beat before finally leaning back, pulling her hand away and glancing off to the side. With a snort sniffle, she runs the sleeve of my brother's hoodie across her eyes, erasing the tiny break that she let herself have.

I'm suddenly not hungry. I don't think I have ever *not* been hungry, but I couldn't eat the rest of my burrito if I were forced at gunpoint. It's not that I feel sick, but more that I feel . . . envious. I was fooling myself thinking that Abby was a passing crush I could easily dismiss. Two months of riding shotgun with her through all things June and Lucas was just long enough for me to get hooked on having her around. But while it's my advice she's listening to, it's my brother's fucking sweatshirt she's dabbing her tears with.

"So, see you at the game?" My move to leave is abrupt, especially after she just bared part of her soul. If I stay, though, I'm going to say things I don't mean out of sheer self-preservation. This is precisely why I don't do relationships. I do flirting and hookups. Feelings, well, they fucking feel.

"What, did you change your mind and suddenly decide that nine-eighty bare-minimum wasn't good enough?" Her nose wrinkles after her insult, but I think I get where it's coming from. She just hit me with a major share, and now I'm bailing. Better to lash out. Her and I aren't so different.

"Something like that," I say, holding up my lunch trash as a wave good-bye.

Abby's face shifts slightly, her wrinkled mouth and dimmed eyes morphing from the snarky expression that accompanies her tease to the look of a girl who just lost her brand new balloon to the sky.

"That hoodie"—I walk backward, pointing toward her chest—"looks good on you." I leave things there with a tight-lipped smile and a nod—a truce of sorts, not that Abby even knew we were in a battle. Hell, we weren't. I'm the only one in a conflict, and it's with my own damn self.

I manage to turn my back to her and toss my trash out without pausing to get one more jab in to fully take things back to our version of normal. For now, I'd like to leave things nice. I wasn't counting on her wanting to leave things that way, too.

"I'll be sure to cheer for you, even if I'm wearing Hayden's number," she shouts.

I spin on my heel and give her a thumbs up, but keep moving away from her because if I turn around, I'll keep trying to win her over. And she's not mine to be won.

6

ABBY

I haven't been to a basketball game since freshman year. Football is easier for me to follow. I guess it's easier to go along with the crowd at those games, too. Our basketball team has always been better than our football team, and it's packed inside. I wasn't about to cram in here alone, and June had to work, so I dragged Naomi and Lola with me. I talked Lola into coming because I knew Cannon would be here, and now that I'm not trying to get with him, she is. *Good luck!* That boy is like a miserable, grumpy ice sculpture focused on only one thing—getting drafted by a major league team right out of high school.

Lola peels away from Naomi and me the minute Cannon walks in with his cousin Zack, and she manages to get him to laugh at something she says when they sit down a few rows away from us. I must admit I'm a little dumbstruck—I didn't make him laugh once in all of the beer-keg party meetups we had. And I'm fucking funny, dammit!

"He's mesmerized by her tits," Naomi says in a hushed

voice at my side. I laugh softly and tap her leg with the back of my palm. She's only trying to make me feel better about not being able to get Cannon to drop his scowl despite weeks of effort.

"Lola's charming. Give her credit," I say.

Naomi wobbles her head but gives in with a sing-songy "Oh-kay."

"But yes, her tits are mesmerizing," I add, both to give props to what nature gave that girl and to let Naomi off the hook after calling her out for shaming our friend.

"Sigh, she does have great tits," Naomi adds in a hum. We both rest our chins on our fists, elbows propped on our knees while we stare at Lola's bright red sweater with envy. After a few seconds, we give in and laugh.

"You have *nothing* to be envious of in that department," Naomi says, elbowing the side of my boob. I wince because *fucking ow!*

"Thanks," I say, adjusting my bra under this giant sweatshirt I'm still swimming in. The plus of wearing Hayden's hoodie is that it's long enough to cover my ass, which means leggings are a go. I can almost endure the carnage drawing on my chest for this level of comfort, plus my fuzzy boots look super cute. My arms are still carrying folds of material, though, and with the heat on in the gym, I'm starting to get kinda hot.

"There's your boy!" Naomi teases, leaning into my side as our team comes rushing onto the floor. They jog two laps around the perimeter of the gym, and Hayden looks up and winks at me as he passes the second time. I hold up my hand and scrunch out a wave with the few fingers I manage to get loose from the cuff of the sweatshirt.

"He's pretty into you, huh?" Naomi's voice is dreamy. All I can do is laugh.

"I don't know about that. Hayden and I just sort of happened. Like it was easy, you know? It's nice to have someone to talk to about all of life's shit." My gaze slides over to the other D'Angelo while I say that, and I note the far more serious face Tory wears compared to his brother.

"Yeah, okay, but . . . tell me about his body, girl. Give me the details! Those boys are so freaking hot, and getting to kiss one is like winning the lottery." Naomi is practically licking her lips, which . . . gross.

I shake my head with a soft laugh and glance from her back out to the floor where the guys are all stretching.

"It's not like that with us." My smile slips a little as that realization sinks in. Hayden's attention slides to me a few more times and I make sure to prop my smile up every time, but eventually I can't hold it anymore.

"Oh, yeah, I'm sure all you do is hold hands," Naomi teases.

"No," I retort, scrunching my face. "We kiss. We kiss a lot. All the time."

We kiss some.

"You're telling me you haven't gotten all up on that boy?"

I turn to face my friend, her eyes wide and chin dipped low as she waits for my answer. All I can do is shrug, which I know is not the kind of story she wants. I'm far from a prude, and I'm not uncomfortable talking about being with guys. I've slept with two boys, almost three. The third and near sex partner was my co-star in the yogurt commercial, and I had the sense to realize that every time I saw that commercial I would be reminded of him. We had zero in common other than being pretty on camera. His name was Jake. There was no future for Jake and Abby. Not that I have a future with anyone. Serious is not really my thing, and forever love is a myth. I have yet to get close to a family that is still whole. Marriages just don't last forever. There's an expiration date, and it always comes due at the shittiest time.

"Wow, Abby Cortez is taking it slow," Naomi says, leaning back on her self-righteous elbows.

I furrow my brow because that's not the case at all. At least, it certainly isn't intentional. I just don't really . . . *want* to move things fast.

"I'm just busy," I respond, turning my head briefly to the side. I let my focus stray back to the gym floor, pausing on Hayden's back, his perfectly toned arms, broad shoulders, long legs. The boy is built for hands to roam around his skin. His hair flops around as he jogs, and I know there are a dozen freshmen girls in this gym just staring at it. I should want to run my fingers through it and grab hold tight. Yet somehow, I just don't. I think it's because Hayden and I know each other so well. At least, we've known each other for so long, and that's almost the same. I see the seventh grader underneath who got gum stuck in his braces and who spilled chocolate milk on my favorite backpack. That history, it's part of the reason I like him so much. Hayden is a comfortable home in the turmoil of my life, and I might just be his safe place, too.

Lola comes back up to join us by the time the game starts, and I can tell by the way her mouth is set tight that she didn't get much more than the one laugh out of tight-ass Cannon. I hold my hand out as she moves to sit on my other side and we squeeze each other.

"Don't take it personally. I seriously think that boy might be broken. You are beautiful," I say.

Her eyes soften and her bottom lip plumps with a pouty expression.

"Thanks, friend," she says, hugging my arm as she slides into the space next to me.

A roaring thunder brings all of us to our feet, and soon we're stomping on the bleachers to join the sound of our boys' squad circled on the floor, all taking one knee and bending forward as they slam their palms against the hardwood and shout out the letters P-R-I-D-E. When they all jump up at once, the crowd hoots with them. I'll get that part down for the next game, but I dig the spirit. It's fun.

Mr. Newsome's brother does the announcing for our school. He's retired military, and has one of those voices that booms. I've only ever heard him do the football games, so I'm not prepared for the fanfare he gives the basketball team. It's clear where his loyalties lie.

"Ladies and gentlemen, welcome to the Madhouse on Main, home of your District Seven defending champs, The Allensville Public Eagles!"

I'm surprised by the volume of my own screamed response. My hands cup my mouth to boost the volume as Coach Newsome announces the players on the other team. We're playing some Catholic school from the city, which means they're either going to suck or kick our asses. There's no in between when it comes to private school athletic talent.

So far, it looks like they have us on height. But every

single player just sorta looks lanky and easy to push over. Maybe I'm projecting my bias.

By the time he gets to announcing our team, I'm on my feet again and stomping along with the girls. Hayden and Tory get saved for the very end, which I'm guessing is a testament to how good they are. The same team chant follows each player's name, but when Tory's name and number gets said, there's a new chant that takes over, a long, deep-voiced *boo?*

"Why are they booing him?" Naomi asks.

I shake my head, having no idea. Everyone is cupping their mouths and making the same awful sound, but they seem so happy about it. Even his team is bellowing, and Tory seems to feed off it, skipping his way down the line of players and pounding fists with every one until he gets to his brother, where he stops so they both can jump high and bump chests.

Tory takes his spot at the end of the line, cracking his neck in both directions while someone plays Jay-Z on in the backdrop of the announcement of the rules and good sportsmanship. He's antsy, like a bull being held behind bars with a steak waving in front of him. His eyes are fixated on the nothingness at the center of the court, almost as though he's playing out the entire game in his mind. Where Hayden smiles, Tory growls. Everything about him is harder, meaner—cut with a sharp edge to keep people from getting too close.

Keep people from getting burned.

I will myself to look away, but before his form leaves my periphery entirely, his movement draws me back in. He reaches over his back and tugs at the collar of his warmup shirt, pulling it up and over his head in one smooth movement, his jersey underneath rising up enough to expose his entire abs and chest, and I feel flushed.

I'm sure the other girls noticed, too, but a quick glance to both sides doesn't reveal either of them to have a noticeable reaction. I laugh silently to myself—*at myself*. It's not as though I haven't admired both D'Angelo brothers before. Hell, half the town has. The reason our football car washes do so well isn't the cheer squad that lines up on the street corners holding signs, it's the two Italian-American boys with *oh-my-God* bods who wash anything that rolls in with their shirts off and their shorts slung low. I'm guilty for dropping several twenties at those car wash fundraisers.

I lean forward, crossing my arms over my knees while I bite on my thumb and bring my flared up cheeks under control. Before I get comfortable, though, the crowd stands for the national anthem, so I'm stuck with the guilty color on my cheeks. I dart my glance in all directions but Tory's, like a petty thief covering my tracks, but I doubt anyone realizes it but me.

The student running the sound set up at the front table slips a few times while moving his phone close to the mic. It's such an embarrassing rigged-up system, no doubt dwarfed by the tech over at the private school we're playing against. But that's what Allensville is—a place where you take what you have and find a way to make it work.

I settle my gaze back on the line of boys as the music finally crackles out of our decade-old speakers. The hot red blood that was pushed to the very top of my cheeks is almost back where it should be when Tory comes into view, sucking the calm from my chest with one glance and replacing it with searing hot sin. I'm overcome with guilt because one body width to his right stands the boy I'm dating, his brother. But my eyes are locked here, and I'm sure Hayden can tell. Tory doesn't blink, not once through the nearly two minutes it takes for the Star Spangled Banner to play. His body vibrates with his home-brewed energy and his chin tips more than once in what I imagine is a silent acknowledgement that he sees me staring at him and intends to remember that I did. I wonder whether it's evidence to hold against me down the road or for his own personal ego gain. None of the nonsense in my head can force me to turn away, though.

Tory's lips part just as the song winds down and a slight curve forms in his mouth, dimpling his cheeks. Rather than run scared, I make the same face at him, because really . . . he's looking at me, too. This forbidden flirting game is a two-way street that we are both driving on dangerously.

I could almost convince myself that I'm imagining this were it not for the slight titter as he clearly nods at me before turning his back and huddling with his team. Once cut loose from his stare, I'm suddenly aware that Lola and Naomi probably noticed my little game of chicken. I have milliseconds to clean it up before it becomes a big deal.

"He is such a punk," I say with a shake of my head, confident my girls will instantly agree.

"He has always wanted to get with you. He's probably just jealous." Lola spills first, standing to adjust her jeans along her hips. She steps down one row to turn and face me and Naomi, her hands on her hips.

"He just likes the game. It's so annoying. Hayden is nothing like him," I add, meaning every word. Tory has always loved the game. I don't think I've been to a single party over four years of high school madness where he hasn't tried to get me to make out with him. A person doesn't keep coming back for the rejection if they don't like to play. And his lame pick-up attempts over the years have been so annoying. Hayden was so adult about it all—so easy. We were hanging out on the bleachers at school having one of our long talks when he reached out and took my hand in his, looked me in the eyes and said, "I really like you." How simple is that? I said it back, we kissed, and when he called me his girlfriend to the lady at the diner the next day, all of the noise in my heart and head just stopped. One two-minute stare down with Tory, though, and a hive of bees are swarming in my chest.

This guy named Danny, who has always been the tallest kid in school, matches up against the big guy for Vanguard (that's the name of the private school, I guess. Or it's their mascot. I can't tell for sure, but it's the only thing people from their school are yelling.) Danny wins the tip-off easily, pushing the ball in the air straight into Tory's hands. This is where everything aggressive in his fabric takes over and drives. Watching him work with his brother out there on the court is like watching a pair of ice dancers. They have this unspoken choreography that plays out on the floor, from one quick pass to another until Tory launches the ball in the air for Hayden to grab and hammer home. People are on their feet as the twins manage to score six straight points in less than a minute, and I find myself shouting Tory's name as he makes a steal and races down the court. Everyone expects an encore of the last shot, where he fed his brother under the hoop and Hayden laid it in with a gentle finger roll, but that's just what Tory wants. Everyone barrels down the court, but he stops short, giving him just the edge he needs to set up and catapult the ball in the air with the smoothest body movement I've ever seen. I'm not sure whether everyone has gone silent or I've temporarily lost the ability to hear, but the only sound that accompanies my view of Tory's ball soaring in a perfect arc is my hitched breath, which I hold midway for good luck. The net swishes with his three-point shot, and the players on the bench go absolutely nuts. Tory's signature smirk crawls up into his cheek as he turns, and for a brief moment our eyes meet and I get an overwhelming sense that he's showing off . . . *for me.*

The complete dominance doesn't last forever, and by the time the first quarter ends, we're only up by six. With my focus back where it should be, I stand and take advantage of the short break between quarters, tagging along with Lola to search for something sweet at the snack bar. I give her money while she stands in line and then rush to the dimly lit restroom, happy to find it completely empty.

It's here, in the last stall of the gym lobby women's restroom, that the first hint of something ominous finds my ears. I only recognize it because of the nightmares I've had most of my life. The deep moan that the wind makes—as though it's alive, when a thunderstorm like this one crawls along the Indiana landscape—is undeniable. The forecast said rain, and it's December, so this sound is unexpected —*unwelcome.* The last tornado to touch down remotely near Allensville in December happened eleven years ago.

It sounded just like this.

I finish my business quickly, rushing my hands under the sink water, and kicking open the door with a flourish that cracks the handle against the wall outside. My pulse is thumping throughout my entire body, but the beat is loudest in my head. It's annoying because right now, more than any time ever in my life, I need to hear. My ears are the one sense I can count on against the dark sky outside.

I pop open the side door and breathe in the moisture, the air thick with dirt and destruction. A rumble echoes along the ground, different from thunder. This sound can be felt; the earth is being moved by nature, and the beast is coming for us.

"Tornado!" I scream over my shoulder, disobeying all the rules of calm civility I've been taught through every storm drill we've practiced at this school. That shit is out the window, because that wind is picking up, and the whistle is getting steadier—louder.

Lola is the first to react, dropping the pretzel and cheese she just spent a few bucks on before rushing over to see what I'm seeing.

"She's right! Shelter!" Her voice crackles with panic. My voice disappears.

The next few seconds happen in blinks. I'm rushing toward the middle of the gym. Players are pushing, and whistles are blowing.

"Hey!" One of the referees grabs my arm, but his grip loosens the second more shouts echo my initial warning. His admonition quickly turns into crisis management as he motions me toward the double doors on the other end of the gym. His whistles morph into the kind that guide people where to go, and order in this chaos still feels achievable.

And then the lights flicker.

That's when the screaming begins, somewhere along my route to the school's storm shelter, a large, concrete corridor with zero windows and emergency lights buried in the walls. A blur of purple jerseys, the ones worn by the Vanguard team, surrounds me as their team runs past to safety, and a stray elbow cracks my nose with enough force that I'm instantly dizzy and on my ass.

The hit was hard enough that I might have passed out if it weren't for the straight-up terror coursing through my veins. I manage to stumble to my knees when I'm instantly swept up in someone's arms.

"I'm bleeding," I mutter, my hand awkwardly assessing my nose. I expect a gush, but miraculously it's only a few spots on my palm.

"You're okay," the familiar voice says.

My hand flattens against the chest of my rescuer, over the emblazoned number 2, damp with sweat with a wildly kicking heart underneath. I look up enough to see Tory's worried eyes scanning for a way in. Too many people cram into one opening, and the lights have completely gone out. The backups will kick on, but not right away.

Tory bypasses the crowd still pushing to enter the tight hallway, running with me against his chest toward the men's locker room. He pushes it open with his foot and weaves around rows of lockers and tiled walls until we're in the center of the cluster of showers. He sets me down in front of a main pipe, and I wrap my hands and legs around it on instinct. He crouches down with me, his body cocooning mine while he reaches around my body and grabs the same pipe with both hands. The heavy weight of his head leans into the back of mine, and for the first time ever, I hear fear in his ragged breathing.

"It'll pass soon," I say, somehow able to get words to leave my quaking lips.

He doesn't give me a verbal response, but I feel him pull in tighter around me. I do the same, and within seconds we're practically one with the metal pipe that runs deep into the ground. The vibration against the palm of my hands is making me numb, but worse—I can no longer hear the screams from other students in the gym or nearby hallway. The storm, it's too loud.

A large branch, or perhaps a piece of a nearby building, crashes against the heavy metal door that leads outside, and I flinch. Tory's hands slide from above and below where mine are gripping to cover mine. His hands are nearly double the size of mine, his fingers filling in the gaps where I wrap around the pole, locking me against the metal. His head shifts just enough to bring his chin over my shoulder, and strangely, he begins to hum. I focus on the sound, learning the tune as he gives it to me in faltering bits and pieces. It's vaguely familiar, and I've found my breathing has started to follow along.

"So, hoist up the John B's sail," he sings in a soft murmur. If I didn't know how scared he was, I'd assume he's nervous. He shouldn't be; his singing voice, even this soft, is really nice.

"See how the main sail sets," he continues, this time the faintest touch of his lip brushing against my ear. It isn't on purpose, but every single nerve in my body tunes in as my skin reacts with a rush of pebbles that trail down my arms and legs.

The wind is crying outside our walls, and panic takes hold of my emotions. I shudder out cries as more debris smacks against the walls outside, but Tory continues to hum his sweet song against my ear. His voice shakes every so often, but nothing deters him from keeping up the rhythm and pace.

And then it happens.

There's a difference in the way his mouth touches my exposed neck. It's purposeful, even if feather light. There's a taste taken with his lips, and he lingers for longer than a second, long enough for him to consider what his lips should do next. I'm frozen, less scared of the storm for this brief moment and more afraid of what's happening and the question beating down my conscience. *Do I want it to continue?*

As if he can read my thoughts, Tory's head tilts just enough to remove his mouth from my skin, the cool spot left from his lips drawing all my focus. The wind seems to be at its peak, a relentless hiss beating its way inside. Fear crawls back inside my chest, and Tory's body rocks me side to side in slow movements, as if we're lost at sea.

"Call for the captain ashore, let me go home . . ." His voice is a little stronger with this part and I blurt out a short laugh mixed with tears at the sentiment in his words.

"I want to go home!" I shout as the building quakes around us and we both start laughing hysterically, a mania taking hold in the moment.

"You know this song?" His voice is loud at my ear.

He seems so happy that I recognize whatever this is that I shout back, "Sure!"

The heavy patter of rain fills in the gaps left behind as the wind shifts direction, the destruction headed somewhere else. As the pounding subsides, Tory shifts enough to check my face, but his arms are still locking me down, his muscles still flexed as if ready to hold us both to the earth.

"You're such a bullshitter," he says, his voice raspy and mixed with laughter that's probably leftover from the massive dose of adrenaline.

"Thanks, and I'm glad you survived, too!" I bite back.

"No, the song. You have no idea what that is," he explains, finally easing his grip and scooting back enough for me to unglue myself from the pipe.

I stand, ass damp from the shower-wet floor, which I guess is a small price to pay for not losing the roof over our heads. I glance down and meet his sideways look and crooked smile as he stills with legs outstretched and palms flat behind him.

"You seemed so excited that I knew it, so I went along."

I smile and extend a hand to help him to his feet, and he studies my palm for a few seconds with an amused look on his face. I'm about to rescind the offer for help when his eyes flit to mine and he grasps my hand, barely using it to get to his feet. His hold is firm, and he doesn't let go right away, the pressure of his thumb against my knuckle bringing the raised bumps back to life along my neck and spine.

"Are you okay?" Tory steps close enough to have to look down at me from his height. My stomach tightens and

I'm not sure whether it's because he's got me feeling strangely nervous or because of the question he just asked. I haven't heard those three words in a very long time, from anyone, about anything.

"I will be," I say, which isn't the answer I meant to utter at all, but it's the one that's honest.

His slight smile remains, even as his lips close tight and his eyes wrinkle at the sides with thought. The bustling of students and parents and players filing out of the hallway adjacent to us draws his attention behind me briefly, and I take that opportunity to glance at our still connected hands. I shouldn't be holding his hand like this. The acceptable time has passed. I'm not fighting to get free, though.

"I liked it, the song," I say, bringing his attention back to me. He shakes his head with confusion and our hands naturally part. Perhaps both of us realize that things were venturing into awkward territory.

"Come on, people will be worried if they don't see us," he says, his hand pressing softly against the center of my back, directly over his brother's number.

"Sloop John B, by the way. That song I was singing? Beach Boys version, not the really old folk version." There's a giddiness in his tone when he talks about the song as we find our way back to the door leading into the gym. I had no idea about this side of him.

"You have a great voice," I say, squeezing out one more compliment before we go back to trading snarky insults in public.

His feet stop briefly and I jump, nervously afraid he's

seen something bad. When I catch the expression on his face, though, I realize I'm the one who surprised him.

"Thanks. My dad played that on the guitar when we were kids. It's the one song he taught me that I really mastered." A proud grin pushes into his cheeks, but it's fleeting as he's still racked with nervous energy.

"Maybe you'll play it for me sometime."

Those are the last words I get out before we open the locker room door and step into the panic and mess. The gym is intact, mostly, though a large section of the metal roof is either missing or bent. It's hard to tell with the harsh glow of the emergency lights. The floor is soaking wet, and people are shouting random names in search of each other. It's chaos, and I find myself drifting silently through the midst of it with Tory at my side.

I don't hear my name being called, but I recognize the way it's formed on Hayden's lips as he rotates slowly, scanning the crowd with his hands cupping his mouth. His face is pale, and his eyes are deep, dark circles. He's like a ghost of himself, a shadow left in the wake of a rare December tornado. When he spots me, he rushes in my direction and instantly folds me in his arms. I can't understand the words he's muttering into the top of my head, and I don't feel settled at all. If anything, I somehow feel more scattered than when the wind was threatening to tear down the walls. I also feel guilty, because the only thing playing through my mind is the slow hum of that sweet song and my inappropriate hope that Tory might sing it to me again.

7

TORY

Hayden and I spend most of the morning clearing the debris from Mom's front yard. Somehow, the damage from last night's surprise twister is minimal. The gym roof is the worst of it, along with flooding in some classrooms, and the shingles on the nearby Coffee Shack. It's enough to cancel school for the day, until they figure out where to put the displaced teachers.

The rest of the damage was sustained by the old maple trees that line the entire main drag through town—fifty or sixty years' worth of growth wiped out in five minutes. When I drove in to meet up with June and Lucas for lunch, I counted maybe six still standing out of the more than twenty that should be. Most of the businesses look fine; the streets are messy as hell.

I'm a few minutes late, and it looks as though my friends have already ordered and gotten their food, which is fine because really, I just came to talk.

I slide into the booth to join them and dive right into the meat of my problems.

"I fucked up."

June and Lucas don't even flinch.

"Did you guys hear me?"

Both of them are staring down at their bowls of pasta. I've been eating at this joint my entire life and I know the pasta here is shit. They're teaming up on me, which is seriously irritating.

"Hey!" I smack my palm on the table between their two drinks. June flinches and drops her fork, quickly running a napkin over her mouth to clean the splatter of sauce left behind. Lucas merely glances up, still masticating the world's worst penne.

"We're listening." June clears her throat and sets her napkin to the side, folding her hands on the table in front of her. After a few seconds she elbows Lucas, and he huffs, but sets down his fork and pushes his bowl away.

"Yeah, what she said. We're listening," he says with a preteen-girlish roll of his eyes.

"Wow. I didn't realize I was such a burden. I mean, it's not like I didn't spend the last three months listening to both of your bullshit." I move to slide from the booth, but Lucas juts out his leg and leans forward with a stiff arm, staring me down.

"Relax, dude."

I glare at him for a hard second, still considering barreling through his barrier and jetting out of here, but then who'd I have to talk to about this? I breathe out long and hard but slide my way back into the booth, centering myself across from them.

"We didn't mean it," June starts, but before her apology gets wings, Lucas makes sure it crashes and burns.

"Speak for yourself," he cuts in. "I meant it. Tor, you've been telling us the same thing for the last five days. It's this endless circle of 'I wasn't really that into her' followed by 'I really blew my chance.' Just . . . pick one."

By the time Lucas is done, June's glare at him does the job so I don't have to. When he slowly turns to meet her gaze he flinches a little in his seat.

"What? You know I'm right."

June just shakes her head then turns her attention back to me.

"Anyway, please, Tory. You can talk to us, or *me* at least," June says. Lucas snorts out a laugh and shakes his head, pulling out his phone to scroll through social media.

June waves her hand to bring my attention solely to her. I take another deep breath and shift in my seat, leaning forward on my elbows and resting my forehead into my hands so I can knead away at my temples.

"I'm guessing you haven't talked to Abby." I stop rubbing my head long enough to raise my brow and glance up at June.

She tilts her head sideways and squints her eyes.

"I have not." Her voice sounds suspicious.

"Okay, maybe I'm not fucked, then," I say, leaning back into the soft, squishy padded back and let my shoulders sag. Damn, they were up to my ears tense.

"You're going to have to give me details if you want my advice, Tory." June's method has always been no-nonsense. I think it's kinda why we clicked all of a sudden. She's helped me get my shit together more than she realizes. We both assist Coach Newsome's class for our last hour, which means we basically sit in the back and do whatever. I don't think June would let me out of that room, though, without checking to make sure I actually did my homework or studied for whatever test is coming up. This might just be the first semester I pull off a 4.0.

"Things got pretty chaotic at the game last night, with the tornado and shit. Everyone was running toward the back hallway, through those main doors—you know the ones?"

June nods, and Lucas puts his phone down—I guess he's over his pouty fit and ready to listen.

"Abby was there watching the game, and in the rush, she took an elbow to the nose. She was a little stunned and getting pushed around so I picked her up and took her with me." I sound like a fucking hero if I stop the story here, and given the way June's looking at me, I'm half tempted.

"Seems like the human thing to do, man," Lucas says.

"And then I took her into the locker room. Alone." I'm unable to finish before Lucas pipes in again.

"Aww, shit!" He laughs, holding a fist to his mouth as if that somehow mutes it.

"Not like that, dude. Just, fucking listen, all right?" I scold him.

"Sure, yeah." He snickers. June gives him another elbow.

"Thank you," I say to her, recalibrating myself to finish the story and get to the hard part. I crack my neck to the side and bring both of my hands together and rest them on the table. "There were so many people cramming through that space, I was afraid we weren't going to get inside in time. It was the first thing I could think of, because of the pipes."

"Okay, might be a bit of a stretch, since those pipes only go down a foot or so, but whatever." Lucas adds his color commentary. I shoot him a look and keep going.

"We were both holding on and she was so freaked out, and maybe I was too, so I started . . . like . . . humming this song that calms me down and shit."

The snort that leaves Lucas's nose is epic, only outdone by the cackling laugh that actually forces him to hold his hand over his chest. June pushes him toward the window, to the other end of their seat, but he laughs right through her efforts. She eventually gives up and leaves her boyfriend's side of the booth and takes my hand, dragging me to a table and chairs on the other end of the diner.

"Oh, come on!" Lucas shouts. June holds up a flat palm.

"I'll deal with him later," she says, her eyes square on mine. There isn't an ounce of judgement in her expression.

I swallow.

"I'm not gonna lie, I was scared, too. The walls were buzzing, and the emergency lights were a joke. All I could feel was her body shaking, and I just sorta . . . started . . . singing."

"You sing?" June whisper shouts.

I level her with narrowed eyes and tight lips.

"Right, sorry," she says, clearing her throat. "Continue."

I squirm a little in my seat because this next part, this is the part that's bad. June is like my church, though, the place I can come to repent and ask forgiveness, so I hit her with the truth.

"I was holding her against my chest, kinda from behind, and her hair smelled like apricots or fruit or something, and her neck was wide open, and it just felt like I should rest my chin on her shoulder."

Her eyes sag and her bottom lip protrudes, her face turning into that one girls make when they have to leave a puppy.

"The first time was totally an accident," I say, skipping ahead.

She shakes her head quickly and twirls her finger, signaling for me to rewind. I sit back in my chair and slink down, stretching my legs out and leaning to one side with my arm slung over the back.

"I was keeping my mouth so close to her ear because I wanted her to hear me. I thought maybe it would calm her or whatever. It was like a graze, I guess."

"A graze," June repeats, her mouth all twisted in disappointment. I may as well spill it now.

"Yeah, that one was a graze. Then I fucking kissed her neck." I shrug under the heat of her blistering glare. "I told you. I fucked up."

"Oh, Tory." Her voice is low, but not angry. It's the goddamned pity again.

"I know." I huff, standing and rounding the chair. I'm about to push it in when a waitress walks up with a glass of water and a straw for me.

"Oh, you're not staying?" The girl looks familiar, sophomore class maybe. I don't want to look like a jerk, so I grab the back of the seat I just left and look down to regroup. I manage to shift my frustrated scowl into something more pleasant, lifting my chin and flashing her the biggest smile I can muster.

"Just heading to the restroom. Give me a burger, cheddar, and skip the side." I keep my mouth locked in the tight-lipped smile while she sets down my water and scribbles my pretty basic order on her pad. I think maybe she's new here; I should tip her good. I blink a few times, silently counting the seconds, until she looks back up at me and tells me my food will "be right up."

There's a happy sway to her hips that bobs her ponytail from side-to-side as she walks away and I laugh lightly before returning my gaze to June. "Why couldn't I get stuck on a girl like that?"

"Because she just got her driver's license and you're narrowing down your college choice," June replies.

I point at her and nod in agreement, then excuse myself to the restroom to follow through with my charade. My hair is a mess, having rushed from yard work to the diner without a break in between. I spend a few minutes at the sink, soaking my hands and running my fingers through my hair, wishing like hell I had a hat. I'd dry my hands on the front of my shirt, but now that I glance down at it, there's dirt all over the front. I grab a towel from the dispenser and pat my hands dry before taking the towel to my shirt to clear some of the dirt off and, *what the—?* My pants are worse. Who am I? I bend at my waist and brush along the seams of my joggers, actual leaves and twigs getting knocked to the floor.

"Ha." I laugh out loud at myself.

I give up when major chunks of nature are no longer

stuck to me, and wad the towel into a ball and toss it across the room into the trash bin. Guilty or not, I do feel lighter now that I've bared my soul to June. I'll just go back and take her lecture or her advice on how to get over crushes—*like she ever did*—and then I'll go home and crash face down in my sheets to make up for the zero sleep I got last night. I tossed and turned with stress for seven hours, and I was pretty close to barging into Hayden's room and begging him either for forgiveness or his girlfriend. The end goal changed every ten minutes.

The bathroom door opens with surprising ease and I almost crack heads with the person coming in while I'm exiting.

"Oh, shoot!"

There's a strange element to being a twin that people don't talk about. Even when you're used to it, it's still surprising to look right back at yourself. I had a slight warning, though, because *shoot* is a total Hayden word.

His palm grasps my shoulder hard, and at first I prepare myself for a fist in the jaw, but he shakes me instead.

"Damn, you scared me," he says, gripping his hand to his chest. He's all cleaned up, a nice white T-shirt and jeans. It's kinda like we traded places during the tornado, like one of those movies, only I'm still stuck wanting his girl and he's still got her. All I got was his frumpy-ass look while he got my style.

"Sorry. Hey, I didn't know you were coming." I scratch at my head as I swap places with him, stepping out while he steps in.

"Yeah, so much for a day off, I guess," he says.

"We've got practice?" My face screws up with surprise because Coach texted us all this morning, telling us to work out and do sprints for the next two days and be ready to hit the gym at the junior high on Thursday. Ours is basically a shipwreck.

"Nah, I picked up a shift, and Mom gave me her car," he says. It's then that I notice the infamous red weenie shirt clutched in his fist. "First official day on the job!"

"Nice. I'll let you change," I say with a quick smile to excuse myself.

My back barely turned, Hayden catches the door.

"Oh, and Abby came with. We were going to hang but then, duty calls! She thought maybe you'd be up for running lines? If not, it's cool. I can take her home."

I don't want to turn around. If I do, I'm either going to tell him that the phrase *duty calls* means he has to take a shit, or I'm going to massively fail at bluffing as I stammer my way through an excuse to avoid being alone with Abby.

"Sure," I say, because of the third option—the one where I *want* to spend time with her and I can play loyal as long as my back is turned.

"Cool. I'll be home around nine, I guess."

I hold up a thumb and walk away, mentally doing the math on the number of hours left before nine. It's barely twelve-thirty.

I get back to the booth where things started, my burger probably still several minutes away from being ready. Abby is twisting where she stands, eyes on the spot where her gym shoe digs at the floor. She's dressed for the gym in tight black leggings and a black workout tee, a white long-sleeved shirt tied around her waist. Unlike me, she's got her hair tucked neatly under a hat, and I can't help but wonder if that's so she can hide underneath the brim.

"I guess I'm driving you back to our place?" My words come out convincingly nonchalant, but June reads below the surface. My friend shakes her head at me slowly, a warning I ignore as I fish out my wallet and toss a twenty on the table. "Just take my burger home. I'm not hungry anyway."

"I'll eat it," Lucas says, winking at me. Clearly, June filled him in on the details he missed. "I'll probably be over in an hour too. I don't mind doing my own thing while you guys study or whatever it is."

"Run lines," Abby corrects. She tips her head up sharply and her eyes shift from Lucas to me, but they're impossible to read. Maybe I'm overreacting, because I could swear she's her usual self, short-tempered and pretentious, and appalled that Lucas wouldn't understand her world.

"Right, study," Lucas says, just to be a dick. I chuckle, mostly to fit in but also because that was funny.

"Ready?" Abby's entire body has turned to face me, and she's completely void of tension, at least it seems so on her end. I, however, am an impossible knot.

"Sure, yeah," I say, picking up my water cup and gulping down half of it. I set it back on the table and clutch my keys in my pocket, nodding toward the door. Abby walks away first, not bothering to wait for me, and I breathe out a laugh as I follow, a little thankful for the normalcy.

"So, see you at one?" Lucas calls after us.

That's hardly an hour. It's less than thirty minutes from now. But I know he should show up. If he's there, everything will stay above board, maybe even my imagination. If he doesn't show, I might get all sappy and shit and pull out my guitar.

"Sounds good, bruh." I hold up my hand as I push through the door, the tiny bell ringing at the top as I leave. I'm pretty sure that means June gets her wings.

8

ABBY

S *tick to the plan, Abby.*

I woke up with a renewed sense of business as usual when it comes to Tory D'Angelo and me. If only he'd participate in said plan. This works much better when he acts like a dog, tossing out misogynistic jokes while acting like every girl wants him.

Every girl does want him.

I sense he's trying, though. His cocky swagger is only at mid-strength. He called the guy with the double-sized spoiler and whirring muffler who tried to race us a douche, then laughed when the guy had to stop short because a minivan pulled out in front of him. Other than that, he's acting as if I'm not sitting here, a foot away from him in his bucket seat.

I kiss his brother sitting in this seat. What am I thinking? What am I doing? Why am I even dating someone? I'm not emotionally equipped for this stuff.

We get to the main drag of town and traffic halts, a line

of twenty or more cars in front of us. Tory rolls down his window and climbs halfway out from his seat, sitting on the ledge. I lean toward the middle of our seats as if somehow, I can see better from here.

"They're removing some of the downed trees. Looks like they're almost done," he says, slipping back inside before I have a chance to move away. His brows draw in a little and his mouth sits on the cusp of laughter as our eyes meet.

"You wanna have a look?" He points over his shoulder and out his window.

"*Pfft.*" I huff, glowering before blinking my gaze back to the windshield and situating myself away from him again. This little tiff almost feels normal. If only I didn't know that his stare was loitering on the side of my face. Every breath I take has thought behind it, knowing he's watching. I work to hold my mouth in check, my face expressionless, despite the burning sensation of his eyes staring at my lips. My pulse is racing, and I'm getting hot even though it's forty degrees outside and the heater in this car is shit. A perfect storm of my mood triggers clashes in my chest, and finally, I just snap.

"Can't you just go around?" I jerk my head to face him, catching the twitch in his eyes. I think he's both nervous I caught him staring and jumpy at my tone. I sounded mean just now. I'm fucking hot, and . . . confused. And I want out of this car.

My hand moves toward the door handle with my panicked thoughts, and on impulse I push my door open a few inches.

"What, are you gonna go help them hurry things along,

lumberjack Abby?" Tory adds in a wry smile and I tug my door closed again, crossing my arms in a humph as I fall back into the seat. His laughter grows, but he glances up at the rearview mirror and then over his shoulder, flipping on his turn signal.

"Hang on. I know a way around." He hangs a quick U-turn, then speeds back past the diner, where June and Lucas are just getting in Lucas's truck. The minivan is gone, so Hayden must have already rushed off to work. He was pretty excited about his first day, and even more excited about a paycheck in a few weeks.

"How come you don't have a job?" I ask.

Tory doesn't answer right away, and at first, I think maybe he didn't hear me, but as he checks the mirror again, I note his grimace and pinched brow. My question came out kinda judgmental, I guess. It's not like I have a real job, either. I have gigs, and all of this sort of fell in my lap. My dad signed me up for a summer acting class when I was six, mostly to get me out of the house, but I got hooked. That little class registration, of course, is the cornerstone of his legal argument for deserving a portion of my company. I think the summer fee might have been thirty-five bucks.

Tory makes a sharp turn into an older neighborhood where most of the homes have front porches and cute yards with huge trees now barren for winter. Flower beds are all emptied for the freeze, but you can see the outlines where they probably bloom bright reds and yellows in the spring. Winding pathways lead to swings and sitting areas where kids no doubt run through sprinklers while parents drink lemonade. I've always wanted to live in a house like one of these. I crave that Hallmark lifestyle. Maybe I just crave a normal family.

"I should be spending my free time on basketball," Tory finally says, drawing my attention back to the driver's seat. His eyes are hazed as he stares at the road ahead, and while my first reaction is to be defensive under the assumption that he's talking about me taking up his free time, I realize he's alluding to something deeper.

"You guys are going to get back in the gym, right?"

There's a long pause before his answer, and I wonder if he's thinking about last night, too. Less about the disaster and more about . . . us.

Tory leans his weight to the side and rests one hand on the steering wheel, wincing.

"We'll be in the junior high gym until the new year, which is lame as hell. You know I dunked there in eighth grade?" He flashes a child-like smile at me, and I get that while he's being funny, he's also sorta bragging about it.

"Wow. Big time," I tease.

Maybe I don't have to be *quite* so cold with him. It feels as if we're in a new place, friendship-wise. It happened with June, so perhaps we're all coming around to each other and maturing.

"It's been hard to focus, with all of the drama. I'm sure you get an earful from Hayden, and I'm fine, so let's talk about you." He glances my way with a tight-lipped grin that tells me his last little bit was complete bullshit. He's not fine at all.

"You know, it's not like I have a set number of hours to hear about people's struggles. If you need to talk, I can listen to you, too," I say.

"Nah, it'd be like reading the same book twice, back-to-back. Who does that?" he says with a snort laugh.

I stare at him and blink slowly, my mind picturing the book on my nightstand that I'm reading right now—the second time through. He does a quick double take when he realizes I'm staring at him, and by his third glance, he gets it.

"Oh, shit. You do that? I'm sorry. I mean . . . that's cool. What do I know? I read *Sports Illustrated*." He shrugs and looks back to the road.

"You look at the swim suit issue," I crack.

His body shakes with quiet laughter and he eventually nods.

"Yeah, I do."

I muse at his humility. It's rather charming, which is the opposite of the objective I set. I'm not supposed to find Tory likeable. The plan is to aim for tolerable. But likeable goes with friendship, so maybe I can shift my end goal.

"Hey, if you want, we can trade. You can run lines with me, and I'll play you some one-on-one." I throw this out there not to flirt, because Tory knows damn well that I am not athletic in the least.

He blurts out a quick laugh.

"Yeah, okay, Abby."

His eyes soften when he says my name, and I feel it in the dead center of my chest. Time to move that goal line back where it was.

With only a mile or two left until we reach his house, we spend the last few minutes letting the radio fill in the dead air in the car. It's nothing but commercials for pot roast sales at the grocery store, snow tires at DJ's Pit Crew, and a laundry list of side effects for some drug that helps you keep your hair. I'm thankful when we pull in the driveway and see Lucas's truck.

He's already pulled a ball out of Tory's garage and is shooting hoops in his driveway as we pull in. A pile of branches and debris forms a mountain near the street, and I survey the new bare spots in the D'Angelo front yard before Tory shuts off his car. His house seems intact from here. We lost a patio cover, but it was basically only a board held up by two crooked posts, so I'm shocked it didn't fly away sooner.

We both get out and Tory jogs over to his friend, stealing the ball from him and palming it in one hand to dunk it easily. He's graceful in the air.

"Dude, how'd you get here so fast?" Tory asks. He punts the ball and catches it off the bounce, then passes it back to Lucas. I lean on the back of Tory's car, dropping my purse between my feet, to watch boys be boys.

"They got Main all cleared right after you took the detour," Lucas says. "We saw you guys drive by. Dropped June off on the way, and maybe, just maybe, I sped a little to beat you here."

"Just a little, huh?" Tory slaps the ball from Lucas's hands again and jogs to the end of his driveway, putting up a shot that bangs off of the rim.

"Oh, so close," Lucas teases.

Tory flips him off, then moves my direction.

"Come on, let's go see what this movie you're in is all about," he says.

I grab my purse, noting how Lucas isn't far behind as we march into the garage and enter through the back kitchen door. I sense that Lucas is trying to protect Tory from me. Or maybe to watch Hayden's back, like I'm some super predator out to double-cross twin hotties.

Shit. Am I?

Tory stops at the fridge, bending over and reaching in deep for a bottle of water. He offers one to me, which I take, then holds up another for Lucas.

"I'm good. Mind if I hit up your PlayStation?" He's already flopped on the couch and turned on the TV.

Tory's glare shifts from Lucas to me and he shakes his head slightly.

"I don't even need to answer that, I guess," he says.

A laugh puffs out as I take my first drink from the water bottle. Tory nods to my purse, where I've stashed the script I have to memorize. I've actually got a lot of the early part down. I read it over and over every night, picturing the scenes in my head. My mind works like a movie in many ways, where I can visualize something as if I've already seen it. It's like memorizing your favorite parts of movies, only this one hasn't been made yet.

I pull the script out and plop it on the counter. Tory spins it around and reads through the direction. He flips through the first few pages, eventually setting his water down and taking the script in both hands as he leans back against the opposite counter. I slide into an open stool and sit on my hands, which are suddenly super clammy.

"So, your character—" he questions.

"Roni," I fill in. "Veronica, but Roni for short."

"Got it." He nods.

I wait while he reads on, getting a good ten pages in before flipping back to the opening scene. I'm the first thing people see in this film, assuming this part doesn't get left on the editing room floor. It's a tough scene, where Roni is smoking crack with two guys from her high school, her inner dialogue about how she's tired of her mom's boyfriend abusing her.

"This is some fucked up shit," he says, pinching the bridge of his nose and squeezing his eyes shut. "I thought you said this was a romantic comedy?"

"It gets funny near the end," I deadpan.

Tory's eyes pop open and he stares at me for a solid second before laughing.

"Jordan Shotcraft, huh? Yeah, I guess I can see it. His stuff is always this mix of serious and light." He drops his chin and his eyes scan the first page again in silence. Eventually, he looks back up at me, a crooked smile playing at his mouth.

"You know you're going to be stupid famous after this, right?" He rubs the back of his neck as he glares at me with one squinted eye. I'm oddly not very good at dreaming big. I take big breaks one at a time, never expecting them. It keeps me sheltered from disappointment. Landing this role was a big deal, but in my gut, I still expect something to go wrong—movie shelved, me replaced mid-shoot, Jordan getting struck with some huge scandal that renders our movie a flop and sends me into obscurity.

I lift one shoulder, signaling a *whatever,* then deliver my first line.

"The drift to sleep comes on sweet and slow, like drinking molasses. I do this so the high erases all of the fucked up things in my life, like tar oozing over gravel."

My gaze drifts off to another place entirely. I'm not

secure enough in my lines yet to be able to look at Tory's face, and I kind of want to take on that feeling of being adrift mentally. After a few seconds pass without him reading anything, though, I'm forced to look at him.

"Oh!" He startles. "Sorry, I . . . just . . . damn!"

"Stop. I don't even know what I'm doing." My chest, though, flutters with butterflies at the compliment. I like that he thinks I'm a little bit good at this.

Tory's gaze sticks on my face for one beat too long, and I get up from my seat to pace, partly to run away from it. I take a few steps around the kitchen island and back while he reads more stage direction. It's an odd juxtaposition with the cacophony of gunfire barreling through the television a dozen or so feet away.

"Hey, Lucas? You mind maybe . . ." Tory cups his ears with both hands. Lucas gives him a blank stare, then jars himself when it dawns on him.

"Oh! My bad," he says, leaning over the arm of the couch and opening a drawer to pull out headphones. It takes him a minute or two to get them synced, and Tory whispers an apology to me while we wait, watching him wrangle with the Bluetooth settings. He gives us a thumbs up and we shoot the same gesture back.

"Jesus, he's a child," I mutter.

Tory laughs quietly.

"Don't tell June that," he says.

"I'm sure she knows. Anyhow, let's start from the cop's first line, yeah?" I pace again, feeling more in character this way, even though on screen I'll be nearly passed out on an abandoned couch in the middle of a fake desert for this scene.

"Hey . . . hey!" Tory gets into character for me, reaching out and shaking an imaginary shoulder.

"Go away, Paul! My mom doesn't want you touching me anymore!" I let loose now that Lucas isn't listening. Strangely, I have no problem watching my own work on-screen later, but having someone hear me deliver lines live and in person makes me sweat like a pig.

"Miss, I don't know who Paul is, but you're under arrest." Tory stands and makes his way closer to me. I freeze at the end of the island and turn my back to him slightly, putting both my hands behind my back, ready for his fake cuffing.

"Fuck you, Officer Friendly!" I slur my words and anticipate a timid touch to my wrists, but Tory grabs them firmly, wrapping one of his hands entirely around both my arms and tugging.

I shirk, both as part of my character and as a natural reaction to his aggressive touch. His hold on me loosens, but I push my arms harder into his palm, encouraging him to keep playing along. Now fully in character, I turn fast and force my face inches from his, my nose close enough to scrape along his cheek. The black in his eyes bleeds into the hazel of his irises, and his nostrils flare with a sharp breath.

"I said I'm done with strange men thinking they can touch me." I speak in a low growl, gritting my teeth and preparing myself to actually bite into Tory's shoulder. Before things get that far, though, his grip falls away from my wrists and he takes a step back, blowing out and running his palm through his hair.

"Damn, sorry. You . . . that was intense," he says,

flexing his hand—the one that held me forcefully—a few times at his waist.

Realizing how into it I was, I blush and retreat back to my stool.

"I'm sorry, I was just feeling it. I guess I know this part really well. We can probably skip ahead—"

"No, no. I just need to get some balls I guess and step up to your level." He shakes with a short laugh and rubs at his forehead while reading through the next few lines in the scene.

"I'm not so sure I want you to bite me, if that's cool?" His brow wrinkles while he reads ahead and gives me his request.

"Fair enough." I laugh out. "How about I stick to my seat and you stay on the other side of this thing?" I tap my long, freshly manicured nails on his counter, and he smirks with a nod.

"Deal," he agrees, jumping right back into the text.

We manage to get through my first six scenes in a little over two hours, and we're so absorbed with the story that we don't realize Lucas has pulled the headphones from his head and put his feet up on the couch to nap. Neither of us is sure whether he listened in for any of the performance, and the only reason we discovered Sleeping Beauty is because he snores like a donkey.

"Oh, my God! June is a saint," I say, slipping from my seat and moving closer to Lucas. His lips are actually vibrating with his breath.

"That's nothing. Back in junior high, he sleepwalked. Fucker showed up at our front door at two a.m. in nothing but these cartoon character briefs."

I cover my mouth to mute the laugh his story evokes.

"You're shitting me," I whisper.

Tory shakes his head.

"My dad took a picture, then drove him home. I still have it somewhere. I save that sucker for a rainy day, when I need to call in a *huge* favor."

"Well, then, you should probably find it," I say, suddenly desperate to see it for myself.

I make my way back into the kitchen, twisting the cap off of the new water bottle Tory gave me a few minutes ago. My throat is dry, and my brain is a little fried. Turns out rehearsing lines *is* a lot like studying.

"Hey," I blurt out, remembering a question I had for Tory but forgot to ask. "Why did you think I knew that song you were singing?"

I promised myself I wouldn't bring up our moment in the locker room, but I'm really curious. Maybe it's how good Tory was with his lines that made me think about him singing. He's amazingly natural at performing.

He smiles with his cheeks full of the water he just drank and holds up a finger while he pauses to swallow.

"You actually said the next line in the song. When you yelled, 'I want to go home'? That's the next line." That same music-nerd smile is back. I like this secret side to him.

"Shut up!" I look at him sideways.

He crosses his heart, but I keep my stare steady and my eyes slitted.

"Sing it again," I say, falling into another trap I promised myself I wouldn't. I shouldn't hear him sing again. Hearing it the first time is what stirred up all the weirdness in my head. Yet, I really hope he does.

"You know what? Come here." He motions his head toward the stairs and jogs up them, stopping midway to see if I'm following. I hesitate for a beat, but the temptation and the possibility that his guitar is upstairs are too strong.

We round the short wall that divides the stairs from a small loft space with floor-to-ceiling bookshelves, and Tory runs his thumb along a row of tightly packed albums. I take this opportunity to nose around his upstairs, a place I've never been, not even for one of their infamous parties. It's a strikingly modest home inside despite the grandeur of the outside façade. I guess it's the large open space in the living room where the fireplace towers up twenty feet, a monument of ivory rock with a massive rustic beam sliced through the middle for the world's most ostentatious mantle. The obligatory family portrait sits atop it, the twins maybe seven or eight in the photograph-turned-painting. I was a little surprised to still see it there when we walked in.

Up here, things are tighter, the space more intimate. This loft area has a built-in desk with a computer I assume Tory and Hayden have to share. Their school bags are both tossed in the corner, and phone cords poke out from a charging station on the wall. To the right is a set of double doors—I'm guessing the master bedroom—and behind me, on the opposite end of the house, above the garage, are two doors divided by a bathroom. I already know what Hayden's looks like. He took me on a video chat tour when we first started talking. His room is spotless, like a military man. Something tells me Tory's is probably on the other end of the spectrum.

"Found it!" His exclamation draws me back in. I step

closer as he pulls a record from a sleeve. There are probably a hundred or more albums organized on these shelves.

"Wow, this is some collection," I say as he tips the lid up on a sleek black turntable. Tory leans to his side and brings his eyes level with the record as he gently sets it down on the player. A small speaker tucked between a row of books crackles when he turns the device on, and he quickly turns the dial to keep the volume low.

"*Shhh,*" he says, holding a finger to his lips, then pointing toward the stairs where Lucas is still sawing dreamy logs.

"I don't think he could hear it at full volume over that racket he's making," I say.

Tory's smile is sweet, and he holds his soft gaze on me for a single blink of his eyes before returning his attention to the record, which is now spinning. He picks up the arm and rests it gently on his thumb, finally engaging it somewhere in the middle of the album. I recognize the melody almost instantly, not that I've heard this song more than once.

"Beach Boys, *Pet Sounds.* Maybe one of the greatest albums of all time." He grins after that statement, maybe expecting me to challenge him. I couldn't. My knowledge of music is limited. I could, however, debate him until Sunday on classic film.

"I think my dad likes this stuff," I say, falling for the sway of the melody. It sounds just as it did when Tory sang it, minus the threat of a tornado and plus the digital mastering of a music studio.

Tory clicks his tongue against his teeth and shuffles his feet closer to me, holding out a palm. I stare at it for a good, long, awkward while, but finally place my hand in his. He threads our fingers together and pulls me in, his other hand gingerly resting at my waist like a gentleman.

"Time for a music lesson," he says, careful to look anywhere but directly into my eyes. I'm thankful. This, so far, feels safe.

"School me, Salvatore," I say, sparking a short laugh from him.

"Your dad likes this stuff because this stuff is good. Music made in the sixties has backbone. Words mattered, and sound was a constant experiment. Most real music fans would list a dozen albums from this era on a best-of list before even touching something contemporary."

While he's looking away from me, I'm drawn to stare at his eyes. I have no idea who this is that I'm dancing with, but this is not the guy who hands me red cups at parties and asks me when we're gonna bang. This guy is . . . strange. He's interesting, and he has passions. Secret passions that beg the question—

"Why are you not doing something in music?" I ask. We rock slowly in an extremely chaste slow dance, and Tory merely flits his gaze to me, long enough to acknowledge my question.

He shrugs the shoulder that's under my hand as he looks away again.

"I like basketball more," he says.

I blink a few times, staring at the lashes of his too-near-to-me eyes while I wait for him to explain further. I realize soon, though, that it's that simple. He has a passion for his game and keeps music as a love.

"Huh," I say.

His eyes move to mine again, then leave immediately.

"*Huh,* what?"

"Huh, that you have, like, hobbies, I guess." I laugh through my nose. A slight shift in my body and a tiny step from him as we both laugh brings us closer, and suddenly my chin is resting on top of my own hand, which is now comfortable on his shoulder.

We turn together, our laughter silences. The song soothes, and if I could manage to hold myself up, I could fall asleep right here. This is not appropriate.

"Show me some of the others," I say, slipping out of his arms and moving my attention to the rows of albums on the shelves. He lets me go easily, probably glad I broke things up. I think maybe music can be a drug. I think maybe surviving a tornado with someone is a bit of a drug, too. That's it.

"What kind of music do you like?" he asks, pulling a few albums out sideways to peer at the covers, standing at the other end of the long row.

"Everything, I guess. I mean . . . I don't know. I guess I listen to what's popular." I kinda feel schooled standing in front of a collection like this.

"Well, when you were little, was there a song, maybe a hit, that you just *had* to *have* so you could play it over and over again?" His finger is teasing the corner of a silver album cover.

I suck in my lip and think back to junior high, and then the years before. I don't think my life really has a sound-track, and that's maybe a little sad. Before I realize it, my forehead is creased from the weight of my frown.

"You know what, let me try this," Tory says, letting me

off the hook. I step closer to peek at what he's pulling out, but he holds up his hand and shoos me away.

"Okay, fine," I relent, sitting down on the thick carpet in the center of the wooden floor. I let my fingertips pet the strands while Tory does his thing, carefully putting the first album away and blowing dust from the new one. He hovers over the player as he lowers the needle, and a familiar beat flows through the speakers. I nod with the rhythm as Tory kneels down and eventually sits facing me. He leans back, digging his hands into the plush cream rug and pulls his knees up, swaying them with the beat. As I stare at the dead leaf stuck on the knee of his pants, I smile; recognition is settling in.

"This . . . yes! My mom used to play this all the time on our way to auditions. She said it was her 'power jam!'" I exclaim. I sing along with a few of the words until I get to the title of the song in the chorus and Tory sings along with me.

"'Rhythm Nation'!"

He exhales a celebratory type of laugh, his head falling back as if he's proud to have unearthed another thing I like. Perhaps I have a soundtrack after all.

"My dad was *in love* with Janet Jackson. She came to the state fair when Hayd and I were like six or something, and he dragged us along. Hayden fell asleep but I stood on my chair and just watched my dad sing every word and stare at her like she was some goddess." His gaze drifts off, caught in his memory, and the longer he's gone away, the more I realize what these albums—what us playing them right now—is all about. He misses his dad, misses being a family.

"It will get easier," I say.

"Huh?" He stirs, shaking away the dust of wherever he'd been as he looks at me. "Oh, yeah, I know."

"I won't say it gets better; it doesn't. It just gets easier." I hold his stare and feel a little sorry that I maybe dashed a flicker of hope. "It's an amazing collection." I change the subject and look toward the bookcase again. Tory follows suit. A heavy breath lifts and collapses his chest.

"All of these are my dad's. If he leaves permanently, they'll go with him. But I won't be here anymore, I guess, so it's whatever." His gaze shifts to me for a beat, then to the floor. He sits forward and brings his hands to his lap as his legs fold together. Right now, we're two kids playing records, but the longer we sit in silence, Janet marching along in the backdrop, simple leaves the situation and complicated seeps in.

"My brother treating you right?" His head cocks his head to the side and his eyes level me with a look that feels like it's hiding more.

"Yeah," I say. Nervous energy jolts at my insides, so I shift my position and tuck my legs under my body, leaning to one side. I'm careful to keep my focus on the floor, on the albums, on my own fingers and knuckles and skin. The song fades out, a new one begins, and I rush around mentally in search of something new to say while also silently begging Tory to ask me easier questions than the ones I fear are dancing around his head.

"He's a good guy," he continues.

"Uh huh." I nod.

My pulse is drowning in my ears, the beat heavy, leaving me dizzy. I spare a quick glance up to meet Tory's gaze, hoping maybe he's looking elsewhere. Or maybe simply smiling, happy to see his brother happy. Me happy. But that's not what I get at all. My chest squeezes when our eyes lock, his mouth a soft smile that hints at regret. My lips part and I draw in a quick breath, thinking for a moment that I'll say something—*anything*—that acknowledges there is something unspoken and heavy in the room.

"Hey, I heard the music."

Lucas's welcome presence breaks the tension, and I take the out, climbing to my feet and putting more distance between Tory and me. Tory stretches out his legs and crosses them at the ankles, tipping his chin to grin at his friend.

"Just dusting off some of my dad's gems," he says.

He and Lucas seem to speak without words, staring at each other with knowing smiles that verge on the cusp of words, as if they're about to trade insults with each other or something.

"Right, well . . . I'm going to take off and thought since I'm leaving, maybe Abby needs a ride home?" Lucas turns his attention to me, his eyes wide in a way that signals I'm to leave now. It feels oddly parental, but also . . . he's right.

"Sounds good, yeah. We got through a lot. Just let me get my stuff in the kitchen," I say, moving toward the stairs. I get a few steps down before pausing and making eye contact with Tory again, his expression erased from any of the strangeness from before. "Hey, thank you, by the way. I feel really solid on this now."

"Don't mention it," Tory says, moving his focus back to Lucas so they can continue whatever weird-ass staring match they have going on. "We can pick it up again Saturday."

My mouth pops open, ready to turn down the offer, but before I'm able to push out the words, something inside me makes me stop. I say nothing and instead descend the rest of the way into the kitchen, shoveling the script into my purse and hooking it over my shoulder in a smooth, brisk move through the rest of the house. I'm sitting in Lucas's truck before I take another breath. Lucas, however, doesn't come down for another fifteen minutes.

9

TORY

I didn't need a lecture. I knew exactly what I was doing, where the line was, and how I was walking all over it.

Lucas gave me one anyway. I guess that's his job, though. I'm used to getting different kinds of lectures from my best friend. Usually, he tells me not to eat something that says *fire hot* or drink one shot too many before jumping from the roof into the pool. Dumb shit.

Abby's a different story. I know what I'm doing, and I know it's wrong. My feelings are wrong, the goddamn dreams I'm having are wrong, and this animosity I'm developing against my brother is wrong. It's not his fault that he figured out how to talk to Abby like a human before I did. Hell, he had no clue I had a *real* thing for her. I flirt with everyone. Abby's just the only one to ever shoot me down, over and over. Me hitting on her and her telling me to eff off became our routine, a one-act show that we perform at every party and in every class we have together.

And then, I don't know . . .

I even liked the rejection. It was attention, a push-pull that was a challenge, yeah, but also, she has this edge that feels, I don't know . . . a lot like me?

I have to stop this cycle, though, otherwise I'm going to spin out. I slept through Wednesday, and I've been about as social as a toad all day at school, but I can't completely turn away from the outside world just because I have a crush that hurts to deal with. It's time to find my groove again, especially since Hayden and I are heading right from practice to our first family therapy session. If I bring this mood in there, nobody is going to make progress, which is what my mom keeps preaching this is all about. *Making progress.* Some fucking family goal.

The junior high moved their players outside for practice, which has all of these twelve- and thirteen-year-olds pissed as hell at us. One kid calls me a douchebag on my way into the locker room I long ago outgrew.

"Yeah, you too, kid," I say back, getting a rise out of Hayden and a few of the other guys nearby.

I dump my gym bag on the bench and change out of my jeans and sweatshirt into shorts and a T-shirt, then take a seat to wipe down the bottoms of my basketball shoes. Hayden drops his stuff next to me and I catch the photo on his phone screen of him with his arms wrapped around Abby. The angle is weird because it's a selfie. Couple shit.

Deep breath, Tory. Deep breath.

"Hey, nice job landing Cortez, man. You tap that yet?" Chaz, whose real name is Chad but insists on forcing everyone to use the stupid z, tabs his shoes against my brother's back as he walks by and takes a seat on the next bench over.

"Oh, ha, yeah. Thanks, man. And I don't-I don't talk about that stuff." Hayden's respectful, but his grin is super evasive and full of innuendo. I drop my shoes to the floor and let them land with a heavy smack against the concrete. Chaz and Hayden both look my direction.

"Sorry." I shrug.

Not sorry.

"That's gotta really piss you off, right?" Chaz's question lingers unanswered. I don't bother to look up because I assume he's just goading my brother about not getting laid or some shit. Frankly, I'm glad Hayden isn't talking about it. If he's gotten to that level with Abby, I'm going to have a really hard time ejecting that visual from my head.

"Ah, I see. Silent treatment, huh?" Chaz keeps going, and I finally look up to catch him leaning forward, arms resting on his knees so he can stare at me like a major asshole.

My brow wrinkles.

"What the fuck?" I glare at him for a full second, then lean forward and slip my feet into my shoes, lacing them tight around my ankles.

"Ha! Baby Hayden sweeping in and taking what big brother thought was his. Yo, your brother hates you right now," Chaz taunts, thinking he's super clever playing around with the meaningless fact that I slid out of my mom's vagina a full minute before Hayden did. What an ass!

I stand without reacting, finding inner strength I didn't

know I had, and stop with my stance square with Chaz. I palm the side of his face a few times with a playful force.

"Why don't you just run along now and get the water for us starters, yeah?" I wink and flash a tight smile before turning and heading into the gym, catching the deep *oooooh* that sounds behind me from my teammates. Hayden's voice better be in that mix.

After jogging a few laps around the gym that once seemed so big when I was little, we all circle up at center court and begin our stretches. The tension left from my little moment with Chaz is still very much present, and there's hardly a sound other than the occasional snicker from someone trying damn hard to keep their mouth shut. Coach Newsome is a nice guy, but he doesn't do drama during practice. He calls stuff like this "playtime" and I've seen him kick guys out of the gym—and once, off the team —for letting girl trouble interfere with the business on the court.

I turn to face Hayden and nod for him to go first for our hamstring stretches. He lies in front of me and lifts his right leg, holding it straight for me to push toward his body. I try not to look down because I know he's staring right at me.

"Hey, thanks for running lines with Abby the other day. She said you were actually pretty good at it," Hayden says.

I blink slowly, tempted to leave my eyes shut. *He's talking. Why is he talking?*

I glance down and nod my chin.

"Yeah, no prob." His focus hangs on to my eyes, a hint

of suspicion in the way they dim. I raise my brows and shake my head a little in question, calling him on his silent question. I know he's got one.

"You do hate it, don't you?"

Fuck.

I sigh and roll my neck and lean forward, stretching him a little more, probably to punish him. He takes it.

"Hayden, I don't *anything*. I'm just trying to get through practice then to this therapy shit that's not going to work so I can go home and go to sleep. That's literally all I have going on in my head right now." I let go of his leg and purse my lips when our eyes meet. His head tilts just a hair, trying to read me better. I snap my fingers, calling for his other leg.

I assume he's letting things go when he gives me his left leg and I look away, repeating the stretch in blessed silence. Once he's done, I squat to lay as he stands to work on me. I give him my leg while my head rests on my threaded fingers and I look off to the side. But before he pushes my leg forward, he grasps my foot in both hands, his fingers squeezing into the top of my foot hard enough that I feel it through my thick-ass shoe.

"Hey," I protest, jerking my foot but unable to break free.

Hayden's jaw is set and his eyes are searing into me, and I wonder if he has a hidden camera near dad's albums.

"You need to take it easy on Mom." This is so out of left field that the only reaction I can possibly have is laughter.

"You're fucking kidding me, right?" I shake my head,

amused. Hayden clearly isn't joking, though. I'm so struck by it because no matter how many ways I bend the truth, I'm still on Dad's side.

"You don't hear her cry at night? Your cold shoulder is killing her," my brother says, finally pushing my leg forward to stretch.

I stare at him with my mouth agape.

"*I'm* killing her." I repeat this as if it might suddenly make sense. It doesn't.

I switch legs.

"Just . . ." My brother pauses, grimacing as he pushes forward on my leg. Hayden doesn't like conflict. He never has. And he's partly right—*though, no fucking way I'll admit that.* My parents have never been picture perfect, and they fought all the time. They also made up a lot, too. Dad went out of his way to make sure my mom had whatever she wanted. She just didn't want him.

"I won't pick sides in therapy. Is that what you're asking?" I chew at the inside of my mouth and wait for him to admit it. He finally agrees, nodding once and letting go of my leg. I hold my hand up, partly for a lift but also for a gentleman's agreement of sorts. I pat my brother's back a few times with a heavy hand and Chaz can't help the commentary.

"Aww, you guys work it out?" he says.

"Yeah, we took care of things while you were over there on the bench," I reply, not bothering to look his direction. My brother snorts out a laugh.

We muddle through practice, as good as practice can be in a gym that feels too small for our bodies and with rims that can be lowered to my height. We work on plays mostly, which is boring for the guys like Chaz who barely have a role, so at least I get to watch him stand around and whine with the irked look on his face.

I was hoping for more of an outlet though, because even after we leave the gym there's a clenched fist in my chest, like I want to scream or hit something. It's the anxiety from this impending doom that Hayden and I are driving toward. He's driving, actually. I'm riding shotgun, preparing mental lists of all the passive aggressive things I'll want to say but won't because I promised.

"You don't have to speed there," I say the closer we get.

"We're late, so . . . kinda do."

Hayden's back teeth are gnashed. I recognize it because I do the same damn thing when I'm stressed. I'm doing it now. We have different reasons, though. Hayden hates being late. I hate having to do shit I don't believe in.

We pull in, parking between the minivan and my dad's truck. How incredibly prophetic. Hayden rushes out of the car, but I take a moment to myself to let what's happening really sink in. I can't remember the last time I truly idolized both of my parents. I still do my dad, I guess. I just don't see him now, haven't really in a while. Even when he was at home, he was never *home*. He travels a lot for work at a job that bought the house we live in free and clear and has kept both of my parents in new cars for my entire life. Hayden and I share because my brother is practical and insists on it. Dad told me on the side that he'd get me my own ride, but it never felt that important. Wish I'd taken him up on it now, though. If I had, I'd still be on my way to this session while Hayden was here right on time, waiting for my ass to show up.

My brother raps his knuckles on my window. I don't bother to look, breathing out hard enough to flap my lips as I push the door open and join him out of the car.

"I was enjoying the last bit of quiet I'll have for a while," I say.

"Like you have ever wanted things quiet," my brother scoffs.

Touché.

Our parents are in the waiting room for the family therapist, Dr. Majestic. I thought my dad was shitting me when he texted me the info for Hayden and me to come, but no, that's really this doctor's name. It's going to take superhero powers to fix the broken things in this household. Dr. Majestic sounds a lot more like a villain.

"Son," my dad says, reaching toward me first to shake my hand. We make the same uncomfortable, fake smiles at each other because neither of us wants to be here. We're a lot alike, stubborn with a veil of easygoing.

"Hey, Dad," Hayden says after a few seconds, nodding to our pops.

"Hey, kiddo."

"*Psh*," our mom sounds.

"What, I can't call him kiddo? I suppose that's babying him?" My dad is on edge, which is not promising for the next fifty minutes. I looked up the fees and at four hundred an hour, I hope my parents spend less time on childish sounds and button-pushing when we get in the room.

None of us are sitting, which is typical. We're the family that, when we go out to eat, hovers impatiently around the hostess stand even if the wait is an hour. We have this unspoken strategy that standing makes other people uncomfortable so they seat us faster. It works.

"Gio? Natalia?" My parents turn in sync.

"*Hmm?*" they both say.

My eyes fall to the floor and I lead the way toward the incredibly tall woman standing with her door held wide open, welcoming—like the gates to hell. I glance up when I pass her and give her a crooked smile. She probably thinks it's my way of greeting her and expressing how upset I am over all of this, but really, I just think it's cool she's my height.

The rest of the family files in after me, the four of us cramming onto a sofa made for three. The black leather is stiff and it squeaks with our weight, a sound that repeats each time any of us moves. This won't be distracting at all.

"I have other chairs," Dr. Majestic says, indicating a high-back recliner pushed against the wall.

"I'm on it," I say, happily volunteering. I grab the chair by the arms and slide it a few feet forward so it's now part of the circle of death. I get in and immediately pull the handle, kicking my feet up and crossing my ankles.

"Salvatore." My mom's voice has that scold-tinge to it, like when I was a kid and made a farty noise in the back seat of the car during a long drive somewhere. I give her a sideways look and consider putting up a challenge. Hayden clears his throat and I give in.

"Fine," I say, lowering the foot rest and sitting up enough to rest my elbows on the arms and fold my hands together on my lap. I'm ready for testimony.

"All right, first . . . I'd like to congratulate you all on this very important first step. I want you to take a minute and

congratulate yourselves, quietly or silently. Thank yourselves for this. I know coming here isn't easy, and the fact
you rose to the challenge means you all have something
invested in this family unity."

My dad breaks first, puffing out a short laugh that he
quickly covers with a cough. My mom gives him a stern
look, which he pretends not to see. I enjoy the show while
my brother shrinks, his head falling into his shoulders as he
sits on the rubbery sofa between them. I can't believe I'm
here.

Congratulations, Tory. You did it.

Yeah, this Dr. Majestic is full of it.

"I'm familiar with your file and I understand the
circumstances, but I've found that the things we report on
paper are often not the *real* story. Why don't we start at the
root, being open and honest. Shall we?" Dr. Majestic scans
the room, getting nonverbal commitments from each of us.
I shrug, just like my dad, while Hayden and my mom nod.

"Good. Tory, let's start with you."

Aww, fuck.

"How has your parents' split made you feel?"

The heat from four pairs of eyes is instantly on me.

"Ha!" I laugh out, mostly from the audacity of the
question. My mouth hangs open, and I look first to my dad,
who is of absolutely no help, his eyes clearly saying he
doesn't want to be here. I move to Hayden next, who has a
poker face that would save any gambler, and then there's
Mom—oh-so hopeful, expectant Mom. She wants me to be
her good little boy.

My head swings back to the front and I deadpan to our
doctor with dim eyes and a sour mouth. "Fine. I guess."

"Tory," my mom cuts in.

"No," the doctor says, halting her. "Let him talk."

I raise a brow and turn my head a hint to the side while staring at her.

"I did talk. That's all I've got." So far, my plan on how to handle this is falling to shit, but I have yet to break my promise to Hayden, so, hey—win!

"Why do you think you answered that way?" She's not going to make this easy. She's needling, chewing on the tip of her pen and leaning in as if I'm about to get raw.

"There are a lot of germs on your pen," I say, pointing to the spot where her teeth have locked onto the clicking part. She lets go, smirking slightly as she leans back in her chair, which matches mine. I wonder if she ever gets to put her feet up.

"I bet you're known as the funny one."

Wow, she's a genius.

"Among other things," I say, winking.

"Tory." This time, the stern warning comes from my father. I shift and release my hold on my hands, exhaling on his command.

I rub my face, digging into my eyes that feel puffy from too much sleep. Resting my face on my palm, leaning on the arm of the chair, I stare in thought at the strands of the very expensive-looking rug that's centered in this room. It doesn't fill it completely, just enough to stretch under the sofa, the doctor's desk and these two chairs. My chair is an intruder.

"I don't know, maybe I'm disappointed." I grimace and glance up to meet the doctor's approving eyes.

"Go on," she says.

I draw a long breath through my nose and shake my head, letting my stare wander off again into the swirling pattern on the carpet.

"He's not the favorite anymore; that's how he feels," Hayden says, his unexpected contribution widening my eyes so much they actually burn.

"Hayden," my mom says, a totally different tone than the one she used with my name. This one is nurturing, and perhaps a bit pathetic.

"That's how I feel, anyway. I feel like my brother was always the king, and now that life at home isn't picture-perfect, he's less . . . shiny." My brother's eyes flit to mine a few times, but he doesn't stick around long. Probably because I'm full-on gawking.

"I was a king?" I laugh at the statement, thrusting down on the chair handle and kicking my feet up again because *fuck this!* "Go on. Please."

My dad's brow is pulled in tight, maybe as surprised by this outburst as I am. I'm starting to think, though, that maybe this is calculated. My brother doesn't back down, holding my stare as long as I hold his. The longer I look into eyes just like mine, the more animosity stews in my belly. Hayden's eyes, however, haze with a sinister fog. That bit in the gym, the stretching of my legs and asking me to be on my best behavior here, it was never about Mom or this session. It was about Abby, and those things Chaz put in his head.

My lips curl of their own accord, my chest gradually bubbling with laughter until it finally erupts and I'm practically cackling, minutes into our family therapy session. Look who's the crazy man in here!

I smile with a wide open mouth and look off to the side, trying to form words.

"Unbelievable." That's the only thing I can say.

"Why do you think your brother was our favorite?" our mom asks, twisting to the side to face my brother.

"Because I am?" I even surprise myself with the words. I don't mean it, but now I'm just pissed.

"Tory," my dad says, only the second time he's spoken since we got in here, and both times it was my name.

I push my feet down again and look my father in the eyes. He doesn't want to make any of this work. He's going through the motions. There's no way he is forgiving my mom for what she did. And there's probably no way I'll ever be able to either. This is where the ride ends. My dad isn't coming to any more of our games, driving in from the city when he's not traveling. He's taking his albums, too. And maybe I'll see him a weekend here and there.

All of those frames in my mind are just bullshit. Me hoisting up my first MVP trophy and him holding me on his shoulder, him placing my hand on the right strings to make a G chord on the guitar, him telling me to be careful who I love because if I pick wrong, she's going to chew my heart up and spit it out. He wasn't talking about me on that last one; he was sharing experience.

"You know what?" I stand, knowing my pocket is light of keys and that my shit is still in the car. I've taken busses before, and it's not that cold out tonight. I could use a walk. "I'm done. You guys figure out whatever you need to in here. I'm going to take care of things my way."

I get to the door before my dad stands to utter my name a third time. I stop him before he does.

"Don't act like you want to be here," I say. His confession is all over his face, his eyes relenting first, followed by the tight line of his lips and the sag in his shoulders. He used to seem like this strong, amazing man. Now he's just a shell.

I push open the door and meet the gaze of the front secretary. She doesn't speak, and she doesn't even look surprised to see someone making a run for it. I bet this happens all the time. I hold up a hand and tell her to have a good evening, then step out onto the cold sidewalk in my practice jersey and shorts, still cold from old sweat. I tug on the car handle, glad my brother forgot to lock our car again, and pull out my sweatshirt, throwing it over my head and slamming the door behind me. I stand at the edge of the parking lot for a minute, looking up and down the street for signs of a bus line. Traffic is steady but light. I look over my shoulder one last time, giving my brother a last shot at redemption, but he isn't coming after me.

I want to choke him, but I also understand this is all coming from somewhere else. Hayden isn't good with change, and this has been a major adjustment. He's lashing out, and I'm the one who can take it. But I won't pretend there wasn't a trace of something else in that long gape he steamrolled me with.

Just start walking.

My legs travel north at first, but unsure how to get around the highway, I end up doubling back a few roads over. I finally find a creek bed that runs underneath most of the big streets between where I am and our neighborhood. I amuse myself for a while with my breath, puffing out thick, icy smoke then slicing it in half with my hand.

That works for about half a mile and then I get anxious at my own lack of direction. I start to run, thankful for my lung capacity, and after about three miles, find myself in the last place I ever thought I would be at a time like this— at the end of Abby Cortez's driveway.

10

ABBY

We look like hoarders. Between legal contracts for some of my residuals, contracts from the production company for the film, travel plans, waivers, and the files upon files from my parents' custody battle, I'm just glad nobody in this house smokes. There is so much paper for kindling, we would go up in flames.

"Abby, babe, I swear there's a knock on our door. Can you . . ?" My mom's glasses are perched at the end of her nose, her fingers dug deep into her temple, and the light above her like a heavy spot on whatever it is she's reading. It's something from my dad, but she doesn't talk about it with me if she can avoid it.

"You need to eat, and then you need to go to bed, Ma," I say, hopscotching my way through the living room over papers and a few scattered pieces of laundry.

"I will. I just have to finish this last—"

"Yeah, yeah. You always say that. Just one more page,"

I tease. My mom looks up at me and smiles with her eyes, her mouth too tired to make the trip.

"Soon. I promise," she says. I wonder if she remembers the pencil she shoved in her hair to hold it up out of her eyes.

"Okay," I holler, turning around while opening the front door.

Tory D'Angelo looks back at me, and he looks like he's been in a fight. Only he hasn't been hit, he's only been emotionally tortured.

"Mom, I'll be right in," I say, stepping out to our front porch to talk with him. My mom hasn't seen either of the twins in years. She doesn't even know I'm dating one of them. All we talk about lately are travel plans and court dates. Seems like a confusing way to bring my love life up to her, what with an evening visit from the brother I'm *not* dating.

"Hey, something wrong?" I lead Tory down to the first step, motioning for him to sit next to me.

"I think I need to stand. I'm too amped up," he says, his feet in constant movement between the two stairs of our porch. He's a constant whirl of up and down, and he looks like he's just finished a marathon.

"You, uh, out for a run?" His hair is slick with sweat. He glances up, straining his eyes, and runs his hand through his hair a few times to push it from his forehead. A crooked smile plays at his lips for a flash of a second.

"This is kinda weird, I know." His eyes flutter closed and he tangles his hands behind his neck for a stretch, exhaling while bouncing on his toes a few times. When his eyes open on mine again, he seems more settled, less like a stray dog who just dodged a shit ton of traffic.

"Let's just say therapy did not go well." A sarcastic smile plays at his lips, tightly closed and pulled up in the corners.

"It never does," I say, making him laugh lightly.

My plan to keep our talk outside falls apart as my mom opens the door and leans against the door frame, holding her own tired body up.

"It's freezing out. Come inside. I'll make some cocoa." She dips her chin so she can peer at me over her glasses, brows raised as she shifts her eyes to my male visitor a couple times, hinting for an explanation.

"Mom, you remember Tory D'Angelo, right? He threw up at June's fourth grade birthday party."

"Come on," Tory whispers in exasperation.

I glance at him and shrug. It's the one thing I know will stick in my mom's memory.

"Oh, yes, the green cake. Glad to see you're feeling better," my mom jokes.

Her reaction manages to pull a laugh from Tory and he drags his tired legs up the step and across my porch, reaching out his hand.

"Much better. You sure about that cocoa, though?" He cocks a brow, somehow able to charm a real hard-ass like my mom with his personality. Her lips pucker with the smile of a blushing school girl, but he doesn't have her completely fooled.

Patting her hand on his cheek a few times, she says, "I'll get you a bib."

My mom leads us inside and Tory glances at me with a wry smile.

"I see where you get it," he says.

As my mom is riffling through our cabinets looking for stray packets of hot chocolate, Tory takes a meandering tour of the state of my home. Our house isn't as big as his, and it isn't fancy by any means, but it is historic.

"It was my grandparents' house on Mom's side. My grandfather built it," I say, feeling the need to narrate his experience. He runs a hand along a wooden sill under a stained glass window that overlooks our dining table.

"It must be a pretty cool feeling to stand back when you hammer in that last nail and see a house you put together." He continues to touch the little details, like the corner nook bookcase that holds my grandmother's dishes, and the chair railing that lines almost every wall, from the front door on to the back of the house.

Eventually, he turns his attention to the table, littered with documents and my mom's two spare pair of reading glasses haphazardly tossed in the mix. It's strange having him here, especially when Hayden usually stops at the door. It's as if I've unintentionally built two worlds, one where the boy I'm dating kisses me in his car and takes me out for burgers, and this one, where shit feels hard. Tory, he can walk in between.

"This is the best I could do," my mom says, walking over with two mugs in her hand, the strings from what look like tea bags dangling from the side. She carefully sets them on the edge of the table before clearing a little space by stacking folder on top of folder.

"You like tea?" I quirk a brow at Tory.

"Love it," he answers, for my mom's benefit, while shaking his head no to me. I pucker a smile.

We pull out chairs and sit, the rounded corner of the table barely dividing us, and I lift my mug to dunk the bag up and down. I wiggle my brows to Tory to hint that he can do the same until my mom leaves. He does.

"Tory, it was very nice to meet the older version of you. Please, if you're going to throw up, the powder room is . . ." My mom points to the door under the stairwell.

"Thank you, Ms. Cortez," Tory plays along.

"Call me Denise," she insists. She turns her focus to me.

"Baby, I'm done. I'll see you in the morning." My mom moves to stand behind me so she can kiss the top of my head. As she does, I reach an arm up and hug her from behind.

"Don't forget the pencil," I say as she shuffles away. A glance over my shoulder catches her pulling it out and tossing it on the small table where we drop our keys. She heads up the stairs with heavy thumps, and when she's out of sight, Tory puts his mug down and pulls off his sweatshirt.

"We like the heat in the winter." I grimace.

"It's fine," he says, his head finally free from the fabric. He runs his hand through his hair a few times to straighten it, then rolls the sweatshirt up and sets it on the table. He's still wearing his practice jersey and shorts.

"Long day?" I look him up and down.

He blows out a long stream of air and stares at me, the amped part of him finally seeming calm.

"Longest ever," he says.

He twists in his chair so he faces the table and pulls my script toward him, the pages now curling from me reading and carrying it around.

"You up for a little reading?" he asks.

I shake my head.

"I don't think you have it in you," I respond.

His lips pout for a second but eventually he nods and pushes the paper away, clearly exhausted.

"You're probably right."

I study him while he scans the contents of my table, all the ugly and exciting things about my life on display. It's like the ingredients for Abby soup, a little sweet and a little sour.

"Want to talk about therapy?" He's staring at the latest argument my father submitted, but I'd rather talk about him than me.

"I'm not sure," he says, distracted and distant.

"Okay, so . . ." I let my voice trail off.

We sit in silence, Tory glancing over the highlights of my parents' divorce while my stomach knots in this shameful squeeze, knowing how much worse I've made it all. I've never quite gotten over the sense that some of their relationship's demise was my fault. The frenzied legal state it's at now is most *definitely* my fault. It's because I'm selfish, and that might be what ruins me—my mom for sure. I have a feeling Tory's in that place now, the very beginning of it. I wish he knew his brother was right there with him. They could help each other. I had to swim through the swamp on my own.

"I should put that on my resume," I say, needing to break the quiet.

"Huh?" He pushes away the page he was reading with a flick of his finger and turns his attention back to me, his hands resting in his lap.

"Bargaining chip. That's what I am in this whole thing. I'm a bargaining chip for my parents. I don't really blame my mom, because she's the one who has also been a parent along with being a manager, but it still feels kinda like—" I cut my words short when Tory interrupts.

"Like every other kid we know gets to grow up normal and we got ripped off?"

"Exactly," I say. My forehead pinches as I consider that for a moment. "Though, pretty much all of our friends are from fractured families, so we really aren't missing out."

"We're missing out," he says swiftly. "They're just missing out, too."

He stands and wanders around my kitchen, moving on to the hallway plastered in framed photos of me through the years. Most of them are headshots, but some are pictures from performances. My favorite is the one of me in tap shoes with a giant heart covered in sequins around my head.

"You were always a diva, weren't you?" he teases, tapping his finger on the glass of the frame. I move in closer to cut the glare and take in my ear-to-ear, full-teeth-showing smile.

"I'm certainly *always on*," I joke.

"Not always," he replies. I look to my right and meet his waiting stare. It isn't that he suddenly sees me, but rather that he maybe always has and finally understands my fabric.

"Therapy . . ." I work to bring things back to him and his needs, but he's having none of it.

"Show me more," he says, moving down the wall and pivoting at the stairs. "Your room up here?"

He points.

"Yeah," I croak out.

He takes the steps slowly, probably not wanting to ruin his good graces with my mom. I follow, noting how he takes time to look at every photo on the way up. The ones here are more personal, family portraits that include people who are no longer alive. My favorite is the last one near the top of the steps, which attracts Tory's attention. He pauses there, waiting for me to catch up to him as I climb the last three or four stairs.

"You in a wedding or something?" he asks.

"No, it was my fifteenth. We went down to Miami for my *quinceañera*. Most of my family is down there, which is why my mom prefers to be up here because my aunts and cousins are nosy, and bossy. But that's also where my *abuela* lived." I run my finger along her form in the photo. I felt so grown up on that day, so celebrated and loved. My father even showed up, and for a full weekend, he and my mom didn't argue once.

"You said *lived*," Tory notes.

I nod softly and turn to meet his gaze.

"She died last year. She was in a nursing home down in Florida, and Mom and I hadn't been to see her in almost a year." I feel the burn of tears threaten to expose themselves, so I clear my throat and move past Tory to lead him toward my room.

Hayden hasn't been up here. My mom is never home

when he picks me up. I never invite him inside, and he never asks, yet more than anything I want to show Tory this personal window into my world.

We're both hushed as we move in the opposite direction from my mother's door. The spare room between is overrun with paperwork and costumes. It was supposed to be our business office, but it's become more of a dumping ground for things that don't require our immediate attention or that don't fit me anymore.

I push down on the door handle to make the click as quiet as possible, then slip inside, Tory knowing he should hurry. I close the door behind him and flip on the small purple lamp next to my bed. It paints my room in color. I don't bother to kick away the clothes I left on the floor or hide the makeup scattered around my vanity, and Tory doesn't even seem to notice any of it's there. He continues his trip through my life in pictures, now standing in front of the corkboard next to my closet door. It's filled with pictures, most of them things I've printed out from my phone.

"Why is June always so grumpy?" He points to the one I took the night of his party a few months back, when June got locked in the garage with Lucas. I laugh and pull my phone from my pocket to sort through and find more images of my friend.

"It's sort of this thing I do with her. I take random pictures of her expressions. I won't lie, I love to catch her when she's pissed off. It pushes her buttons, and maybe I like the negative reinforcement." I laugh, handing him my phone.

He takes it, sliding through a few of them and wincing at the ones that are truly bad.

"I know," I say, covering my face in fake shame. "But it's not like I print all of them."

"June knows you do this?" He turns the phone to show me the one in which her cheeks are puffed out and her face is red. She was about to punch me in the shoulder for that one.

I smile and nod.

"She does. I give her the right to rip them off the board if she hates them. She knows they make me happy, though."

Tory's face scrunches and his brows lift as he shakes his head, not totally understanding my most important female relationship. He doesn't have to. I'm sure he has weird traditions with Lucas or his brother, and I *so* don't want to know about them.

He hands me back my phone, but on the exchange, my hand covers his, and we both jerk back, like we touched a hot skillet mid-air. My phone tumbles to the floor, and I giggle with embarrassment while he apologizes profusely and we both bend down to retrieve it. We stop when our heads are an inch from banging into one another and I brace myself, grabbing his shoulders and falling forward to my knees.

"Whoa," he hums, steadying me with his hands on my hips.

My adrenaline-fueled smile mixes with a breathy laugh until I look up and we come face-to-face. Every molecule between us is palpable; the air has a taste to it, somewhere between sweetness and intoxicating liquor. My lips part with a breath and his eyes flit to my open mouth. We're slow dancing without moving, facing each other on our knees, alone in my room, which I purposely cloaked in mood lighting. I can't lie to myself any more. I'm painfully attracted to Tory D'Angelo. I'm also regrettably committed to his brother.

We're young, and relationships at our age are so fluid, and if it were anyone else, this would just be a life lesson, a moment of growth or an innocent mistake fanned by teenage hormones. But it's Tory, and then Hayden.

I swallow hard. His gaze falls to my throat and back to my eyes.

"What happened at therapy?"

In his world, it's the worst possible time for this question, but it's also probably the best. Things are going on between us that need time to sort themselves out, just as I'm sure there are things happening in his head that need attention. I'm not sure if he realizes it or not, but Tory needs someone to listen.

"No judgement," I continue.

We're inches apart, a breath away from making dangerous decisions.

"Why are you with my brother?" His stare is unrelenting. My stomach is sick but at the same time, my heart is pounding. I am the center of a tug-of-war, the part of the rope that is fraying. I don't know how to keep it from splitting, but I do know that his question cuts to the very core of it all. He reaches forward and tucks a strand of hair behind my ear, and his hand never leaves, his thumb tracing the small inch of space along my temple, then making a slow pass along the cut of my jaw toward my lips. I turn into it and let my eyes close, waiting for the alarm to sound in my head that makes me stop.

"Don't," I say, getting to my feet and shaking my head. "You're just avoiding the question, and I know you're struggling, too. We can be friends, Tory. Just like June and you are friends."

He falls back on his calves and positions himself like a catcher, arms resting on his knees, head cocked to one side and a faint yet intensely confident smile playing at his lips.

"Abby . . . you and I can't be friends like that, and you know it." He blinks once, slowly, and I'm tempted to push him off balance and watch him land on his ass.

"I told Hayden I'd call him. You should go," I say.

A quick inhale flares his nostrils and his body shakes once with a short laugh. He gets to his feet, his eyes making a slow drag around my room as if he's memorizing it to infiltrate the space at some later date. He nods eventually and moves toward my door, stopping to look at my board of photos one more time. He tugs one loose and pinches it, holding it close to his face for a long second before tossing it on the floor between us.

"You tell me we look like friends in that photo," he says, leaving me with a short, challenging glare. He pats his hand on the edge of my doorframe as he leaves my room and peers over his shoulder.

"I'll show myself out."

I remain frozen until I hear the click of the door downstairs. My space still smells like him, my skin still vibrates from the place his hand touched my skin, my heart still pounds so hard I feel it in my throat.

My phone vibrates in my pocket and I pull it out,

knowing I'll see the image of Hayden's smile to show that he's calling. I glance at the screen just long enough to swipe to answer, then fix my eyes on the Polaroid of me and Tory at last month's school carnival. I paid ten dollars to smash a plate of whipped cream into his face to raise money for the basketball team, and I got to keep this photo as a memento. Have I never really looked at it before? Or was I just ignoring it all along.

"Hey, Abs. Sorry it's so late. Our session was . . ." He pauses to let out an exasperated breath. "It was kinda brutal."

"I heard," I say, the words coming out on autopilot, the logical answer rather than the smart one. My attention is on the photo Tory tossed to the ground. I kneel and pick it up, turning it right-side up so I can absorb the way we're looking at one another. His face is covered in cream—minus the two holes I wiped for his eyes because I felt bad—and the enormous smile formed by his laugh. I'm laughing hard, too, truly happy with red cheeks and a dot of cream on my nose. The evidence is in the nuances; not only our display of happiness, but the way our hands happened to be wrestling with one another, threaded together so comfortably in a perfect fit. His eyes are soft and affectionate, looking at me not like the girl he makes sure to hit on at a party, but like the girl he stares at in class.

"Abby? You there?"

I stand with the photo and move back to my board, startled into movement by Hayden's voice. I push the sticky side back against the board, putting it back in its place.

"Yeah, sorry, I was balancing my phone while doing something else," I say. I'm vague.

"Oh, I asked how you heard?" There's a bite to his question and I wince, realizing what I said.

"June and I were texting. Tory stopped by her house."

I just lied. I lied and I feel like shit for it, and at the same time I am terrified that Tory won't back up my lie and I don't even have his phone number to call him and tell him to. I don't fix it, though. I leave that lie where it is and let it buy me time.

"Oh," he answers, the quiet after his short response telling me he doesn't fully buy it.

"You wanna talk about it?" I kick off the fuzzy shoes I wear around the house and slip my feet into my unlaced tennies in anticipation.

"If you're not too tired." I'm sure he's already driving toward my house.

"Of course not," I say, flipping off my light and quietly closing my door.

"You want to start telling me about it now, or wait until you get here?" I ask, anticipating his response.

"I'm almost there," he says.

Hayden opens up better in person. He also only really opens up to me. That happens when someone finds you on the wrong side of a bridge railing with an incredibly steep drop over some very jagged rocks, drunk from too many shots at a party you didn't want to go to in the first place.

Not Hayden.

Me.

"I'm at the end of the block," he says.

"Okay," I say, making my slow descent down the stairs.

I'd gotten the call for the audition, and I went to the party in the woods to celebrate. Sean McCaffey's parties are legendary. He's rich, and he owns the land he throws his parties on—massive bonfires and expensive-ass booze. I went alone because June swore she'd met her party quota for life, and she's turned Lucas into a homebody. Naomi and Lola weren't around to play my wing woman, so I went expecting to know a few people there and with the understanding I would only stay an hour.

The guy I met that night was cute, and two hours passed with many drinks and a lot of talk. I was feeling a good buzz, and we hooked up. I didn't go all the way, and I was fully aware of my choices and consent. What I wasn't aware of was his motives.

He left that party with three photos of me—three *compromising* photos. On his phone. It only took thirty minutes for the bribe to hit my phone. What's crazy is I knew I was too drunk to drive; that's why I was walking home in the first place. The idea to climb out over the bridge railing was an impulsive one. A destructive choice would have kept my keys in my hand and my ass behind the wheel. All I could think about, though, for those four miles I wandered in darkness, throwing up twice, was that my dad was going to use this against my mom.

Hayden found me before reason left my head and I jumped. He brought me home, and when I woke up in his car sitting in my driveway, I spilled my guts. He spilled his. We cried, and not a single night has passed that we haven't talked on the phone just to give each other an out, an excuse to mess up and hate ourselves for a little while.

"I'm out front," he says, my hand cupping the phone to my ear.

"Be right there," I say, ending our call and grabbing the sweater hanging on the finial at the bottom of the staircase. I slip my arms inside to stay warm and rush to the dining table to pick up my keys. I stop dead in my tracks, though, because sitting right next to them is a black sweatshirt that someone left behind, and I can't help but sense that he did that on purpose.

11

TORY

"Did you sleep out here all night?" Lucas flips up the tailgate on his truck with a thrust in case I didn't hear him blare out his question.

I pull my feet up and lift my knees, rubbing my eyes from the bright-ass sun. My hat must have fallen off because my hair feels ratty like I was raised in a cave. Goddamn, I feel like shit.

"Only half the night," I say, rocking myself into a sitting position. Lucas tosses his backpack into the back of his truck and rests his arms against the frame, looking at me like I'm a toddler in a baby pool.

"Oh, well, that makes sense, then," he cuts, his mouth a tight light.

I rub my face to help focus my eyes, then crank my neck right and left, trying to work out the kinks before flattening my wild hair under my black hat.

"Therapy didn't go well. Kinda hate Hayden right

now. I maybe went to Abby's last night and made things all fuckin' weird, and I hate that I have to live with my mom. That a good enough reason to sleep in your truck for six hours?" I lift one brow and hit him with a sleepy stare.

He holds my gaze for a second then nods.

"Yeah, that seems right. Come on, get in." He smacks the side of his truck to rile me more.

I stand and kick my legs over the edge of the bed to jump to the ground, then slide into the much more ergonomic passenger seat and recline back as far as it will go.

"Are you going to sleep on the way to school?" Lucas asks, cranking his engine to a roar.

"No, I'm going to sleep on our way to the gas station where I plan on getting a forty-four ounce Dew." I look at him, one eye shut.

"We're gonna be late," Lucas argues.

I shrug and silently dare him to come up with a better excuse. He can't, so I tip the brim of my hat lower to shadow my eyes while he drives the four miles to the gas station near our school. We both run in and grab donuts, and I fulfill my Dew destiny, chugging a quarter of it from the exit to the passenger door.

"Better," I breathe out.

Lucas chuckles and backs us out of the lot, taking us the rest of the way to school.

As much as I need the caffeine jolt, I have an ulterior motive for being late to school this morning—I want to avoid running into Hayden. I've gotten tired of conflict. Lately, it feels that's all my life is, a connect-the-dot puzzle from fight to skirmish.

Seems Hayden has his own reasons to walk into class late, though. He knows I won't skip completely; I take my sports eligibility seriously during basketball season. Lucas backs his truck in so my side is butted up next to my brother in the driver's seat of our car. Abby is sitting next to him, and she's doing that thing where she only looks my direction but not actually *at* me.

This day is going to be epically bad.

"You want me to just lock you in? You can sleep on the jump seats in the back," Lucas kids.

While he thinks he's being funny, I take a second to actually consider the idea, looking over my shoulder and assessing the room. It's a tight fit, but as tired as I am, I'm pretty sure I wouldn't even notice. I glance back to my friend, who's looking at me sideways.

"That was a joke," he explains.

I know.

I grimace and pop the lock on my seat belt, leaning forward and resting my arms and head on his dash to stretch out my lower back. I managed to slip into our house to get a shower and a change of clothes, but sleeping in a truck bed didn't do much for my wardrobe. My long-sleeved shirt is wrinkled, and there's a line of dirt on the side of my jeans from the back of Lucas's truck.

"Go on in. I'm gonna get this over with," I say, wiping my palm down the side of my face and over my mouth. I open my door and make a slow trip toward the passenger side of the car, opening the door for Abby.

"Can you give us a minute," I say, pinching the bridge of my nose and doing my best to not crowd her.

"Sure," she says in a whisper.

I look her direction just enough to catch her give Hayden a look and ask if he'll be okay. What does she think? That I'm a monster? I wonder what version of events he told her.

She turns her body to the side and her bare legs cut in front of mine. She's wearing a long, tight skirt and a blazer, as if she's ready for a job interview. I open the door wider to give her space and she stands, straightening her skirt and jacket. Her hair is pinned up in loose curls, and she smells like candy. I saw her car, so I know she drove herself here. She's just been waiting for me with Hayden, keeping him company, making sure he gets all the attention he can because, apparently, I'm some attention whore who has ruined his life.

I'm determined to pay no attention to Abby but she makes it impossible when she clears her throat and shuffles in her heels to face me, adjusting the collar of the shirt she's wearing. She stares into my eyes with a terrified gaze and swallows.

"How do I look?"

My cold stare breaks down and my eyes narrow with inexplicable guilt. She looks beautiful. Her permanently golden brown skin is flawless, her lips pout and glow, her eyes are dewy but still the most stunning mix of brown and gold. She looks scared, yet also strong.

"Court today?" I assume, my eyes sloping with empathy.

She nods.

"How do I look?" she asks again. I scan down the lapel of her jacket to the spot where her hand is needling at a button near the bottom. She drops it as soon as she sees I've noticed. I move my focus back up to her face.

"You look ready," I say. My response draws a hesitant smile from her and she gives me a tiny nod.

"Be nice," she whispers, careful to keep her words between us.

I agree with a slow blink and wait as she grabs her bag from the floor of the car and pulls it up on her shoulder. I don't allow myself the pleasure of watching her hips sway as her heels click down the walkway into the front office, but I imagine it. I get into the car as soon as she disappears into the building and close the door behind me, knowing Hayden and I will probably sit here for a while.

Neither of us is ready to talk. Hayden has yet to kill the engine, so the car hums enough to keep the heater on and the speakers at a low buzz. I lean forward and turn up the volume to see what he's playing, expecting his usual barrage of R&B. It's the one place where my dad, brother and I differ in our tastes. I don't mind it, but I never got into that part of my dad's music obsession the way Hayden did. I think my brother spent an entire summer memorizing every lyric to, like, fifty songs.

I'm a little surprised to hear the song I sang for Abby spill through the speakers, and I narrow my eyes as I look at his phone screen.

"Branching out?" I ask.

My brother shrugs.

"Abby wanted to hear the Beach Boys this morning," he says. My stomach tightens, a little bit hopeful and a little bit sick. Hayden's hands fall from the steering wheel to his thighs and his head rolls against his head rest, his eyes making the slow, suspicious trip to mine. "She said you showed her Dad's record collection."

"Huh, yeah. Didn't think she cared that much," I say, trying to pass off what was a memorable thing as a meaningless one. I sense by the long, silent breaths Hayden takes while staring at me that he isn't buying it.

Whatever. I'm not the one who threw his sibling under the bus at therapy. I think maybe it's my turn to talk, and give him a long look.

"Oh, and hey . . . what the fuck was that shit you pulled yesterday?" My temper isn't even a little bit controlled. I've gone and blended my love of sarcasm with my own boiling rage at how unfair life is being. My brother's reaction is completely unsatisfying.

"You know how I get with conflict. I wanted to say something to end the bickering—"

"That's bullshit," I cut in.

His mouth shuts into a hard, straight line and all of the pretend sincerity he was trying out fades away. He shifts his head, his eyes moving to the stereo controls. After a few long seconds, he finally lifts his hand and pushes in the power button, shutting off our distraction.

"You know what's bullshit?" he says. "What's bullshit is that you and I are basically the same person physically, but for whatever reason, Dad has always preferred your version of us to mine."

Wow.

"Dude, you're way off base," I reply. Hayden quickly laughs me off.

"I'm right on base, Tor, and deep down"—his gaze

shifts back to mine and he bites the tip of his tongue, actual hate simmering in his smile—"you know I am."

My brow drawn in, I shake my head and laugh quietly, mentally shuffling through so many times in our lives when Dad was equal with us to a fault. I'm a better player than Hayden. It isn't even a question, and if I asked him right now, he wouldn't be able to lie and argue with me about it. When it comes to the court, I am dominant. He is decent. But my entire life has been held back to his level because Dad didn't want the "dynamic duo" to be split up. He didn't want Hayden left behind. I know in my heart that my dad just wanted Hayden to feel equal, but I always felt I had to carry him, which slowed me down.

"You do know that you and I are two different people, right? I mean, we look alike, but that's it. I am me, and you are you." It's a harsh response but I'm growing tired of working so hard to make sure Hayden is happy. I love my brother, but damn, sometimes my parents were too obsessed with the idea of coddling his sensitive ego.

"Oh, I'm well aware." He shifts in the driver's seat, turning to the side and folding his arms over his chest. "Think about Dad's bookcase. There's a row of albums, and then the top shelves are all of your special moments—your first place triathlon plaque from junior high, your invitation to Duke's high school basketball showcase, the photo of you, Dad, and Phil Jackson. And where are my things? They're on the bottom, Tor. They're on the goddamn floor."

I picture the space in my mind, conjuring some detail that will prove my brother wrong, but there isn't one. He's right. I can't believe any of it was intentional, but at the same time, the split is so obvious that how could it not be on purpose?

It seems insignificant to apologize. It also doesn't seem the right fit for the situation; it's not my apology to make. I've been holding my dad on this pedestal because of my mom's affair, but really, they both are flawed people. We're all flawed.

"You want some room on my shelf, maybe?" I squint, looking into the morning sun, and Hayden laughs.

"Sure, I'll take some shelf space."

We look at each other briefly, the new awkward truth sitting thick and heavy between us. He's still mad, and I'm still pissed off about therapy, but I also feel really shitty about the stuff he just said. I can also tell that he feels bad about the way it came out.

"I should have saved that for another time. Maybe I need some one-on-one sessions with Dr. Majestic," he says.

"Can we talk about that name for a minute? Really? Our family therapist is named Dr. Majestic?" This is my way of accepting his olive branch. Avoidance and humor—this is something we both definitely got from Dad.

"Right?" Hayden finally turns our car off, and I take the signal as it's finally safe to get out and go beg for late slips instead of detentions from the front office. He gets out of the driver's side, and with our bags slung over our shoulders, we walk in tandem, mirror images in many ways, opposites in others.

"Not gonna lie, I was picturing, like, major octopus tentacles to pop out of her shoulder blades or something," Hayden continues.

"Why does it always have to be octopus tentacles? Every bad guy—full-on tentacles."

"Why does it have to be a bad *guy*? Why not a bad *woman*?" he argues.

"Touché, brother. Touché."

We slip in the office door and put on our most charming smiles, bashfully wincing when Maggie, the best front office manager a high school senior could ask for, spots us. She was the queen of orange slices when Hayd and I were kids. I don't think we played a single game without her showing up with bags full. Her son, Nicolas, is in our grade, and he played most things with us when it was all about participation and less about athleticism. He's horribly uncoordinated, but dude is going to graduate high school with something like forty-eight college credits out of the way, so who cares if he can't throw a ball. Pretty sure he's going to build rocket ships.

Maggie spots us while she's on the phone and leans her head to one side, eyes hazed enough to admonish us. She writes out our slips while talking to the person on the phone, then puts them on hold when she brings them to us.

"If I ever find out you two are late for doing something stupid like smoking pot or robbing a liquor store, I'm going to whoop your tooshies, you got it?" She points at me instead of Hayden when she says that, which makes my brother laugh.

"Yes, ma'am," he says, taking his slip.

My brow knit tight, I bunch up my face and pinch the edge of my late slip between my fingers. Maggie doesn't let go right away, keeping her other hand pointing at me as she tugs the slip to bring me in closer.

"That's right, Tory, I'm talking to you. Of you two, I know you're the one I've got to keep my eye on." Her smirk breaks through just in time because I was about to get irrationally butthurt over her opinion. She finally lets go of my slip and pats my cheek in her overly coddling Midwestern mom way. "Oh, I'm teasing you."

"Thanks, Maggie," I say, my pulse beating fast from my emotional roller coaster.

"But I'm serious about the pot. No pot, you two!" She lectures over her shoulder on her way back to the phone. Hayden salutes her and pushes through the door into campus with his back. I follow along and wait until we get outside before I react out loud.

"I mean, it's kinda late about the pot. Been there, done that, over it," I say.

"Over it, huh?" Hayden says, slapping my back.

I'm pretty sure he and I both lit up a month ago out at one of McCaffey's parties. I guess that's recent to some people, but for me, shit I did a month ago is in an entirely different lifetime.

"Yeah," I sigh. "I'm over it."

He gives me a sideways look, daring me to prove him wrong. I lift a brow and reach out my hand to shake on it and he takes it.

"All right then. I'm gonna hold you to it," he says.

I shrug it off as if it's no big deal, but in reality, I just haven't been to a party in weeks. I'm the king of both enforcing and caving to peer pressure in those situations. Hayden has the resolve of stone, so for him this really is no problem. I might have to become a permanent introvert.

"Oh, hey." He stops me just before we split up and

head toward different buildings. "Abby's birthday is in a few days. I want to do something special, but I'm stuck. This place is kinda void of special things. Got any ideas?"

Instantly, all of that good will we just forged collapses in my chest. I manage to keep that feeling from exposing itself on my face, though, and bundle it all up into a thoughtful expression. What kind of man am I? This is one of those forks in life's road. I decide to take the path I know will make Abby happiest.

"You know what? You said she really liked that one song you were playing. Maybe you should learn it on the guitar, play it for her," I suggest, the petty child that lives in my gut kicking me.

"Oh, I don't know, man. You're a way better player than I am. I could never really get it down," he says, over-whelmed at the idea. Thing is, that song is really easy to play. And Hayden and I sing about the same. He's just a lot shyer about stuff like that.

"Nah, I'll teach you. It'll take an hour, two tops." I cross my fingers over my chest and feel the scorch of my decision.

"Seriously?" There's a flavor to Hayden's surprise that reeks of suspicion. My brother isn't stupid, and while our little talk this morning focused on his envy over my rela-tionship with our dad and my ignorance to it all, I can't forget that his first words to me were about how I spent time with his girlfriend and made an impression.

"Sure," I say. "What the hell else do I have to do? Go to McCaffey's and smoke pot?"

His lips purse into a tight smile and one brow ticks up.

"I swear, it will be easy. She'll love it, and you can talk

about how many hours you put in to learn it just for her and blah, blah, blah." I want to throw up just thinking about her reaction. She'll think it's sweet and thoughtful, and she'll instantly realize how my brother picked up on her clues of liking the song but I didn't. He'll come away as the good guy and I'll be the chump. As it should be.

12

ABBY

A nymore, I don't really know how to judge whether or not things go well with the lawyers. It might be my new hardened belief that court mediators and custody lawyers are greedy bastards. It's probably not fair to lump them all together like that, but my experiences have been so tainted that it's hard not to.

Sitting in that room while my mom and our lawyer hashed out what seemed like a fair deal for my father's investment—*in me, the daughter he left*—was demoralizing. Add in his claims that he spent nearly a hundred thousand dollars making some sordid photos of me disappear, and today was basically an out-of-body experience.

I wasn't the girl in those blurred-out photos that my dad's lawyer kept referencing in his argument. I was dressed for business, a professional with a huge future only a few weeks away from beginning. That man made me sound like a wild party girl who shows up in tabloids, even hinting that there's no guarantee there aren't *more* photos of me like this flying around. "Or worse, video," he said.

I've told my mother everything. I promised her it was just this one time, which it was—I've never been so stupid as to flash my flesh for the camera. But I was drunk and feeling invincible because I just landed the part of my dreams. I was feeling carefree and romantic with a mysterious guy who was paying so much attention to me, and it felt good. I hate that I keep blaming myself for this mess. My mom keeps nearly convincing me that I'm not the one to blame, that the guy who took advantage of me is. Yet all it took was that one seed of doubt planted by my dad's calculated lawyer to fuck up everything.

Or worse, video.

That one tiny phrase is on repeat in my head, as is the sick expression that weighed on my mother's face, sagging her eyes, souring her mouth and tightening her body where it sat. She shifted her feet when he said those words, her heeled shoes scraping along on the floor beneath her chair like chalk on a board as her ankles uncrossed and crossed again.

Our car ride home was quiet. That's usually a sign things didn't go well. When my mom leaves one of those meetings feeling confident, we stop for smoothies. Today, we drove straight home and she took a bath—for an hour.

She's back at it now, hunched over at the table, emailing statements back and forth with our attorney until she gets the wording just right.

"I'm sorry," I say, paused at the coffee maker, the bag of grounds in my hands.

She blinks up at me, one pair of glasses on the tip of

her nose, another pair tucked in her hair. I point at it and she looks straight up at her brow, feeling around the top of her head until she uncovers them.

"Oh." She laughs, pulling them from her twisted-up hair and tossing them on the table. "I spent an hour looking for those."

"Found 'em," I say.

She gives me a very tired, slightly crooked smile. Both of our bodies are numb from the emotional beating we took today. It kills my mom to have to talk about me like I'm a commodity, especially when I'm in the room. Even worse, it's probably hard to have her parenting judged on my mistakes, especially when the other parent couldn't even bother to fly in for this meeting.

"Stop saying you're sorry," she says, finally, resting her chin on her fist.

I shrug.

"But I am."

My mom slowly shakes her head.

"Well, forgive yourself, then, because I have no reason to. My daughter is perfect. Mistakes are part of growing. As parents, we are here to guide you and support you through your highs and lows, even if there's a financial responsibility tied to it. Your dad . . ." She straightens her spine and draws in a deep breath.

That's another thing my mom is good about. She limits the bad things she says to me about my father. I did not inherit her ability to take the high road. I like to battle in the trenches and go low. Mostly, though, I do it to stand up for my friends who are like my mom and won't get ugly.

That's how fights are done—ugly.

"Okay, well, how about this? I'm sorry I didn't make him pay for the privilege of taking my photo in the first place." It's actually a thought I've had a lot, about how this guy didn't even earn what I gave him. I'm starting to think the only reason I made out with him was because his name was Jake and he reminded me of my yogurt commercial crush with the same name.

"If that makes you feel better." My mom chuckles.

She pushes her glasses back up her nose and continues with her work while I begin a pot of coffee. A light rap at the door catches my attention and I look over my shoulder to see if my mom heard it too. She's so deep in her work, though, that I dump the water in the coffee maker and wipe my hands on my way to the door.

Hayden is standing close enough that his nose looks way too big for his head through the fisheye lens on the peep hole. It makes me laugh, and I continue being amused while I open the door.

"Were you trying to look through it the wrong way?" I ask, playfully pushing at his chest. He's dressed for practice, and I'm not sure why he isn't there now.

"I was, but it doesn't work that way." He tips forward on his toes and kisses my forehead. He hands me a single rose from behind his back and my face heats from the sweet gesture, knowing that my mom will make a big deal about it. I may as well bring her into the loop on my dating life.

"What's this for?" I ask, pushing the door open wider to invite him in.

"Early birthday gift. I have something better planned, but I wanted to stop by and give you this on my way to practice," he says, clearing up my question on where he's headed.

"Still at the junior high?" I assume.

"Yeah." He sighs as he steps into the house, and my reactions are too slow to undo the trouble I see coming.

"Back so soon? You must really like tea," my mom says, slinging one arm over her chair.

A squiggle forms on Hayden's forehead.

"This is Hayden, Mom." I make eyes at her, silently signaling all of the complicated shit I have to say about him, his brother, and that she got to see one of them all grown up before the other, when it probably should have been the other way around.

And . . . shit. This is bad.

My mom's brow lowers and her mouth bunches as she pulls her glasses from her face.

"Ah, yes. Reading glasses made you all blurry but I can see the difference now." She's joking, but Hayden isn't in on it. It takes a while to get a grasp on my mom's humor.

"Very funny, Mom. Yes, they're still twins," I say, placing my palm on Hayden's chest as if he's an exhibit. I glance to him and whisper, "I'll explain this later."

He laughs out "okay" and continues toward my mom with his hand outstretched.

"It's nice to see you, Ms. Cortez. It's been a few," he says.

My mom's head tilts to the side as they shake, her mouth hung open with questions just waiting to spill out. She looks from him to me, to the rose in my hand, then back to him again, and her mouth curves up in an amused smile.

"Nice to see you again, too," she says, that smile growing into a full grin. "So grown up."

I turn my back on the situation because she's about to get nosy and pushy, and embarrassing. I find a tall glass in the cabinet and fill it with water for my rose.

"So, tell me, Hayden. How long have you two been sneaking around behind my back?" Again, my mom is kidding. This is her way of both making Hayden shit himself and getting dirt on the stuff I haven't told her. I exhale and turn to face them with my back against the sink.

Hayden falls right into her plan, stuttering his way through some semblance of an answer. "Oh . . . I didn't mean to disrespect . . . Not that I'm disrespecting your daughter, but I meant your house . . . or rules. Yes, rules!"

My mom finally gets up and places her palm on what I am certain is Hayden's wildly beating chest.

"Relax, child. I'm messing with you. I figured you'd tell me more about my daughter's life than she does," she says, shooting me a glare that only I can see. She's joking in front of Hayden, but deep down she's upset that she had no idea that a *we* existed between us.

I haven't had a real boyfriend, well, maybe ever. It's a topic my mom and I talk about when we watch romantic comedies or teen movies where all girls seem to want are boyfriends.

"Where is your boyfriend?" she always asks.

My consistent response: "I don't have one."

She pushes me about it because deep down she's afraid that her and my dad's ugly relationship is ruining my perspective on love and matters of the heart. And honestly? It is. When I think about love, I can't help but associate it with animosity, jealousy, regret, hatred, destruction. My list is endless and so very negative. But I can't tell her that. Besides, I'm not so sure it's a bad thing that I got to see love for what it is—a dangerous gamble, high on distraction and low on reward.

There's no risk in dating Hayden. He's kind and I know I can confide in him, and I like that he needs to lean on me right now. But I know I don't love him. I don't think I could. I'm not sure I'm capable of it . . . at all. I like him a whole lot, and he likes me. But love? No. The only danger I've found in being with Hayden is one that I've only recently realized. And I don't understand why it's happening.

"Tory." My mom says his name and it shakes me from my thoughts, bringing me back to the conversation unfolding between Hayden and my mom.

"Right, that's your brother's name," my mom says, snapping her fingers as if Hayden just filled in a gap in her memory. My mom is playing along now for my benefit, which means she picked up my silent plea. She doesn't forget anything. It's half the reason we've been able to fight my dad's legal team so well. My mom has a photographic memory, and she's a touch of a hoarder, saving every remotely important piece of paper on the planet to back up those memories. There's no way Tory's name slipped her mind.

"You know, it's amazing how damned near identical you and your brother are," my mom says. I kind of wish she would drop the comparison conversation because lately it feels as if Tory and Hayden are doing plenty of it on their own. And I'd rather quit thinking about one of them.

"The only difference is I'm a little better looking," Hayden responds, his joke getting a short chuckle from my mom.

The slightest hint of a smile remains on her lips long after Hayden turns his attention back to me. I find myself caught in the look on her face, trying to decipher it while Hayden is talking.

"Earth to Abby," he says, waving a hand in front of me and cupping my shoulder. I jerk and reengage with the world.

"Sorry, you were saying something about Saturday night."

He laughs at my pathetic summary.

"Umm, yeah. That's your birthday. I was talking about taking you out. To celebrate?"

My mom has suddenly given us space, disappearing into the mudroom in the back of the house, folding things I'm sure are already folded and staying just close enough to the door that she can hear every word we say.

"I'm simple. We can just go to dinner or something." Truthfully, after the day I've had, my birthday feels completely insignificant. I looked forward to the independence of being eighteen, but it's looking more and more as though my dad will be an unwelcome business partner until I'm successful enough to pay for lawyers who can fire him.

"Okay, well, it might be a little better than simple, but I promise you'll enjoy it," he says, pulling me into arms that have been nothing but safe and a home for my restless mind. This time, though, his embrace does nothing to stop my racing thoughts.

"Hey, is that Tory's?"

My stomach drops at his question, my mouth watering in reaction to the dose of adrenaline injected into my veins. That fucking sweatshirt! He left it here like a Trojan horse and it will put me right smack in the center of whatever bullshit pissing contest is happening between him and his brother.

"Oh, yeah. I'm not sure why I have it, but—"

"I'll take it to him," Hayden says, grabbing it forcefully before I can come up with a lie as to why it's here.

"Great."

I'm too weak to elaborate. Too scared to invite more conflict. Too afraid to lose this other version of myself that I get to be with Hayden. And that's what this is all about. It sinks in suddenly. With Hayden, I'm the girl who can have a steady relationship and a person to call, and I'm the person who solves someone else's problems. My problems are in the background, easier to ignore tucked neatly in the shadow of something normal—like just being a high school senior planning to celebrate her birthday with her boyfriend.

Hayden leaves for practice with the token left behind by his brother in hand, such a trivial piece of clothing to spawn such an intense shift in my world. One more hug from arms that feel a little colder than before and leave me feeling nothing, and Hayden is gone.

13

TORY

I've texted my brother six times with no answer. I hung out with June and Lucas after school so I had them drop me off and told Hayden I didn't need a ride. I didn't hear back then, and the five texts after have all gone unread. Normally, I'd lie for him about being late to practice, but I think I've made enough concessions in the last twelve hours to hold me over on favors for a little while. He can come up with his own excuse for this one. Besides, it's not like he or I would ever get benched. Coach sits us and he might as well spot the other team twenty points.

I toss my phone into my temporary locker and fling the door shut, jogging out the door to begin warm-ups with the team. Our shoes squeak a little more than normal on the junior high floors, and we set a playful rhythm as we jog our laps around the gym. I'm comfortable in the pattern, laughing with Chaz, who actually isn't being a dick for once, when something quickly throws our rubber sole musical off beat.

"Hey!" My brother's fast pace is accompanied by screeching steps that spin me around as I run. I take a few steps backward before my own sweatshirt is thrown at my face, followed by my brother's fist.

"You left something at Abby's house, you fucking snake!"

I'm still a bit wobbly from the first punch, struggling to get my feet under my weight as they scurry. Hayden seizes the moment, shoving me backward completely, and I fall on my ass. Hard!

"What the fuck, Hayden!" I run the back of my hand across my nose, getting a streak of blood on my skin. The bright red fuels my own rage. So much for high roads and forgiveness.

I scramble to my feet as my brother charges me with his shoulders lowered, like a bull seeing red. I brace myself for impact, catching him around his midsection and lifting him in the air before throwing him to the ground. Our bodies tangle, a fury of awkward punches and flails. He smacks my ribs and sides so hard I get the wind knocked out of me, but I'm undeterred. I'm finally able to get my knees on his arms, pinning him to the floor as I straddle his body. I'll only be able to hold him like this for a second, three tops.

"Hayden, what is going on?" I hold his wrists to the ground and lean all of my weight on him as I look into his raging eyes.

"You tell me, brother. You tell me!" He thrusts me off and grabs the sweatshirt from the floor, once again throwing it at my face.

I know what it is. I know why he's pissed, but this reaction—in front of everyone—feels a bit excessive. It's not like anything happened. *Not that I didn't try.*

Maybe his reaction is more on target than I give him credit for.

"Abby get cold or something and you just need to warm her up? Or you leave that over there when you were sneaking around behind my back?"

Chaz snickers in a low breath, loving this drama between me and my brother. We should both forget about our issues and take out Chaz right now.

"Hayden, I'm not sneaking anything. And if you don't know your girlfriend well enough that you have these kinds of trust issues, then maybe you need to step off and deal with that." I toss my sweatshirt into a corner then tug down my jersey before testing the blood on my nose again. My cheek is puffy, and I'm sure there's a bruise forming under my eye.

"We about done here?" Coach Newsome steps into the space between Hayden and me. My brother and I are maybe eight inches taller than the man, and we each outweigh him by forty pounds. His physical authority isn't intimidating, but he has this disappointing tinge to his expression that tends to dominate whenever he needs to use it. He's using it now, his mouth a flat line and his eyes drooping with disgust. He tucks his clipboard under his arm to clap. I've seen this move before too. He does this to referees when they blow calls. Hell, he's gotten thrown out of games for mocking them like this. Pretty sure Hayden and I don't have the authority to throw him out of anything.

"Sorry, Coach," Hayden says, getting to his feet.

"Yeah, sorry," I reiterate.

His clapping continues, long enough for us to feel truly uncomfortable.

"You two figure this shit out. You're done here today. We're going to work on some defense, and since you're both shitty at defense, you'll just be in my way anyway. So, go on. Get out of here. Maybe Monday will be a different story. Last game before the holiday break, then our invitational tournament. Try not to ruin Christmas, yeah?"

He glares at both of us over the top of his black-rimmed glasses. His brows are thick caterpillars that meet in the middle when his eyes narrow like this, and it makes him look meaner. His method works because I feel like an asshole, and I can tell Hayden does, too. His shoulders sag, and his body drags as he walks over to the place where I threw my sweatshirt. He picks it up and shakes off the dust from the floor, then holds it out for me without making eye contact.

"Thanks," I mutter.

We both head into the locker room like puppies caught chewing the new couch, tails tucked between our legs and chins buried into the nooks of our neck.

Neither of us says a word as we switch out our shoes and stuff our belongings into our matching gym bags. Dad bought these for us for the start of the season last year. I'm not sure why they feel so symbolic now, but the fact they're exactly the same seems important. Inside, they are so incredibly different.

I sit down on the bench with a heavy exhale and stare at the empty locker in front of me for a few seconds while my brother zips up his bag. Eventually, I get the courage to swivel my head in his direction. His jaw is tight and his movements are rigid. He's still mad, and now that the heat of the moment has passed, I realize he probably should be.

"Dude, I'm sorry," I say in a low voice.

"It's fine," he says, tugging the strap of his bag up his arm and popping his gaze to mine just long enough to show me that he's no longer in the mood to talk about this.

I breathe out and get to my feet, stepping in front of him before he's able to just walk out the door. I hold the side of my fist against his chest and he looks down at it with narrowed eyes.

"Don't do that. I mean it. Abby and I are . . . friends. That's it. And I'm sorry if it seemed disrespectful." The words feel like acid on my tongue.

Hayden covers my fist with his hand, wrapping his fingers around it then tossing it from his body. His eyes shift to meet mine and we stare hard at one another, each of us knowing there is a layer of bullshit coating the things we're saying to each other.

"Like I said. It's fine," he grits out.

He makes his way to the door and I wait for it to slam closed behind him before I scream out *"fuuuuuck!"* so loudly that the word bounces off the walls around me. I follow his footsteps through the door, expecting our car to be long gone, but it's not. Hayden is idling near the curb by the exit.

I get in and Hayden begins driving before I buckle up. We ride the few miles in silence, and he pulls into the driveway at an uncomfortable speed, taking the bump in the curb hard enough to scrape the chassis of the car. I shoot him a glare because we share this thing, but he doesn't seem to notice.

"Get out," he finally utters.

I don't immediately, instead subjecting myself to the hot fumes of his temper and letting them reignite my own. But for once in my goddamn life, I manage to not engage.

"Whatever," I say, kicking open the door and dragging my bag out from the floor. I slam the door closed behind me and Hayden speeds backward a beat later, tires squealing when he shifts back into drive and peels down our street. I stare at the space he vacated for a few seconds and replay the last thirty minutes in my head.

My mom is home. She almost always is. She's had the same part-part-time job at Craft Mart for years. She works, and when they get in new displays, her job is to build them then do the sample craft for people to see on the tables by the entrance. Her degree is in elementary education, but I think her emphasis was on crafts. Hayden and I always turned in the best projects in grade school. Mom did every single one of them.

In a fantasy family, I would be able to walk in, call her name out then go tell her about my problems. She'd be able to help me work out a solution. Instead, she's part of my mess. Hayden talks to her a lot more than I do. Now that I think about it, I don't think my mom and I have spoken for maybe a full week—perhaps even two—not counting therapy, of course.

I glance through the van windows on my way into the house. There's a pack of cigarettes in the center cupholder, the top ripped open and the end of one poking through the hole. She's smoking again. She's tried to quit about a dozen times. My dad hates it, so she keeps it to the van. I can't help but think she's stress smoking in the van out of respect for him, and her delusion that he's coming back.

He's not. I knew the minute he moved out. I guess even I clung to a thread of hope, though.

The kitchen is messy, bread left out from toast my mom must have made, so I dump my bag in the laundry room and spend a few minutes cleaning the house. This is another one of those things my father took care of, despite the fact my mom hardly works and has always had time to keep up with the house. He's fastidious; Hayden got this trait. I'm normally more like my mom when it comes to neatness. I'm trying to shed any quality we share, so might as well start with tidying up.

The more I dust and straighten, the more caught up I get in making this place look as if Dad were still living here. I tuck the cord behind the coffee maker the way he would. The mugs in the cabinet all get turned with their handles facing the same way, and the random bags from shopping that my mom has just thrown into a drawer get neatly rolled into balls to save space.

I continue making little changes around the living room, dragging the dust cloth up the stair railing after I finish with the tables and shelves downstairs. My dad would use this wood shine stuff in a spray bottle when he did this. I couldn't find any downstairs, but the rag smelled like it so it will have to do. I cleanse our space in the scent of something familiar, clearing away the layer of dust that's formed on the record player top and along the spines of Dad's albums. I pick up one of my trophies from the end of the book case and run the rag around the dusty base, pausing to read the inscription.

MOST VALUABLE PLAYER

I set the rag down and kneel, looking for the matching statuette on the bottom shelf, finding it quickly and holding them both in my palms side by side.

LEADERSHIP AWARD

Those are the words on Hayden's statue. It's not even a real thing that teams give out. It's a made-up recognition to make sure our family wasn't sent home with one trophy in a house with two boys.

Fuck, he's right.

I pull out more of his things, reading the engravings and certificates more closely than I ever have before. Every single piece of hardware out on display is the equivalent of second place, a make-up award. When we were little, it probably didn't register with him, *but come on!* There's no way that by the time he was eleven or twelve he didn't see the difference in our accolades. I can't believe it's taken him this long to act out on it.

My eyes glaze over, staring at the neatly lined up set of awards with my name on them. My mom's TV hums in the background, the noise muffled through her closed doors. She's probably taking a nap.

I pull trophies and frames down from the top shelf —*my* shelf. I'm gentle at first, but the farther down the row I get, the less I care about these gold-painted plastic pieces of junk. By the time I get to the middle section, I'm done with it all, and I run my forearm along the rest of the space, sweeping everything to the floor in a clattering mess.

The space now cleared, I refill it with Hayden's things.

My movements grow more and more manic until I'm basically throwing his things up on the shelf while my eyes burn with a cocktail of anger and guilt. The top shelf becomes crowded with these trinkets that helped form the animosity my brother now exhibits against me.

Even his photos were kept down here. I lift up the one from our freshman year, his skinny arms barely filling out the varsity jersey, and as I hold it up to study, a folded piece of paper slides out from the back of the frame.

Setting the photo in the very center of the bookcase, I straighten out the paper, instantly recognizing the logo on the letterhead. I applied for Olsen Training Academy in eighth grade. It's a boarding school in Texas where sports are treated with the same weight as math and science. It's a factory for elite athletes, and more than half of the athletes that go through the program end up playing in the pros for whatever sport they specialize in. Almost all of them play in college. Dad helped me apply, and I bugged my parents every day for three months asking if they'd gotten a call, an email . . . *a letter.*

I fall to my ass and sit, holding the letter in both hands as I imagine this life I could have had, my *almost* life.

Provisional acceptance.

I was one visit to the campus away. An interview that I no doubt would have aced. There's no way my dad knew about this, because he was the one who encouraged me. He was ready to travel with me, to buy a second home or a condo near the campus so my family could visit. It was my motherfucking dream!

There's no way to fashion a second-place trophy for

this. If I went to Olsen, I went alone. Hayden stayed behind. I went top shelf and he went bottom.

Without pause, I take my phone from my back pocket and glance to the still-closed doors behind me, my mind vacillating between who to blame—Hayden or my mom— while I listen to the rings sound. My dad answers by the fourth ring.

"Tory, hey. Something wrong? Aren't you in practice?" He knows I should be.

"Dad, I think maybe I need to come stay with you. For a little while at least. I just . . ." I break down, swallowing hard and feeling my lungs tighten as the air leaves them and my body grows numb. This is what betrayal feels like to the utmost degree. This is how he felt when he found out about Mom's affair.

"You're going to have to drive back for school on your own," he says, giving me the only roadblock to the plan. I have a thousand dollars saved from various birthday and holiday gifts and shitty summer job I took at the local pool.

"Okay," I agree, getting to my feet and moving to my room to pack my things. "Can you pick me up soon? Like . . . now? I'll buy a piece of shit car."

"On my way," he says.

I end the call, not sure whether my dad likes the win that comes with me choosing address sides or he senses the urgency in my voice. Maybe it's the aftermath of our pitiful therapy session. Whatever the motivation, I'm glad he's coming. And I'm glad I'm getting out of this place. It's suffocating me.

14

ABBY

I t's been a while since I've felt like myself. I told June all I really wanted for my birthday weekend—because yes, I get an entire weekend, and yes, Friday nights are weekend-eligible—was to do something that felt like the old me.

"Anything you want," she said.

She regretted it the moment the last word left her lips. She could read *party* all over my face. I don't care what she says, though. Deep down, June needs tonight, too. She misses us.

"Are you sure you don't mind driving?" She doesn't, but it makes me feel polite to ask. I like getting ready at June's house. There aren't papers all over her table, and her mom is in a pretty good place. Mine is buried in the fight to give me a life without my father's greed picking away at it. Tonight, I want to forget that version of myself.

"I'm not going to drink, and the van has plenty of

room," she says while running a brush through her hair. I smile because she's repeating my talking points.

"Exactly," I say, leaning close to the small mirror on the back of her door so I can perfect the shade under my eyes.

It feels nice to dress up like this. I've been a lot of versions of myself lately—the girl who wears her boyfriend's oversized sweatshirt, the business woman who gets accused of having a sex tape, the actress who doesn't know what her character is supposed to look like. It's nice for once to just be me. My makeup, my skinny jeans and cut-off sweatshirt—my body, my rules. I can feel my confidence coming back already. It's amazing how much your own unique look can make you feel at home in your skin. My look isn't everyone's, but it's mine.

June's mom holds the door open for us as we leave, hanging out the door as if we're still the same little girls she sent off to walk to school by themselves for the very first time in second grade. I'm tempted to hold June's hand in solidarity.

"Don't do stupid things!" Mrs. Mabee shouts. She says that to me a lot.

"Nothing you wouldn't do," I shout back before getting into the passenger side. She shakes her head at my usual response.

Again—normal.

We head to Naomi's to pick her up, then stop at Lola's work as she finishes her shift. She's a server at the Pancake House, this truck stop joint open twenty-four hours a day, which means she has unlimited access to bacon. I don't care who a person is, if they say they don't like bacon I immediately throw them in the *sketch* category. Because of birthday weekend, Lola swiped me an entire to-go box full. I'm already five pieces in.

"Abby, if you don't slow down you're going to be vomiting before you even get close to a shot of tequila," June says, turning right on the old dirt road a few miles out of town.

"Well, guess what? I'm drinking beer tonight," I say, winking as I take a bite of my sixth piece. June takes it out of my hand and finishes it for me, part for my own good and part because, well, it's bacon.

It's barely ten at night and the party is already crowded enough that we can hear it with June's windows down. I crack my window and breathe in the scent of burning wood. There's a huge clearing on McCaffey's property and he always has these huge bonfires. It's an amazing sight to break through the trees and see the bright orange flames off in the distance. June spots Lucas's truck quickly, so she pulls the van up next to him and we all get out.

"Happy birthday, Abs," Lucas says, pulling me in for a side hug and handing me a cup full of beer.

"Just what I always wanted. Thanks," I say, taking my first gulp and feeling the tension in my neck and shoulders ease.

Tonight, there is no lawsuit. I'm on the brink of stardom. And there is nothing in my life to bring me down. I almost believe these words when a lifted red truck pulls up across the clearing, the chrome bumper catching the flicker of the flames as Tory hops out of the driver's side and Cannon and a few other guys climb out of the back carrying a keg.

Tory stops and leans against the front of the truck, one

knee bent as his foot rests on the bumper, his hands sunk in the pockets of his jeans. He's wearing a red and black flannel over a black shirt, and his normally perfectly sculpted hair is windblown and messy. I recognize his dad's truck, which makes me wonder why he's driving it.

I bring my cup of beer to my lips and taste it with my tongue, tipping it back slowly while staring at Tory over the rim. He's not even pretending not to look at me. It's like a dare, to see if I can handle the attention. Well, I can. And he can keep on looking from over there. Hayden works tonight, which means I am one-hundred percent about my girlfriends. I plan on spending the night gossiping mercilessly, dancing to music under the stars, and telling dumb stories without endings that make me and my friends exhaust ourselves with buzzed laughter.

"You heard he moved out, right?" June says, bumping into my side.

"Huh?" I pull my cup away and shift my gaze to her.

I'm already breaking my rules. I'm not supposed to care. But Tory moved out and Hayden hasn't said anything. Seems kinda weird.

"Oh." She winces. Her mouth gets tight and she forces that pretend smile on her lips, trying to convince me that it's not a big deal.

I lightly punch her arm.

"Don't do that. Spill it," I say.

She wiggles her head side-to-side and shrugs at me.

"Hey, I'm gonna go talk to Tor for a bit. I'll be right back," Lucas says, kissing her softly and glancing at me mid-kiss. I can tell by the awkward bend in his brow that there's more to this story than just Tory moving out. I let him get several steps away before I grill my friend.

"What's going on?" I ask.

June's mouth twists up.

"June," I beg.

"I guess there was a sweatshirt or something?" She shrinks into her shoulders as she talks, and I immediately roll my eyes.

"Oh, my God," I say, waving my hand in the air in a big circle. It lands at the bridge of my nose and I pinch.

"Tory came by once for a visit, just to talk, while he was out for a run a few days ago. He took his sweatshirt off and forgot it. Hayden saw it today and said he was going to give it back to him. I had a feeling he was getting the wrong idea."

"Abby, he sucker punched him in the middle of practice," June says.

My head pops up and my mouth hangs open.

"For real?" I challenge, hoping she's exaggerating.

She nods toward Tory across the field.

"Go check out his eye. It's purple."

I look back toward him, squinting to see if I can make anything out from the light of the flames. It's too dark to see for sure. I knew something like this would happen. I had the worst feeling when Hayden left, and he's been off today. We've barely talked, other than him telling me he had to work tonight. I just figured he was stuck in his feelings, and I didn't want to push.

That's become the problem. He's always in his feelings or my life is chaotic, so instead of having the tough talk about what we're even doing together, I just kick the can down the road for the next day, and then the next.

"So, he moved out because they got in a fight . . . over me?" I look back to June and her expression isn't definitive, one eye scrunched and her mouth twisted up along with it.

"Sorta?" She says it like a question. "I don't think it's a permanent thing. He told Lucas he was driving here from his dad's tonight. I think he's just staying there until things get sorted out, or until graduation, or—"

"Until graduation?" I blurt out.

I hand June my beer and roll down the sleeves of my sweatshirt to cover my chilled knuckles. I hug myself to keep the midriff of my shirt from blowing up in the cross breeze as I cut in front of the fire. The warmth feels good, and moves into my cheeks, injecting more of that confidence I've been missing in my spine. I catch Tory mid-conversation with Lucas and Cannon, and something about the way I march up must signal to the other guys that they should leave. They split without me even having to ask.

"You wanna tell me why you're living with your dad?" I cross my arms over my chest and stare at his smirk. Shit, his eye is pretty fucked up. The bruise is worse on his cheek. He can tell I'm staring at it, so he reaches up and touches it lightly with the tips of his fingers.

"It doesn't hurt anymore. Sometimes, I almost forget it's there." His hands drop to his pockets and he lowers his gaze to the ground, glancing back up at me with his eyes more than his face. "Hayden didn't like that you had my sweatshirt. That's basically all there is to that story."

His gaze lingers as he chews at the tip of his tongue, his lips curved with a hint of a drunken smile.

"You drive after a few?" I jut my hip out and stare at him with judgement.

"Just one beer. I'm fine," he says.

My eyes haze and I hold them on him until he has to look away.

"What? Fine, okay, maybe two. And I just rolled up to McCaffey's house to haul down the keg. No main roads. And I'm sleeping here, so just . . . don't worry about me, birthday girl." He leans forward and touches the tip of his finger to my nose, then walks away.

I'm left there all alone, wondering how I got here, to a place where I'm both livid that he belittled me and care that he's upset with me. This is Tory D'Angelo. I walk away from *him*, not the other way around.

Determined and pissed, I follow in his path and slide up next to him at the keg, waiting while he fills a cup. I partly expect him to give me the one he's working on, but he doesn't. Instead, he turns to make space and holds his hand out to signal it's my turn as he takes a long gulp. Seems the old Abby *and* the old Tory are both making appearances tonight.

"Where's your boyfriend?"

He says it with such animus, I wonder if he found out Hayden knew about his mother's affair when it first started. This rivalry brewing between them has to be about more than just me. Hayden has been struggling with major guilt over hiding his mom's secret for so long. Nobody knows he knew. He saw them together at football camp their freshman year, and a few unexplainable lunch-time visits when he ran into Lucas's dad at his house fanned his hunch that the fling was not a one-time occurrence. Since his parents' relationship blew up, Hayden feels his lack of action made everything worse. I've tried to tell him it didn't, it only postponed the inevitable.

I finish filling my cup and take a few steps back, opening space between us so people can get through.

"Hayden's at work. He know you packed up and moved out?" I take a slow sip, smiling with my lips against the cup.

We stare at one another while two freshmen come up and fill their cups between us. It's amusing to watch them blush and act out for Tory's benefit. So hungry for attention.

"Ladies," he says, throwing them a bone.

"H-Hi," one of them says while the other giggles. They're barely fifteen. No way they're finishing a whole beer. I wonder if the daycare camp bus dropped them off here by mistake.

"Careful, ladies. He's all talk," I say, shrugging with one shoulder as I cash in my win.

The girls rush away, whispering to one another. Tory and I just gave them a story to tell for the rest of the year. He's the hot guy and I'm the bitch.

"All talk, huh?" He tips the rest of his beer back, chugging it in one smooth movement then tossing his cup to the ground. I hold my ground even though he's getting closer, even though people are watching us, even though I shouldn't. I'm daring him right back, and a little part of me wants to. It's the beer thinking.

Tory runs his finger up my cheek then tucks my hair

behind my ear. He leans in and dips down, pausing at my ear as if he's about to share a dirty secret. My body tenses, and shivers run up and down my skin. I straighten my posture and shift my feet slightly, hoping he doesn't notice the nervous movements. With his lips close enough to my skin that he could taste me if he wants to, I listen to only his breath. It's warm.

"You look absolutely beautiful."

His mouth hovers there, dangerously close for a full second that feels like several more. He backs away, letting his eyes seer into mine as he straightens tall and walks backward, leaving me where I stand—frozen and oddly heartbroken.

I have zero comebacks. Worse, I can't rectify how badly it turns out I wanted—no, *needed*—to hear it. Mr. All Talk just said the perfect words, and a tear forms in the corner of my eye. I hate crying, but I've suddenly realized how absolutely miserable I have become. My life is a mess, and I'm trying to make it better by being some guy's girlfriend because as messy as I am, he's worse. This is co-dependency at its absolute worst.

"You all right?" June slides her arm through mine and I swipe the back of my hand over my eyes and nose.

"Yeah," I say, smiling at her—performing. "Just cold. Let's get some of that fire, yeah?"

She grins, then escorts me to a flat log parked near the open pit, a perfect spot for me to curl up my legs and think. So far, this isn't the girls' night I pictured, but maybe it's the girls' night I need.

15

TORY

Two things happen when you have about an hour to buy a used car. One, you don't really pick based on the right set of criteria. You scan the lot by price point and then narrow things down based on mileage and the little car know-how you possess to get a sense of what might break and what you can fix. And then two, you get mercilessly screwed by the dealer.

I had a thousand bucks of my own, two with the grand my dad pitched in. Shocker—this piece of crap old cop car rang up just under the cap. I have just enough left to fill the tank. I promised my dad I'd get a job as soon as the season's done so I can take on the insurance. Hayden pays a portion of the Subaru's, and I can't let him better me.

The strange look I get from my mom as I pull into our driveway tells me the body of this car is as bad as I thought. You can almost read the word POLICE on the side; the buffing job and primer cover-up was an afterthought. The one thing this car has going for it, though, is the engine. I'll be able to leave this place fast when I need to.

I came back because my dad said it was a good idea. Our family has a lot of drama happening, and a split like this—two against two—sets up a real roadblock for any hope of peace in the future. I didn't tell him about the letter I found Thursday afternoon. I'm still processing it in my own head, and like he said, I'm not sure if adding more fuel to our dumpster fire of a family is best right now.

I'm not here for all selfless reasons, though. I also came back because Abby's birthday is today, and June is throwing a party for her tomorrow. I want to be there for it, even if my brother spends the time secretly plotting to push me out a window. I'll go back to Dad's next weekend. Space is necessary for me and Hayden. I don't want to hate him, and right now . . . I do.

"Wow, that's . . . some ride," my mom says as I step out of the car. The heavy door squeals as I shut it.

"It gets the job done," I say, stopping when my feet are squared with hers. We face off for a few seconds, my arm weighed down with my bag of clothes that I intend to shuffle back and forth. I see how unsure she is of what to do in her eyes. They keep scanning me, making sure nothing's broken and that I'm as she remembered. Thing is, though . . . I'm not. I've changed in the last two months. And the old me will never fully come back.

"You have laundry?" Her voice is hopeful.

"I was gone for a day, Mom."

"Oh, right," she nods. She steps forward and squeezes my biceps, her attempt at some sort of affection. She hugs Hayden all the time.

"Are you hungry?" She lets her hands drop from my arms and heads in through the garage. I follow behind her.

"No. I ate at Dad's."

"Oh," she says. I can hear the disappointment in her tone.

"He had muffins, so I grabbed one," I say. That's a lie. Dad made me bacon and eggs, but for whatever reason, it seems that would be showing off.

"Well, I can make some sandwiches for lunch, or maybe we can go out?" She turns to face me, hope widening her eyes. I don't think I have ever gone to lunch with just my mom. She's trying so hard, though.

"Maybe. I'll see if I'm hungry," I say, popping her hope balloon with a pin. It's already noon, and I'm not planning on leaving my room.

"Hayden should be home by three." She must know something about our fight. She hasn't mentioned the purple line under my eye, and she has to suspect something made me rush out of this house and head to Indy.

I only nod at her information, and after a long, painfully quiet stare, she moves on, apparently deciding to drop it.

"Well, I'll be down here, going through some old things in the garage. If you decide you want that lunch . . ."

I've already begun my trip up the stairs.

"I'll let you know," I say.

I'm being cold. I'm also being civil. I can't be both warm and polite right now. The two qualities are mutually exclusive.

My bedroom looks like I left for college. My mom must have come in and cleaned up. The only reason she knows I left for my dad's is because he told her. If he hadn't, I sorta wonder if she would have noticed.

I toss my bag to the floor and faceplant into my comforter, pulling my pillow down to bury my head. My dad's rental isn't set up for guests yet. He wasn't planning on Hayden or me coming, so when I got there, my only bed option was the crappy couch that came with the place. Staging furniture is a lot like hotel lobby furniture. Stiff as fuck.

I didn't wake up hungover, which is a refreshing change after a McCaffey party. I didn't get back from the woods until two in the morning. I quit drinking after my short talk with Abby. Instead, I sat in my dad's truck for four hours and watched her have a good time with her friends. She laughed, and I haven't seen her do that in a long while.

She isn't who she's supposed to be when she's with my brother. And yeah, that thought is steeped in jealousy on the surface, but what makes it honest is I don't think she would be who she's supposed to be with me, either. While we're all growing up, Abby's already there. She has her life mapped out and is full of ambition and drive. I'm broke because I blew my birthday money on an old squad car.

Before the urge leaves my mind, I pull my phone from my back pocket and prop myself up on my elbows over my pillow, scrolling through my contacts until I land on June's info. I'm not sure whether she'll think this is a good idea or a bad one, but she must know that things in my life are chaotic at best. I haven't filled her or Lucas in on the latest revelations. I need to process them on my own first.

ME: *Hey*.

I let that message sit there for a while like a test to see if she's even around. I know she's normally at the bowling alley at this time on a Saturday, but since it's Abby's birthday weekend, maybe she took the day off. She writes back after a full minute.

JUNE: *Well hi, stranger. You in Indy?*

I rub my eyes, still puffy from the long night and face still sore from my brother's punch.

ME: *Long story, but no. Trying to keep some peace.*

I pause while she types, but before she can send her reply, I get my real motive out of the way.

ME: *I need to call Abby. Number?*

All signs that June is responding stop, so I drop my chin to my pillow and stare at the message screen with the weight of rocks in my stomach. It finally rings and I cringe. I'm so much better typing than I am talking. At least it's June.

"Look, I just want to apologize to her." I don't bother with hellos because I know June doesn't plan to, either. She'll dive right into how I told her I would be okay and that I was over it and how I'm clearly not. I keep telling her she needs to consider psychology in college. It's not that she's good as much as she loves to dig her hands into other people's heads and find out their business.

"I wasn't going to say anything," she says, a playful lilt to her voice. She's such a bad liar.

"Yeah, right." I laugh.

"Fine. I just don't want to see you get hurt."

"Well, too late," I respond, rolling to my back and pressing my fist against my head.

The line is silent for a few long seconds, and finally I

hear her breathe out a mixture of concession and pity—there it is again, goddamn pity.

"Just try not to make things worse for yourself, okay?" She's serious about her position, and all I can do is laugh because of course I'm going to make things worse. I'm going to torture myself endlessly until I get over whatever this infatuation is that has its hooks so deep in my skin that it actually burns.

"Fine, got it. No making things worse." My response is snarky, and I can tell June is not amused.

"*Hmmm,*" she hums into the line.

"All right," she finally gives in. "I'll text you her contact. But only because I admire you not dropping into her DMs like some creeper. Oh, and hey, you know we're having her birthday dinner here tomorrow, right? You *are* coming to that, aren't you?"

"I guess that depends on how this phone call goes."

"Tory! You can't not come. It will be weirder if you're not here. And my mom made cake, and she has these games planned, and it only works if we have enough people show up—"

"I'll be there." I say it just to shut her up. She's spiraling and Lucas is way more equipped to deal with that than I am. "I promise. I'll be there."

I promised. *Shit.*

"Okay, well . . . good luck."

"Thanks," I say.

We end our call and a few seconds later, Abby's contact info shows up on my phone. I let my finger hover over the call icon for several minutes, running through all the reasons I could use as an excuse for calling. I told June

I want to apologize, but that's a lie. I just want to hear Abby's voice, and maybe talk for a while without all of the noise that comes between us. I want to hear about her court case, and about her in general. I want to do nothing but listen.

With my eyes closed, I let my finger fall to the phone, and then hold my breath as it rings. I move to my side so I can rest on the phone and keep it close. I'm about to give up when she finally answers.

"This is Abby Cortez."

Instantly, my lips twitch with a sharp smile. She's so professional. Much better than my "Yo, what up" greeting.

"Hello, Miss Cortez. This is Salvatore D'Angelo. I was calling with some important information." I put on a deeper voice, expecting it to make her laugh, but there isn't a response for several seconds. Finally, she sighs.

"What do you want, Tory?"

Ouch. She doesn't want to know all the things I want. They aren't mine to have. And while I thought, for a while there, that maybe there was some reciprocation in her feelings, I'm pretty sure it was all on my side.

"Sorry," I say, going with my lie to June. Seems I do need to apologize to her after all. "I just . . . I wanted to call and apologize. I made you uncomfortable, maybe more than once, and I'm just . . . I'm sorry."

"How's your eye?" She doesn't miss a beat in responding.

I breathe out a laugh and roll to my back again, touching the tender skin with my free hand.

"Hurts like a motherfucker." I laugh out.

Quiet takes over again, and my smile falls back to the flat line that's taking up permanent residence on my face.

"I told Hayden it was just an innocent thing. I don't think it had anything to do with you; I think he's just having a hard time lately." She's giving my brother an excuse. One, my sweatshirt being at her house was not innocent. I was a breath away from kissing her that day. And two, she's wrong about Hayden. His issues with me are deeply personal.

"Right," I say, letting it rest there. She doesn't need my baggage. And when it comes to my brother, I'm going to be the bigger man for as long as I can. My anger will come out when it's good and ready.

"He's taking me out tonight," she says. My stomach rolls with a sick envy. I forgot that I told him to play her that song. I never got around to teaching him how.

"Oh, that's right. Happy birthday." I feel like an asshole.

"You told me last night," she says right back.

I did. I also told her she's beautiful. No matter what she is to me, or to my brother, I don't take that bit back. She deserved to hear it, and I had a right to tell her. Admiration is not a breach of loyalty. It is, however, a poisoned knife that cuts deep into my chest. It hurts to admire her so much.

"So, hey, how's the script coming?" I put on my best light and happy voice.

"It's . . . coming," she says, hesitantly. I was supposed to practice with her a lot more than I have. It's my fault we haven't.

"I bet it's better than you think. Why don't you give me some lines," I say.

"What, like . . . now?" Her tone is so offended it makes me laugh.

"No, like maybe later, after you film. Like an encore," I joke.

"Ha ha, Tory D'Angelo."

I catch myself grinning, a happiness taking over my body that I haven't felt in eons. I like the way she says my name. She's always done that when we spar. I think it's her way of showing she's my superior, yelling at me like a parent or teacher would.

"How about we read a little now," I suggest.

"What, on the phone?"

I pause with my mouth open, about to make another smart-ass remark, but I pivot.

"Yeah, why not. Maybe shoot me a few pics of the scene and I'll put you on speaker and we can read. I'll even lock the door so nobody will hear how awful I am and how great you are." I sit up, hopeful she's game.

"I don't think I'm allowed to send pictures of it," she hedges.

"I'll delete them as soon as we're done. Cross my heart." I wait while she mulls it over, and I can tell she wants to.

"You trust me?" I add.

Her pause is brief.

"Yes," she whispers.

I feel that one small word in my chest, and I'm grinning. There's something special about her trusting me, even about something like this. June was right to warn me —this is gonna hurt.

"Okay, send it my way. I'm locking the door now." I don't pretend but actually do it, mostly because I don't want my mom coming in unexpectedly just because she's nosy.

My phone dings with her delivery and I put her on speaker so I can open my images and expand enough to read.

"Got it," I say. "So, you want me to be Jordan Shotcraft?"

"Tory . . . nobody can be Jordan Shotcraft except Jordan Shotcraft." She has a point.

"Okay, smartass. I mean, isn't that his character, this Max guy?" I thumb through a few of the lines, getting the sense that most of the work will be on her. This should be easy.

"Yeah, this is the one section I'm struggling with." She sounds stressed. I'm glad she's letting me help.

"Okay, then. Let's go. Ready?" I have the first line, but I don't want to start reading until she's ready for it.

She draws in a sharp breath before whimpering a tentative, "Yes."

I sit on my bed with the phone cradled in my lap, my legs folded and my hands suddenly sweaty. I can't imagine doing this in front of an audience. No wonder my acting career peaked with junior high and community theater.

"Look . . . kid . . ." The script says pause for dramatic effect, so I am . . . I think. "I'm not really good at this father thing. I think you'd agree, so how about this. Give me a number."

"A number." Abby bites out the line, a near growl to her words.

"Yeah, you know . . . an amount. I'll set you up with whatever you think you need. I can give you money. You'll be good. You don't need me—"

"Money!" Her anger is thicker this time. "Ha! Yeah, sure, fine. Go ahead and cut me a check. Cut me out of your life. That's how things work for Max Stewart. Buy your way out of responsibility."

"Christine, you know this is for the best." I feel like such an amateur reading with her. I'm barely finished with a line when she begins hers. The conversation feels so real, so raw. It also feels vaguely personal.

"Yeah."

There's a long pause, and I wait through it. It's meant to be there, but the longer it drags on, the more on edge I get. Something's off.

"Maybe it is. For the best, I mean," she croaks. It's not quite the line as written, but it's close enough.

"It is," I hum.

"And maybe, maybe you'll regret it one day. Maybe I'll be so famous that you'll wish you took the job of dad when it was yours to have. But it won't be there anymore. That job is closed, no more applications being accepted. Eliminated."

She's definitely veering now.

"Abby, do you want—"

"And then you can swoop in and play hero just so you can get your foot in the door, earn off of your investment. Those are your words, not mine! Your fucking investment. That's all I am to you!"

I can hear the tears through her words, and I get why this section has been so hard for her to get through. I've read ahead, and while it's nothing like the words she just spilled out from her soul, it does ring very familiar. This story has a happy ending, though. I know it does because I looked ahead when we read the first time. Abby's relationship with her father, however, is just one big loop.

"I'm on my way," I say, not giving her a chance to tell me no.

I grab my keys and wallet, and stuff my phone in my back pocket, jetting down the stairs, out the door and by my mom without a word. I fire up my shitty squad car and test out the engine, getting to Abby's house in less than three minutes by blowing one stop sign and rolling through three others.

At her curb, I slam the car in park and dash through the lawn and up her steps, pounding my fist on her front door. She opens it after only seconds, and I step inside and take her into my arms, and let her cry big, fat, ugly tears into my chest.

"I know," I say, running my hand over her head and through her hair, rocking her softly while we embrace in the doorway.

"I can't do this," she fights. I assume she means the movie, and that's just crazy talk. She's too good to let this emotional hump stop her.

"Yes, you can. Don't give him that much power over you. Your choices, your decisions," I say.

She goes quiet, breathing hard, her mouth open on my cotton shirt. She's making a wet circle in the middle of my chest with her spit and tears. In all my years of knowing Abby Cortez, I don't think I've ever seen her truly cry.

"Someone took nude pictures of me, and he paid them off. I owe him," she says, her voice raw and embarrassed. She hides her face against me, turning inward even more. I'm glad because I'm sure the expression on my face is violent and frightening. I feel hot, and it's a struggle for me to keep my touch so gentle while my muscles are flexing, ready to rip someone's head off.

"You don't owe him jack shit, Abby. Taking care of you is his job." I'm probably a little more forceful than she needs to hear in her fragile state of mind.

"He's moving here. To fucking Allensville. He's moving his whole Miami life, his whole Miami girlfriend, to the town he called a shithole and pledged to never step foot in again." She pushes off from my chest just enough so she can form fists with her hands and level them against my chest. I can take it. I hold her elbows while she beats against me, letting out her rage. "He's coming here so he can get a better handle on my business. He thinks my mom doesn't do enough. I should be earning more! He's coming to milk me dry, not to be a dad!"

I bend down enough to look her square in the eyes, my palms cradling her face. I swipe away the tears collecting on her cheeks and wait for her breathing to slow while she sniffles and focuses through her blurred vision. She nervously steps side-to-side in my hold.

"Abby, listen to me. You . . . deserve better. You hear me?"

She shakes her head. It's going to take more to make her get it. I tighten my lips and shake my own head.

"No, you need to listen, to hear! You are worth a thousand suns. Your dad screwed up, and not like a business man, but like a human. He screwed up the day he wrote you and your mom off, and he doesn't get a second shot at that. He's not the man for the job. Hell, you and your mom —you don't *need* a man. Look at what you two strong women have done! You . . . you're going to be in a fucking Jordan Shotcraft film! Like, in theaters, where I'll have to buy some twenty-dollar ticket or some shit."

She laughs through lighter tears and sniffles.

"That's right. Smile, Abby Cortez. Let him try to steal your spotlight, take dollars out of your pocket. He's just using you to fill his empty void. And he did it to himself. He gave up the chance to have a real heart, a real life, the day he took off for Miami. He can move here and fight you in court so he can get paid and it will never be enough because he won't have you. Not having you . . . it is fucking torture, Abby Cortez."

Her eyes blink away tears and open on mine, and I swallow hard. That last part, that's about me. There's no way she doesn't know it. She has to know.

"Abby . . ."

My attempt to get back on track is cut short when she steps up on her toes, clutching my now damp shirt in her hands, and presses her lips to mine. I'm frozen from the touch, my hands falling away from her face but never going far, hovering in shock somewhere around her shoulders until I regain control over them. I move them to her neck, burying them in her hair, my fingers curling at the sensation of her silky hair between them. I've dreamt this exact feeling.

Her mouth is salty from tears and her lips are soft and quivering, but they don't back down. I coax her head to the side to deepen our kiss, and our tongues connect when she opens to me. A sweet hum escapes her throat, and it makes my lungs crash in disbelief that this is happening. Her hands have moved up my body to my neck, gripping at my shoulders to lift herself higher, to bring us closer, and then without warning, she falls several steps away and covers her mouth with the back of her hand.

Her chest is heaving with labored breaths. Mine is too. That kiss, it was forbidden. We crossed the line that took us from good people to the selfish kind. She was weak, and I took advantage. I should have told her no; I should have stopped her. But I wanted it, too. I wanted to kiss her even if that kiss was only about making her feel better right then, for a moment. I wanted to be her medicine, to be the thing that made her smile and made her believe she really is all of those things I said she was.

She is. But now, she's not going to believe it. One kiss took it all away. She'll think I said it solely for the outcome, which, while I'd kiss her back time and time again, my intent was only to give her back her fire.

"I'm sorry. Abby . . . I'm . . ." I hold out my open palm, the sting of my bruised eye burning more than before. Her lips are puffy and smeared with the same pink that's probably on mine. I run my wrist across my mouth to erase it, so she doesn't have to see what we've done. Still, she turns away.

"I'll let you go. I hope you have a happy birthday." My gravelly voice betrays me, and there's no way to hide the hurt.

June was right, and I get my phone out to call her on my way back to my car. I can't do it, though, and while I drive away, I toss my phone into the passenger seat and stew in my own shame. I'm no better than Hayden. He took something from me, and I just took something from him.

16

ABBY

I'm such a fake.

Hayden is standing in my doorway, dressed so nice —*in a suit!* He told me to wear something fancy, so I put on my last awards show dress. It's black and plain, and feels kind of simple now that I see him downstairs, clutching the rest of the roses meant for my birthday.

I kissed his brother.

I suck in my bottom lip at the memory; the tingle hasn't left for hours. It was wrong to kiss him like that. Things were so raw and he was saying all those words that just made me *feel.*

I'm going to break his brother's heart.

I can't hide up here all night, and maybe I'll go downstairs and feel differently. Maybe my heart will swell, Hayden's kiss suddenly feeling different—feeling like Tory's.

Nothing has ever felt like Tory's kiss.

My mom left Hayden in the doorway while she got

back to her work, and he's fidgeting. My dad's news about moving back to Allensville really threw things into a frenzy for her. It's easier to have hope when the problem is several hundred miles south of you.

My father will hate it here. He'll leave, eventually. This is the best plan I have come up with so far—wait him out. Some plan.

Unable to avoid my fate much longer, I make my way down the stairs, catching Hayden's gaze about halfway down. He looks at me like I'm something special. Why can't it light me up inside?

"Wow," he mouths. I tighten my smile.

"You sure this is okay? You're in a suit, and this thing was on double clearance at Boutique Bin," I say, fanning out the skirt to one side.

"You could make a paper bag look good," he teases, tipping my chin up with light pressure from his thumb. His lips hover over mine for a beat, and he smiles just before kissing me. It's sweet. It isn't Tory's kiss. I need to stop comparing.

I need to stop *thinking*.

"Everything all right here?" He motions toward my mom after handing me my flowers. I hug them close to smell them and glance over to my mom, who is making piles out of the piles.

"My dad's moving here," I say with a shrug. It's an inevitable obstacle that I'm going to have to accept.

"Your mom is letting him in?"

I scrunch my brow and flash my gaze back to him, taking a second to realize he's confused.

"Oh, no," I laugh out. "Not for a million bucks. No.

Besides, his girlfriend is coming too. It's part of his plan to be 'more involved.'"

"I'd let him have the floor for a million dollars," my mom hollers from a room away.

My lips bunch in skepticism and I shake my head silently at Hayden, because as tempting as money might be, my mom knows the trade-off would be letting the devil inside. You don't invite them in. You wear garlic and shit.

"Let me put these in water," I say, handing him the small purse I packed for the night with my phone, wallet, and keys.

I slip past my mom and move toward the cabinet to find a vase. I flip through a few, the noise annoying her, and she finally joins me, digging one out from beneath the sink. It's a tall, slender, blue glass cylinder, a gift that came with flowers from June a couple of years ago when my mom got home from the hospital after a car crash resulted in a broken wrist. She's basically ambidextrous now because she refused to stop working. She booked me two national ad campaigns in that cast.

When the vase is full of water, I dump in the flowers and move it to the center of our dining table. My mom quirks a brow at my choice of placement.

"Just trying to liven up all of this," I say, waving my hand around the mess.

"Ah, yes . . . it's much lovelier now. Thank you," she jokes. "Now, go on. Go enjoy your birthday."

"Birthday weekend," I correct as she moves around the table and places her palms on my cheeks. She squeezes them enough to force my lips to pout and she plants a big mother-has-the-right-to kiss on my lips.

"Weekend. Correct," she says, giving Hayden a side-ways look to make sure he's on board.

She moves her gaze back to me, and before she lets her hands fall away from my face, she stares at my eyes with a questioning look, her eyes pulling in to the center and her lips pinched, on the verge of speaking.

"What?" I ask.

Her eyes flit to Hayden and back to me quickly, a silent clue that hits my stomach hard. I'm not sure what she's insinuating, but my mom and I are very close. There's every possibility that she can read my thoughts. At the very least, she can tell that my body language with the twin I am dating is very different from the one I'm not.

"Be good to yourself, baby girl. Be selfish." She pats my cheek lightly.

My gut rolls with the weight of guilt because I *was* selfish. Very selfish.

"Can I take your jacket?" I quickly switch the topic, never reacting to her advice, but she can tell I heard it, knows it sunk in. She's always been able to read me like that.

"Sure," she says, backing away and moving toward the mudroom where she keeps most of her winter things.

She comes out with her black wool pea coat, which is probably the nicest thing she owns. Her letting me wear it is a sign of trust. She let me borrow it once before, to a party, where I stupidly left it hanging on a hook in a house full of pot smoke and underage drinking. I went to retrieve it the next day, thankful it wasn't covered in spilled drinks or worse, but the moment I got it into my car I knew it would never pass her inspection. It reeked. I took a hotdog ad for Twofers just to pay for the dry cleaning.

I slip my arms inside as she holds it open for me and pull the belt around my waist, knotting it in the front. There's a small chance of snow tonight. If it happens, I don't want the little black dress to be all I've got.

"You ready? Reservations are at seven," Hayden says, holding out his arm like a gentleman.

I glance to my mom one more time, and she continues with the same begging look she had when she told me to be selfish. I ignore it and wish her a good night as I let Hayden walk me out to his car.

"This one's all mine now," he says.

I already know. I saw Tory's junker earlier. Hayden doesn't need to know any of that, though.

"Oh, yeah? No more sign-up sheet for who gets to take the car?" I joke as he opens the passenger door for me and I slip inside. He smiles at my joke, but that's about as big of a laugh as it gets.

I figure we're going somewhere nice for dinner, but I don't expect the rooftop grill on the way to Indy. Hayden keeps me guessing for most of the trip, but I figure it out when the only other option is driving completely into the city. He pulls into the lot, tucking his car neatly between an Escalade and a Porsche. He can't afford this.

"Hayden, this is very sweet, but we don't have to go here," I say.

"I know we don't *have* to, but I want to give you a special night." He leans toward me and runs his thumb along my cheek. All I can think is how I wish it were Tory, and how I'm basically using him for a nice dinner because I'm too big of a chicken shit to end this.

"Thank you," I croak out.

He gets out and rounds the car to open my door for me, taking my hand and leading me inside. A glass elevator takes us up to the roof where he's reserved a table in the corner that overlooks the downtown lights. I don't know what he had to do to nab this seat, but I feel as though I'm becoming a way overpriced date. This is too much.

"Madam," he says, putting on a silly voice as he pulls out my chair. Before I sit, a hostess steps in and takes my jacket for me, draping it over an open seat nearby. Heaters hang over our heads from cords strung across the patio amidst the zigzagging lights. It's warm, but maybe I'm warmer because of how uncomfortable I am with this entire situation. My eyes dart around in a paranoid fashion, and I don't even hear when the waiter steps up to take our drink orders. Hayden must have answered something for me.

"You're in shock?" He reaches forward and holds out an open palm, a crooked smile showing his teeth.

I put my hand in his and hope to feel *something*. He closes his fingers around my hand, and it's as if I'm dead. My heart is pounding but only due to this sensation of feeling trapped.

"So, confession time," he begins.

"Huh?" I shoot my gaze to his, my eyes wider than a cat caught in a hound dog's path.

He chuckles and squeezes my hand a little, shaking it against the table softly to work out my nerves. I'm sure he thinks I'm just caught off guard by the fancy restaurant, but that's not it. I've been to dozens of restaurants like this, meeting with casting directors and agents. As stressful as those dinners may have been, they were nothing compared to this one.

"So, my confession," he starts again, and I'm so terrified that he is going to blurt out the L word that I interject with a confession of my own.

"I don't think I can do this anymore." My mouth goes dry, my voice cracking on the last word.

"You . . . can't do *this?*" His touch on my hand has relaxed, his fingers unfurling and letting go. I squeeze back because I care about him.

"Hayden, I'm not . . . I don't want . . ." My jumbled words are not enough. I am no good without a plan, and this is about as spontaneous as I've ever been. I don't know what to say to make things clear, but I do know it's killing me to see the cracks forming in his happiness. His smile has disintegrated, and the dimple in his cheek has become a deep divot between his brows.

"I'm so sorry," I say, tears pooling in my eyes. I shake my head and kneed at his hands, trying to bring life back into them. They've gone cold.

His focus is off, as if he's looking through me more than at me. He leans back in his seat, finally pulling his hands away completely.

"Tell me, is it *him?*"

My insides twist and burst with pain. I don't know how to answer this because the right answer is both yes and no.

I shake my head lightly, my bottom lip trembling.

"I don't know." I won't lie to him. I've lied enough already.

He slumps even more and looks off to the side with a sharp laugh. Our waiter walks up with a tray, holding two sparkling drinks, and Hayden holds up a hand.

"I'm so sorry, but something's come up," he says to the man.

Hayden stands and paces around his chair, catching the attention of others sitting nearby. He pauses behind his seat and grips the back with both hands as he bends his head down with a derisive chuckle.

"We can go," I say, jetting to my feet and grabbing my jacket.

"Yeah. Sure," he says, his focus still on the floor.

I'm too warm to wear my mom's coat. My skin is on fire, so I layer the jacket over my arm and stand perfectly still, my hands gripping tightly at one another underneath the wool while I stare at Hayden, waiting for him to make his next move. He laughs again, a light, ominous sound tainted with the bad blood between him and Tory.

"I brought my dad's old guitar, the one he left behind. It's in the trunk, and after dinner . . . I was going to play that song for you, the one you had me play in the car." His head pops up and his eyes meet mine. There's no hiding the red sting and glossiness taking them over. "It was Tory's idea."

I gurgle out a small cry, biting hard on my lip to stop it from progressing.

Hayden nods, puzzle pieces coming together. I am a terrible person.

"Come on, let's get you home, birthday girl," he says,

and even though his voice is still sweet, there's a note that rests below his tone that carries a brewing mixture of hurt and anger. He's been dealing with it for some time, but I may have just added the final ingredient. Call me the master chef of broken hearts.

Hayden ushers me out ahead of him, and we are both deathly silent for the elevator ride down. It takes several minutes for the valet to retrieve his car, and I note every five-and ten-dollar bill he's doled out since we arrived. His eyes remain straight ahead on the road and mine on the blur of life that passes by out my passenger window. The radio is set on some news channel, the volume low so the only sound to pass the time is a mumbling noise that's broken up by the occasional commercial.

He speeds a little to cut the time, obviously as anxious to leave me as I am him. If I stay in this car with him any longer, I will fold and profess that I was wrong, that I need him and want to be with him, and the only reason would be because I don't want to see him suffer. But that is not heeding my mom's advice.

Be selfish.

My mom was never selfish. She stayed with a man who cheated on her numerous times, and made sure he came home to a perfect house, with clean laundry, a hot dinner, and all of the bills paid. My mom was the first to go to college in our family, and her business degree was squandered as a housewife. Most of my dad's investments turned into money pits. He mortgaged our house—the one my *abuelo* built—to pay off his own debts, so my mom took on an accounting job to pay it off. It's in only her name now, but what was once hers free and clear still has more than a hundred thousand owed. All this, yet my dad is the one who feels he's not getting his due.

My mother was selfless to a fault. She was naïve, and she was a doormat. I don't think she's ever really known love. But I—I might.

Hayden pulls into my driveway but stops short. He's already in far enough. I understand.

"Hey," he says, stopping me before I get out. I pause with one leg out of the car, my purse and my mother's coat clutched in my lap. "He's going to break you, just so you know. My brother?" He shakes his head, his mouth a tight line. "He doesn't know any other way," he says. "Happy birthday, Abby."

I smile and nod, not able to find words to reply to everything he just said. My chest aches and my lungs hunger for me to scream, but I'm too weak. I shut the car door behind myself and wait at the end of my driveway as Hayden pulls out. He doesn't speed away, and he even signals at the end of the street. He's heading toward his home, and I can't stop the barrage of thoughts rushing through my head of what he's going to do when he gets there. I don't know whether Tory's home or not, but it's only a matter of time before the two of them collide again. This time, it's all my fault.

17

TORY

I haven't shot pool with Lucas in ages. It's what I needed tonight. He knew it.

We got to Eight Lanes when June's shift began, and we've racked up maybe forty games of nine-ball in three hours. Because June's here, we're not taking advantage of our usual *look-the-other-way* pitchers of beer. I have to respect the way Lucas respects June. She doesn't like him breaking rules at her place of employment, so he waits until she's not around. I mean, a free pitcher is a tough thing to give up entirely.

I won the last round, so I offer to buy Lucas a slice and refill our Dr. Pepper at the counter while he racks up to break the next game, but June's off work soon. I'm officially third-wheeling. I've done it enough that my Spidey senses alert me. He's waffling in his response because the good friend in him wants to say yes, but he's got a girl to spend time with. They've missed out on enough time as it is.

"Actually," I say before he has to find an excuse. "I'm pretty tired."

It's eight-thirty. He knows this is bullshit.

"A'ight man, you sure?" He's grateful I gave him an out.

I fake a yawn and pick up the empty soda pitcher.

"Yeah, I might head back to my dad's. He wants me to stay here and keep the peace, but I'm not doing a very good job of it." I walk backward a few steps, grimacing. Lucas knows things with me and Hayden are bad. I told him about the camp letter I found, and he was as shocked as I was. He remembers how excited I was when my parents let me apply. It cost three hunny just for the shot. I did not, however, alert Lucas to the details from earlier—the kiss. I'm not in the mood to be judged tonight. He won't mean to do it, but he will. The dude's poker face is shit.

"You gonna come back for the party tomorrow, then?" he asks.

I wince with a tight smile and waggle my head side-to-side before setting the pitcher down at the register near June.

"Tory!" June grunts from behind me. She leans over the counter and pulls on my shirt, tugging me back with a short choke. Her mom's put a lot of work into the party, and yeah, yeah . . . games. But the thought of being in a circle that tight with her and my brother just burns my throat. I don't think I can do it. Call me a pussy, but I just . . . can't.

"You know I wanna be there," I say, which is a very non-answer answer. I grab my collar and tug my shirt out of her hand and straighten it on my body as I turn to face her. I love this shirt, it's all black and says the word DOMI-NATE in the center in dark gray. Now it's all kinked.

"Tory," she repeats my name, this time a little more forgiving.

I take a deep breath. It's hard to say no to June. She has this way of making people do things they don't really want to do, like buy flowers for a girl who will never be theirs.

"I'll try," I say. I'll probably cave and show up briefly just to make June happy. I really don't want to, though.

"Okay," she says, leaning over the counter and throwing her arms around my neck. As I lean in, she kisses the top of my head.

"That was all her, dude. You saw it," I say to Lucas, holding my hands up innocently. He laughs because he thinks I'm joking, but lately I've been hit enough over women that I'm not taking any chances.

"I'll see you guys," I say, grabbing my beanie from the counter and stuffing it on my head. It's crisp outside, the sky clear and full of stars. It's a no-moon night, so the glitter in the sky shows off a little more than normal. It also makes the drive home pitch black.

I go slow, taking a route that passes Abby's house because I'm a sucker and the torture reminds me that a part of her wanted me, too. Her car is gone, which maybe means her mom finally caved and took it in for new tires. Things for her are about to get really hard, and as messy as my parents' relationship is, the one between her mom and dad has years of complications woven into it. She's only shared the tip of the iceberg with me.

I stayed locked in my room until Hayden left, but I saw him haul out my dad's guitar, so he's at least going to try.

Even his poor skills on the thing are going to make her swoon. I get in our driveway, parked in the place where our —I mean *his*—car normally rests, and sit there for a few minutes with my engine off.

Maybe this is all I need to get myself to grow up. I need to take ball more seriously, and I have to send some emails to coaches on my own. My dad was doing the work for us, but it's probably not on his mind right now. I want to get out of this place, go somewhere warm maybe. Basketball in California sounds nicer and nicer.

I leave my car, renewed about my direction. I'm so wide awake and sober on a Saturday night that I might get started making my plans tonight. I practically skip through the garage, my mom's van unmoved for the entire day. I find her already asleep upstairs, her TV on low and a box of things she brought up from the garage on the bed in front of her. I recognize my Little League jersey right away, and pull it loose from the pile. Hayden's is snagged on it, so I bring them both in my hands, noting how they're both Youth mediums. He's number one and I was number two, which makes me smile and laugh to myself. I bet he loved being number one just this once. I remember how excited he was when dad threw the jersey at him. I'd asked to be number two, but not to be nice. I wanted to be Derek Jeter.

My mom lets out a light snore, so I set the shirts on the bed and pull her blanket over her arms. She's still wearing the same clothes she had on earlier. She's probably been cleaning all day, or reliving better times by going through boxes like this one. The sight makes me both happy and deeply sad.

I back out of her room and pull her door closed, not

wanting to disturb her. Hayden's door is wide open, and I think about closing his door too, but instead pause at the entrance and look at all of the things inside to remind me who he really is. His closet door is open, exposing his perfectly hung shirts and pants. Who hangs their joggers? Hayden does. The space smells clean, like lemon, and not because mom whisked through with her laundry basket, grumbling while she picked up socks and boxers, but because Hayden actually cleans things. We have matching quilts; they're made of old jerseys that we wore throughout the years. His is tucked in and even, ready for military inspection. Mine has a peanut butter stain on it from a protein bar I ate two weeks ago, and I don't think I've ever folded a thing in my life.

I'm smiling as I back out of his room, somehow a bit of the hostility I've been clinging to easing. But the carefree moment is quickly replaced with the tight squeeze of suspicion when I step into my room and find Dad's old guitar resting on my bed. My light smile drops, the corners of my mouth like arrows pointing to my feet. I stand over the instrument and run my finger along the D-string, making it vibrate with an eerie buzz. I know Hayden took this with him. At some point, though, he brought it back. He left it here for me to find.

Glancing back over my shoulder, I half expect to find him standing in my doorway, waiting to punch my other eye out. The hallway is dark and silent, though. A quick check on social media brings Hayden up blank. He's turned his location settings off, which usually means he's out at McCaffey's place. Nobody shares their location out there, mostly so the people who aren't invited don't know their way in. Hayden is probably drinking, or maybe taking advantage of McCaffey's side business—the cat sells the best weed in the county. I shouldn't care what Hayden does, *but damn it, I do.* The guy can hold his beer but that's about it. I fish around in my bag for my keys and toss my beanie on my desk, hurrying down the stairs and through the garage toward my junker so I can just get eyes on him. I'm nearly halfway across the driveway when Abby's headlights flash off and on and catch my attention.

Shading my eyes, I take cautious steps down my driveway as she kicks open her door and throws it closed behind her. She's parked across the street in an open alley space like some undercover cop on surveillance. She's wearing a black dress that swings around her knees, her feet stuffed in bright white tennis shoes, and her arms covered in some obnoxious pink sweatshirt that she's only pulled over her arms, the front left bunched across her chest.

"This is your fault," she says, her voice raw as if she's been crying.

I figured tonight did not go as planned when I saw the guitar on my bed. I can understand why Hayden would be marching toward me with a hot fist and fire in his eyes, but Abby? She kissed me. Yeah, I kissed back, but this, for once . . . this isn't my fault.

"Abby, I know you're upset, but now is really not the time."

I don't get a chance to say more before she levels me with both hands in the dead center of my chest. She pushes me so hard that I fall back a few steps and she legit ricochets.

"I broke up with him. Are you happy? I'm a terrible person and I just ripped your brother's heart in half and threw away so much trust. You satisfied?" She comes at me again, this time grunting on impact. I don't budge, but only because I see her coming and brace myself.

"Abby, you aren't a horrible person. I think Hayden's at McCaffey's. I'm just gonna make sure he's—"

Another shove knocks the wind out of me.

"Goddamnit!" I grab her wrists as she lunges at me again.

She literally growls and tugs down hard, my grip quickly releasing as she rips away from me. She takes off one of her shoes and throws it at my head and I swat it away, but not in time to block the second one. It hits me square in my still-black eye.

"Abby . . . stop!" I whisper-shout.

She's swaying forward and back, her arms dangling in front of her, the sweatshirt bunched around her wrists. She has to be freezing with her bare shoulders and bare feet. I can see her breath, it tangles with mine in the air as we both pant.

"Just stop." I hold my hands out flat, like I'm ordering an audience to be seated.

She blows at the stray hairs that have fallen in her face. Sniffling, she runs her sleeve along her nose, yanking the sweatshirt up her skin only for it to slide down to her wrists again as she stands there a total mess, body rocking with this unleashed rage that I think is meant for me. Her head shakes and she points at me, only lifting her arm halfway.

"God damn you, Tory D'Angelo." Her words quiver,

either from the cold or from the fumes of emotion left in her tank.

My hands are balled into fists, and I'm incredibly uneasy. My world tilts more by the second just from staring into Abby's eyes. It's so dark that it's impossible to see the golden hue, but I spot the red in the whites. Her features are heavy, a pairing of exhaustion and fear that I only recognize because maybe I feel it, too.

"Why did you break up, Abby?"

I touch the inside of my wrist to my lip that feels fat from where her shoe hit me. She blinks at my question.

"You know why," she says, her voice low and discreet. If none of the neighbors have come out to see what's happening after the shoe bit, they aren't coming out now. I think my mom might have indulged in a little wine during her walk through memory lane, so we'd have to practically be murdering each other with screams for her to come look.

"No, I don't. I have learned that I don't know shit, Abby. I can't afford to pretend or assume. I need you to tell me." My hands flex from outstretched to fists and back again. My legs tingle, either ready to collapse or to carry me on a marathon. And still, Abby stands out of arm's reach and rocks, and stares, and lets that one tear run down her cheek and fall into the small divot on her neck above her collar bone. It's lit by the stars, like a diamond gliding along her smooth skin.

"Why did you break up with Hayden, Abby?" My mouth quivers in anticipation, and the longer she stands facing me, her mouth unable to say the words, the more I want to reach inside her and pull them out.

She finally shakes her head.

"You know why," she repeats.

I shake my head, prepared to say *I don't*, but words fail me as she takes one step, followed by another, until she's nearly standing with her feet on top of mine.

Her tiny frame fits under my chin, and as I glare down at her she raises her face to the sky, her hair sliding out of her face like ribbons, her bare shoulders covered in bumps from the cold air. Clouds are beginning to move in, killing the only light we have, but before the stars are completely gone, I run the back of my fingers along the side of her bare neck, over her shoulder and down her arm. I lift her hand in mine, doing the same with the other as I duck low enough to tuck my head underneath the sweatshirt that tethers her arms together in the sleeves. Her hands rest on my shoulders and she steps up on my feet, her lips soft and fragile, timid and scared. Open. Ready.

My head falls to rest on hers just as she lifts her chin, and our lips touch just barely. Electric. It's as if I've been stung.

"Why did you break up with Hayden?" I repeat again, this time only a whisper, my lips brushing against hers as I speak.

Her head tilts an inch or two to the right.

"You know why," she breathes, and that's enough. Because I do.

Our lips connect as if they're starving for the life only we can give to each other. I lift her up and she wraps her legs around me while I walk us both back into the garage, our mouths never once breaking their hold. This is how I've wanted to kiss her since the first time she shot me down. I've dreamt of this kiss during our late-night talks with June and Lucas. I stared at these perfect lips and imagined what they taste like.

Honey and peaches.

Her skin is cold, so I smack my palm against the garage door control, closing it behind us. I set her down on the hood of my mom's van long enough for her to toss her sweatshirt from her arms and for me to run my hands up her jaw and into her hair.

We pause to breathe, teeth clinging to each other's lips as we peel apart, chests heaving and fingers clawing into our clothing. Abby lifts her chin, her eyes flitting upward to meet mine under the haze of her long, thick lashes. She's classic pin-up, even dressed down. The girl was born to be a star, and it makes me so angry that her father is trying to chip away at her brightness.

She studies me with a serious face, lips parted enough to take needed breaths, her breasts lifting with each intake of air. I glance down at them just enough, the allure impossible to ignore. Abby reacts by lifting her chest higher and sliding closer to me, her knees parting until I stand between them.

Her nervous lips grow more confident, sneering at me as she lifts her chin enough to give me her neck. Like a hungry vampire, I take the bait, pulling her body against me, opening her legs wide, and running my hand down the length of her hair until I've found enough to grip and pull her head back with a gentle tug. She whimpers when I do, her hands grabbing the loops on my jeans and pulling me close to feel how hard I am for her. I grunt at the sensation and the idea of being so ready against her softest parts.

I dust kisses along her jaw and neck, and she arches as I move lower, her breasts pushing up toward me, begging me to taste them. My tongue traces along the fabric of her dress, across the curve of her tits, my teeth grabbing at whatever cloth I can, wanting to tear away her dress. I settle for placing kisses over her clothes, nipping the curves until my lips find the hard peak underneath. I bite through the material, and her shoulder blades lift from the cold metal of the car.

Unable to do everything I want here in the garage, I pull her into me, my cock straining under my jeans, wanting to bust out and plunge deep into her like the barbaric asshole I am. My hands grab under her thighs and lift her up, swinging her around toward the mudroom door. The house is dark, so I'm careful not to move too fast or run us into anything that might wake my buzzed and sleeping mom. I'm not about to let her go, though. I've kissed this girl before and when she pushed away, it nearly broke me.

"Do you want to see my room?" I ask against her mouth in a whisper. She nods and licks my lips, taking the top one between her teeth and clamping down with seductive pressure. I hope I can carry us up the stairs without passing out from the things she is doing to me.

We both hold our breath at the upstairs landing, passing by the albums and empty shelves where my trophies used to sit. I threw them out, though I saw that my mom saved the bag from the trash and left it in the garage.

I'm quiet with my door, letting it click slowly and twisting the lock behind her back as I hold her up against it.

Her legs relax their grip around my waist and she

slides from my body, down the door, and for a beat, I'm afraid she's about to tell me this is all a big mistake. Not that it isn't. It's a clusterfuck on the scale of mistakes, but I'm already in it. I was in it the moment June talked me into buying flowers and Abby showed up with my brother.

Hayden would probably say I've been handed everything in my life, but that's a lie. I've worked my ass off for every honor I earned, fought my way through expectations and my own failures to show I have grit. Abby was never mine to easily have. I don't deserve her. But damn, do I plan to fight for her, to fight to keep her, and prove to her there's something worth being with inside of me.

With lust-heavy eyes holding me hostage, Abby brings her hands up her body, crossing her arms over her chest, and walking her fingers up to the thin straps of her sleeves. She slides them each over her shoulders at the same time, her dress slipping down her body until she catches it just over her breasts. A coy smile paints her lips, the bottom one caught in her teeth.

Fuck me.

I cover her hands with mine, coaxing her hands to let go of the fabric. The silky material slips from her fingers slowly, revealing a new inch of her skin a second at a time until it slips down to her hips all at once. It's not the kind of dress you wear a bra with, and I knew that when my mouth ran along the smooth material, but it's still a control-altering sight to see Abby like this.

Vulnerable.

Never—not once—is that a word I would associate with her. But she is right now. She is for me, baring her skin and extending her trust.

Taking her hands one at a time, I lift them above her head, pressing the back of her wrists flat against the door as I step in close, my chest pressing against hers. She leaves them above her head, letting me trace slow lines down the tender skin inside her arms, over the nape of her neck and down her breasts until my thumbs find the aching peaks of her nipples. I gently stroke them in circles, and she reacts by scratching at my skin. I pause long enough to tug my shirt up and over my head and toss it to the floor, and my touch returns to her pink tips within seconds.

I gently roll the budding nipples between my thumbs and fingers to start, adding pressure as her body reacts. God, I bet she's wet as fuck.

Stepping up on her toes, she nips at my chin, and I drop my head enough to take her mouth with mine, my hands working her breasts while she runs her palms along my sides and to my back, finally reaching inside the back of my jeans and tracing from the curve of my ass and hips to the front. Her fingertips graze along the tip of my dick and it flexes from the slight touch, causing me to growl against her mouth. Her lips smile against mine. She's proud of her control. So much for vulnerable.

She easily unsnaps my jeans, pulling on the open waistband to bring my zipper down fast. When her hand reaches in and wraps around my width, I shiver in response, my cock flexing again. Lowering myself in front of her, I kiss my way down her neck and the center of her chest until my mouth finds the perfect hard tip of her breast. I clutch it with my teeth, rougher than I probably should, but she seems to like it. My tongue flicks against it a few times before my hands snake around her legs and lift her ass so I can spin her and carry her to my bed.

With one hand, I reach to toss away my total bachelor-style blanket before setting her down atop my deep blue sheets. Her body is like snow against the deep color, like the stars that were just moments ago bright in the navy sky. I allow myself a pause to look down at her, one knee on the bed between her legs, her arms bunching up the pillow above her head while a wanting smile turns up the corners of her mouth.

She hums.

I obey.

I've never had a girl in my room. I've *had* girls, but never in a way that was so slow and perfect and matching every fantasy I've had. I want to take my time, but every nerve in my body wants to rush. And then she groans and rocks her hips, still cloaked under the rest of her dress.

Not wanting to ruin her trust, I step to the table next to my bed and take out a condom. I hold it up, meeting her gaze with a question. She reaches out to take the foil packet from me, tears it open and hands it back.

I'm genuinely nervous. Every ounce of bravado that has ever come before is gone; the only thing left is a nervous young man standing before the most beautiful girl in the world, desperate to be hers completely on her birthday.

Moving back to the end of the bed, I hold the open packet in my teeth while I push down my jeans and boxers, stepping out of them before pulling out the condom and rolling it on. My heated gaze begins at her breasts and trails down to the space between her knees, which open when I look at them. I lower myself to my knees and run my palms up her bare thighs, collecting the fabric of her dress along the way. Once I reach the top along her waist, I curl my fingers and drag the black cloth down the length of her, her curves like the soothing waves of a crystal ocean, kissed by the sun. Her black lace panties barely hide a thing, her skin smooth and shaven, a small gold stud fitted in the skin below her belly button.

I touch the stud with my finger, then travel lower until my hand runs along the edge of the lace, dipping lower along the soaking wet cotton strip between her legs. I push it to the side and dip my finger inside her, reveling in the way her body curls from my touch. I push into her again, causing her to moan and her hips to rock.

Unable to stand not being inside her any longer, I slide both hands to her hips and curl my fingers into the lacy straps along her hips, rolling her panties down her hips and legs until she's able to kick them away. Her pink skin is swollen, dusted with a small strip of hair that begs to be kissed. I bend down, holding myself above her hips, just so I can press a kiss against her soft center, dragging my tongue along her swollen pussy just once before pulling her legs down the length of the bed so she's poised and ready for me to enter.

"Tell me you want this," I say, needing to hear it for my own ego.

"I want *you*," she moans, and that's all it takes for me to push forward and drive through the center of her.

"Ahh," she cries out, grabbing the pillow above her head and covering her face to muffle her cries from pleasure.

I slide out of her completely, wanting to feel the same sensation again, and her reaction is the same, a muffled cry as her body pushes against me, urging me deeper. I do it again, and again, until I'm no longer able to leave the warmth of her pussy, the sweet tightness and the way it hugs my cock. My hands grip at her legs, pulling her into me with every thrust and eventually, she pushes her own body up, sitting on the end of the bed while I push my dick in and out so hard that I'm afraid I won't last more than a few seconds.

That, however, is not Abby's plan. Now sitting before me, she pushes me back until I'm on the floor and she crawls on top of me, lowering herself on my throbbing cock and riding me cautiously, her hands pressed against my chest to pin me down while she controls every single sensation I'm allowed to feel.

My hands reach up to touch her, but she stops them as her hips rock, pinning them to my sides as she leans over me and rolls her hips in the most intoxicating motion, her body sliding down mine and taking all of me before almost letting me leave her completely.

Her hair has fallen all around us, hiding us from the outside world while our bodies take what they want from each other. My hands beg to touch her, and I fight against her willingly until she relents and lets me run my palms along her breasts and back, cupping her ass and pushing her into me hard until she pulses and squeezes around me.

I push myself up with one hand so we're both sitting while she rocks her hips against me and I penetrate her again and again, filling her completely, until she leans back and bites her knuckles in a breathy cry of pleasure. I pull her body into me, close enough to bite at her neck and quiet my own sounds as I come hard, throbbing with every wave of pleasure.

She falls against my chest, her hair damp with sweat, my body beading with moisture, every bit of me sticking to every part of her, and she stays just like this, with me inside, for long minutes until soft laughter brings her eyes to mine.

"I cannot believe I finally let Tory D'Angelo have me," she jokes, referring to every single time I've hit on her without expectation that this—that *us*—could ever be real.

"You've always had me. Only seems fair," I say, my response not as funny as she expects.

Her amused smile shifts to something else entirely. I don't think she was expecting such honesty from me, or such adoration, and frankly, I'm a little surprised to have said it. But it's true. Every word of it. Also, there is no way I'm giving her up to spare my brother's feelings. He can have the fucking basketball academy. I want the queen.

18

ABBY

I knew what I was doing when I left my house and drove to the D'Angelo's after Hayden dropped me off. I knew he wouldn't be home. How could he go home? Too great a chance that Tory would be there.

And Tory would be there, eventually.

I sat in my car and vacillated between wanting to scream and tell him to leave me alone forever and wanting to wrap my everything around his heart and smother it until it was mine. I seem to have leaned into the latter.

I didn't want to leave. He didn't want me to go. Everything about the way he touched me was so different from any touch I had before—*from Hayden's*. My heart was different. What we committed was a sin—an indulgence—but it was also what both of our hearts wanted.

It was selfish.

I left in the early morning hours, one final kiss from him as I wrapped myself in one of his T-shirts and an old pair of sweats, and with the shoes I threw at him during my tirade. Even now, as I lay wide awake after only a few hours of sleep, I feel him everywhere—*still*.

It's my party at June's today. I can smell the menudo on the stove downstairs. My grandma always made it for the holidays, so it's become one of my birthday favorites. It's really the only thing my mom mastered from my grandmother's kitchen. Warm soup is one of the very few good things about December. I guess now I have two good things.

My neck is covered in love bites left behind from Tory. I noticed them when I got home, so I laid my turtleneck dress out for the day, knowing I'd need something that isn't suspiciously modest. It's a sixties style, a dark orange short swing dress that I pair with knee-high brown leather boots. I might have worn it even if I didn't have guilty marks to hide all over my skin.

After a quick shower, I lock myself in my room to dry my hair paper straight and put mascara on my lashes to distract from the major sleepy puffs I sport on my face.

I make my way downstairs with a watering mouth, anxious to take a taste from the pot I know must be near ready. I'm stalled at the bottom of the steps, though, when I see my father's back as he stirs over the stove.

"Get away from my soup," I bite out.

In the courtroom, I'm a quiet girl. In person, though—I'm me. There's no judge here to keep tally on the way I disrespect my father. He's disrespected me my entire life by basically cutting himself out of everything that doesn't make a profit.

I flash my gaze to my mom who stands behind the table, thankfully cleared of all of her homework to fight the man in our house. She's dressed and ready to go to June's house, which means he is an unexpected guest.

My father turns to face me, holding a fat spoon in front of his lips, blowing across the steam. I hate the way his lips pucker. I hope mine look nothing like his. He opens wide and floats the spoon over his tongue, his mouth closing over it like a child waiting for the airplane full of oatmeal.

"*Mmm*, Denise. This is just like your mother's." It's disgraceful to hear him talk about my grandmother, knowing how he could have helped her or checked in on her in Florida but refused since she was no longer his family.

"Thanks. We have to leave, so—" My mom swings her open palm toward to door, ushering my father out.

He drops the spoon in the sink and runs his sleeve over his lips before reaching into his coat pocket to pull out a thick envelope. Neither of us are naïve enough to believe there's money inside.

"I just wanted to drop by to give you this," he says, tossing the envelope on the table. "You can read it if you want, but basically, I own fifty percent." He winks at me, as if I'm supposed to be pleased that he owns half of my soul.

My mom rips the envelope open and unfurls the papers, scanning quickly as my father heads for the door.

"Judge said it was the easiest ruling he's ever made," he says.

My mom collapses into the nearby chair, not even bothering to respond to his smug remarks as he leaves.

"Is he right? Is that . . . *it?*" I ask.

She brushes her hand in my direction to hush me, her

eyes pinched with worry as she reads. She flips through the papers at a maddening pace, then finally gives up, tossing them into the center of the table.

"I give up," she says, shrugging. Her eyes lazily focus on the pages. I move close enough to read some of the language, but it's so *lawyer-ized* that I can't get through the first paragraph without getting lost.

The soup rolls to a boil, so I rush to the stove and turn it off, stirring to keep the rich ingredients from burning. It'll be too hot to put in the car for a few minutes, so I move it to one of the empty burners and leave it there to cool while I return to my mom, stepping in behind her to squeeze the tension from her shoulders.

"Baby girl, no. It's your birthday. I'm fine," she says, patting my hands. I don't budge, and eventually she lets me continue massaging.

"Your muscles say you aren't fine," I say.

She shakes with a quick laugh.

Normally, something like having my dad show up and drop a bomb like this would ruin my day—definitely my birthday weekend. But I'm different today. Optimistic, and maybe a bit . . . bold.

Selfish.

"You know what?" I stop rubbing her shoulders and gather up the papers, twisting them into a kindling stick that I march over to the stove. I turn the burner back on high and hold the paper against the coils until the end catches fire. My mom leaps from her chair and rushes to me, but I hold the papers up high, keeping her at bay long enough for the flame to take hold and eat away half of whatever the fuck this shit stack is that my dad left. I drop the smoking pages into the sink and run the water over what's left, scooping the soupy mess out and tossing it in the trash like a rodent I just killed.

I wash my hands and glance over my shoulder, meeting my mom's wide eyes.

"Oh, like he doesn't have a million copies. And like his lawyer didn't send one to ours. That . . . that felt good." I shut the faucet off and dry my hands on a towel, tossing it to the counter with a bit of zest when I'm done.

The shocked awe on my mother's face shifts into pride after a few breaths, a curve taking to her lips.

"You told me to be selfish," I say, knowing she'll appreciate the credit. Though she doesn't realize just how greedy I've been.

T

June's house is already full by the time we pull up. I park us in the street and my mom hefts the pot from the back seat of my car. She gets halfway up the driveway before Tory runs out and takes it from her. Our gazes meet for one intimate glance.

"Thank you, babe. Not too much cake for you today, okay?" she teases him, knowing which of the two she's dealing with this time. My mom doesn't miss clues, which means she'll probably sense that something is up when Hayden shows up, if he even does. If he doesn't, well, everyone is going to wonder what's going on.

His car is the only vehicle missing. Lola and Naomi both parked in the garage. They spent the night with June baking and preparing for my day. I was supposed to stop in to help after my date, but well . . .

"There's my girl!" June's mom, Kristen, rushes over to me, her hands shielded by oven mitts. She gives me a half hug, not wanting to get flour and frosting on my sweater dress. Her arms are covered in ingredients.

"You look adorable," she says, looking me up and down. I sashay in acknowledgement just as Tory comes back into my space. Our eyes meet again, and I catch the knowing grin on his lips. He's very aware of the reason I'm wearing this dress.

I follow everyone through the kitchen into the main room that the Mabees have set up to be wide open for whatever silly games June has planned. There's a long table pushed all the way against the wall opposite of the fireplace, and it is filled with every type of frosted cookie and cake I can imagine.

"The maple cupcakes are surprisingly good. The oatmeal cookies . . . eh." June wiggles her palm in the air.

"Noted," I say, moving right in for one of the cupcakes. I reach for the perfect-looking desert on one of the tiered plates, another hand reaching for it a blink afterward, resulting in a near tug-of-war.

"What, you think because it's your birthday you can come in here and swoop the best cupcake?" Tory's finger grazes mine where we touch, a hidden token to let me know he's thinking of me—of last night.

Neither of us gives in right away, precariously holding the cake hostage over the Mabees' wooden floor.

"I tell you what, I'll split it with you," he offers.

I shake my head and smirk.

"Uh uh."

He puckers his lips into a tight smile, enjoying our playful spar. This is always where we were at our best—sharp tongues, poised for flirting.

"You want it all, huh?" His finger strokes along mine again.

"Always," I reply. His eyes dare me for a few seconds until others arrive to scour the table for treats near us. He lets go one finger at a time, and I casually bring the treat to my lips, unwrapping the paper from the bottom before I take a bite.

"Worth it?" he asks, one brow raised.

"Totally," I say, licking my lips.

Rather than look frustrated, he chuckles, hesitantly reaching an outstretched finger toward my face. I follow the tip of his finger, crossing my eyes as it lands on my nose and he wipes off a small dollop of frosting I left behind. He sucks the frosting from his finger, leaving it between his lips then showing me his teeth.

It's hot. And I no longer want to be at this party, but instead in his messy-ass bed with his body against mine. Naked. So very fucking naked.

My mom and June's have taken over running the kitchen, lining up sandwiches and my menudo, and with everyone else distracted, I take advantage of the perfect moment to slip away and pray Tory follows.

Tearing my cupcake in half, I hold out a bite as an offering for him. When he leans forward to take it in his mouth, I pull it back and pop it in mine, a suggestive smile on my closed lips as I chew. I wiggle the remaining piece in front of me, then draw him close with a finger as I walk backward to the small hallway that leads to the powder room. I lead him all the way inside, and he shuts the door behind him, locking it.

"You want my cupcake, Tory D'Angelo?" I hold it out for him, and he lets out a breathy growl as he rushes into me, taking my arms and pinning them out against the wall, the cupcake falling somewhere on the floor. His mouth covers mine possessively, his tongue tasting me, our teeth scraping against each other's hungry lips. He runs his hands along my arms and down my waist, bending down so he can continue the trip to the back of my thighs, lifting up my skirt enough to cup my ass.

"You are so much fun to touch," he whispers against my ear, biting the lobe and sucking it hard.

His hands are digging into my ass, palms to skin, and I want nothing more than to unzip him here and now and have him push me against the wall. That's not going to happen, though. I might be a terrible, selfish heartbreaker, but I'm not about to defile my best friend's powder room.

Ten bucks says she'd do it to mine in a heartbeat.

"I like this dress," he says, licking up the side of my neck and then covering my mouth with his for one last raw and needy kiss. I push him away, needing air, and we pant while dirty thoughts run rampant through both our minds.

"I had to wear this dress," I say, pushing the light switch down before we open the door. "You left your mark all over my body."

He bites near my ear as he wraps both arms around my stomach, holding me to him from behind. I can feel what our kissing has done to him, and it makes it difficult to leave this tiny, dark room.

I crack the door, though, knowing I have to be present for my own party, and when I'm sure the coast is clear, I slip out, spinning and meeting his confused eyes.

"You leave in about five minutes. Deal?"

He blinks a few times, then nods, shutting the door while I straighten my dress and the panties he basically hijacked up my ass.

We didn't talk about it, but I assume we're both on board with keeping this thing between us private . . . for now. I don't think Tory's family could handle a girl coming between him and his brother, though I did, and I am. With my dad finally in town, I'm not prepared to handle the backlash from our friends, either. No matter how you position *us,* we're the bad guys.

I'm funneling through the various scenarios, mentally making plans for how and when Tory and I *will* come out when the reason why we shouldn't stares me right in the face.

"Happy birthday weekend, Abs," Hayden says.

My eyes jet about the room as I'm hit with the sensation that I'm riding the Tilt-a-Whirl and I'm not buckled in. Hayden's palm finds my elbow, steadying me as he leans in and kisses my cheek.

"I'm not going to make you uncomfortable," he whispers. "I didn't want you to have to explain."

I straighten my spine and mentally flog myself for being the asshole that I am. I can't believe he's doing this to make sure *I'm* not the one who has to explain things and save face.

"Hey, June? It sounds like maybe there's a leak in—"

Tory stops after taking only two steps into the room. All eyes zoom to him, Hayden's carrying the most intent.

"Hey, bro," he says. The hostility in his tone is apparent, but it's to be expected. Their recent struggles to get along aren't secret. *I'm* the secret part, on so many levels.

"You came," Tory says, a tight grin stitched on his lips. He nods and avoids looking me in the eyes. Hayden's hands are on my shoulders, and though he said he came here as a kind gesture to me, his friendly touch isn't meant to be kind at all.

"Of course. Can't miss my girl's party," Hayden says.

I catch the crinkle on Tory's brow as he turns to take a few more samples from the desert table.

"Cool. Well, I'll be in the kitchen, helping the moms." He pops a candied pecan in his mouth from the few gathered in his palm and glares at his brother, saving a small bit of that look for me as he passes.

Shit, shit, shit, shit.

I can't even talk to June about this right now. I haven't caught her up, and I'm not sure I even want to. I'm not proud of how I handled all this, but the thought that Tory thinks Hayden is here under any pretense other than to just show up and play the part is ripping at my guts. He's assuming that we aren't really broken up, or that somehow Hayden was mistaken. I look like a massive player just toying with two brothers, which, ugh, maybe I am.

"Hayden, good to see you," my mom says, walking by with a platter of sandwiches in one hand, tugging on Hayden's sleeve sweetly with the other.

This is awful. I want to crawl into a hole, any hole. I'll

take a keyhole, smoosh myself inside and just live in a fucking doorknob.

June starts clapping—it's her annoying method of getting attention—and we all turn to face her.

"Thank you, guys, for coming together today to celebrate our favorite diva . . ." She fans a hand out toward me. *I guess I'm the diva?* "Abby, you're a woman now."

"She's been a woman for a while," Lucas says under his breath. June swings an arm at his chest and he spills a bit of punch on his shirt. *Good.*

"Now, we said no presents because let's face it, Abby's got enough shit," June jokes. She's right, my closet is packed and I don't really do trinkets and things. Mostly, though, I don't like the awkward attention that comes along with getting a gift. The giver watches you open it, holding their breath and waiting for this perfect reaction. I don't think I could ever give someone the absolute perfect reaction and the pressure of it stresses me out. Even on Christmas, I ask for cash. Cash is easy to react to. *"Hey, thanks for the cash!"*

"But I did a little thing," June continues.

Shit. A gift.

"It's nothing extraordinary, Abs, so don't expect much. But I may have gotten a little help from your mom to borrow a few things from your room for this occasion." June walks over a large manila envelope, holding it in her flat palms as if she is presenting me with the crown. I quirk my lip up in a half-hearted smile.

"Should I be nervous?" I am nervous. She took shit from my room!

"I don't think so," she answers. Yeah, that's a vague answer.

With a deep breath, I take the envelope in my hands, straightening the clasp to pull the flap free. I reach in and feel the coils of a spiral notebook, and for a brief moment, my heart stops at the thought that she's somehow dug up my fourth grade diary.

My center of gravity shifts a little with the dose of panic, but things right themselves when I slide the booklet from the envelope and see exactly what my friend has done. It's a calendar—of June's various pissed off faces.

Damn it. I love it.

My mouth hangs open in search of the right reaction, but June fills in the words for me.

"Right? It's your most favorite thing, isn't it?" She flips the cover open for me and points to January. It's a photo of her chewing, her eyes all screwed up and angry that I'm taking her pic. There's a dab of pizza sauce on her chin."

"Aww, the memories," I say teasingly, covering my heart and looking my best friend in the eyes.

"It's literally the one thing I knew you needed in your life—a humiliating collection, sorted by month, of pictures of me." She's wearing a wry smile, and without pause, I reach for my phone from my back pocket and snap what is probably a blurry shot of her face.

"Already starting on the next calendar, I see," June says in a flat tone.

"I think we could sell these," I say, flipping through the rest of the months while my birthday guests crowd around. *Most* of my guests, at least.

Tory's taken a seat on the sofa on the other side of the

room, a clear invisible wall between him and his brother—between him and *me* and his brother. It feels thick and ruled by silence. I lift my eyes to his, finding him waiting, staring. I try to form a smile, but it's faint and sad. It matches the one he gives back to me.

June claps again and as she wrangles everyone's attention, I walk my new favorite calendar ever over to Tory, handing it to him and being careful to keep a friend-type of distance between us even though every cell in my body is battling to make contact with him.

"Did you know about this?" I ask, remembering how he looked around my room at my photos of June, and the one of him and me.

"Nope. She did this all on her own," he says, looking up with a half-smile. We stay locked in a stare for a full breath, both looking away when the noise of the room makes us realize we aren't alone.

"Tory, I need you to be a part of this," June hollers.

"She's like a teacher," he says, twisting up his lips and pulling in his brow.

"That's what I've always said!" I step back to make room for him as he leaves the sofa and rounds the small coffee table. I'm careful to keep extra distance between us, walking slower than him, and curving to the other side of the room. I feel confident that I have everyone fooled—everyone but Hayden, whose glare at his brother is marked by a notable heavy brow and dimmed eyes that look like a predator ready to strike.

"So, before we eat," June says, these first few words receiving a collective groan from a room full of hungry bellies. "I know, it smells good. It's almost ready! Just waiting on the wings."

June went all out, making all my favorites. Other than the soup my mom made, everything else in this spread falls in one of two categories—bakery item or bar food.

"Everyone take a paper. Mom is passing them out."

My chest constricts because games are not really my thing, but June seemed excited so I told her it was fine as long as it's not something hard or a pain in the ass to organize. When I take the paper from her mom and read through the first few questions, I wish I let her set up kickball instead.

"Now, no cheating. We have a timer, so you cannot start writing until I say *go*." June's directions are background noise while I scan the list of personal questions about me. My birthday, which everyone should get right. My favorite thing at Holiday Theme Park—*easily the glitter cotton candy*. My favorite color, favorite time of the day, favorite thing to wear, first crush . . .

I swallow and fold my own paper, moving over to the dessert spread to pick at a few more treats while I wait for June to finish this game. I'll be shocked if anyone gets more than two. I'm not sure even June knows all the answers. My mom doesn't, and that thought makes me sad. Over the last few years, we've been so consumed with my career and fighting for our independence from my dad that the personal things have sort of fallen to the side.

"And . . . go!"

Instant silence follows June's directions, and I turn while I nibble on a chocolate pretzel to see everyone feverishly writing answers. June has her paper flattened against a wall so she can write quickly, which . . . *why didn't she just cheat and do it beforehand? She picked the damn questions.*

Hayden and Lucas seem to be teaming up, making each other laugh over their answers. Lola and Naomi seem to be working really hard, and my mom and June's mom are concentrating and giving thought to each answer. Even if they get them wrong, I bet there will be some element of rightness. Tory is hovering in the back of the crowd, his paper folded in his hand. He slips it under some mail in the nook space by the refrigerator where the Mabees keep their keys and phone chargers, then opens the fridge to pull a cold water bottle out from the bottom drawer. He glances my way as he turns, but his attention doesn't stick. He's either good at pretending or detaching himself on purpose, trying not to get hurt.

What June said would be three minutes of time feels as if it stretches on for ten, but finally, she tells everyone to put their pencils down and she collects the papers. She begins reading the responses, and a lot of them are funny. This part of the game . . . it's okay.

"Abby's favorite time of day is any time that Abby is right," June reads.

"That's kind of true. Give that a half point," I say.

"Score," Lucas shouts, pulling in a fist pump.

My mom ends up getting the most right, even more than my best friend, which soothes me some, but I'm curious about the one paper that wasn't turned in. I wonder if he tried at all.

"Okay, food is finally ready," June's mother announces.

Everyone files toward the table to collect plates and

bowls so they can filter down the line and stuff themselves in my honor. Tory is near the front of the line, and I smile to myself at the sight of him filling a large bowl of menudo. He'll love it. It's impossible not to. Waiting my turn, I back up a few steps into the kitchen while nobody notices and walk my fingers over to the paper Tory tried to dismiss.

I pull it into my hand and open the fridge, bending down to act as if I'm getting a drink or searching for something down low. It's silly that I feel like I have to hide just to read his answers, but I do. And as I read on, I'm even more certain.

He's gotten every answer right. My favorite color is pink, but not just pink—pale pink. My favorite glitter cotton candy is jotted down. Sunsets are my favorite time of day, and my first crush was Peter Pan. I liked the idea of someone sweeping me away for an adventure. Hearing my name mentioned, I quickly fold the paper up small enough to tuck it in my hand and pull a water bottle out for myself, shutting the fridge and moving back into the room full of people.

"Do you want to tell everyone the right answers?" June asks. I discreetly stuff Tory's paper into my purse and set my water down on the floor by the chair I've chosen to be my throne for the day.

"No, I think I like the mystery. Besides, maybe some of you have answers I like better." My response gets a laugh, and Lucas pipes in to take credit for changing my mind on some things.

I fill my bowl with my mother's soup, knowing this is probably the only other thing I will eat today and I will eat servings until it is gone. I take my seat again and nudge my purse under my chair with my foot, glancing up to see Tory staring at it. His eyes flit to mine and we lock gazes for a quiet moment when everyone else is too busy to notice.

"Thank you," I mouth.

His lips curve up slightly at the corners and he blinks slowly with a careful nod. I don't know how he knows me so well, but perhaps he's been paying attention. I'm starting to wish I had been all along.

19

TORY

This is hard. Loving a girl is hard. I'm in love with a girl, with Abby Cortez.

And it is fucking hard.

My brother and I drove in separate cars this morning. We left the house a minute apart, to give each other space. It's all starting to feel so trivial. And wasteful. Gas is expensive.

Something has to get figured out between me and Hayden before our game tonight. I've never actually seen Coach this upset at us. At other guys? Sure. But Hayd and I are exceptions. I guess getting away with four years of shit is finally catching up to us. Either that, or maybe this time our problems are too much for a team to take.

We play St. Agnes today. It's a big game, the first in our division. If we can run up the score against them, we have a good chance of taking the holiday tournament and maybe coming out the top seed in our division for state. We won't beat St. Agnes if Hayden and I aren't in sync, and it's less about the team and more about how much it's affecting me emotionally. I hate hating my brother. I can't do it anymore.

Part of making amends is going to mean letting go of Abby. I just don't see a way that she and I can be something without it ruining everything else. I promised myself I would fight to keep her, but maybe the honorable thing and the best way to love her is to let her go. Maybe in another life . . . another time and place. This round, we are just off. The world isn't ready for us.

It's hard to commit to being honorable when I read her texts, though. She wants to know how I knew everything about her on that birthday list, and I have to shake my head because I don't really have an answer. I just do. I know so much about her, more than I realized. All from watching her, from paying attention to her little details, the things that make her tick. She wears more pale pink than any other color, and when she wears it on her lips, her smile is always brighter and her laugh a little more real. I knew the Peter Pan thing because she mentioned it once in fifth grade, that she thought Peter Pan was cute. Some of the boys in our class laughed at her; she punched one of them. She got sick eating the damn glitter cotton candy during our eighth grade trip to Holiday Park, but she said it was worth it when she threw up. I've been watching Abby Cortez for years; I just didn't realize that the lens I was looking through was one of love.

I leave my last hour early. I told June to tell Coach I am going to get things right with Hayden. She was glad to hear me say it, and since we're both his assistants for last hour, she said she'd handle it.

Hayden has study hall this period, and unfortunately the teacher in there is a former drill sergeant. I don't say that to make commentary on the woman's demeanor, I'm being real—she was in the Army for fifteen years. How our school was lucky enough to land her, I'll never know. I had study hall last year, and she and I . . . let's just say we don't gel.

I see my brother's backpack dangling from the back of a chair, so I know he's within earshot if I can manage to get his attention through the small crack in the door. She'll be closing it soon.

"Hayden," I whisper, giving my voice enough volume to carry but not gain unwanted attention. It does zero good.

I look both ways and move in closer, smooshing my face through the door to whisper it again.

"Psst, Hayden!" I move away fast and flatten my back to the wall. My heart is thumping. I swear, this woman terrifies me.

I crane my neck to peek through the open part and catch my brother's eyes as he leans back. He grimaces and waves his hand, shooing me away.

Goddamnit.

"Come here," I whisper a little louder, again darting away. I think that's all I've got in me. If I try one more time, she'll grab my tongue mid-speech and lord knows what that woman will do to it. Probably nothing, but something about her glare instills that kind of fear in me.

I wait with my back against the wall for almost a full minute, and I'm about to give up when the door opens and my brother steps out. He walks past me, toward the restrooms.

"Come on," he says over his shoulder.

I follow. We get inside and move to the window along the back wall where people put out their cigarette butts and snuff out the ends of their blunts.

"What's up? Something wrong at home? You need money? What?" He can barely make eye contact with me while he talks, and he keeps pacing, clearly not wanting to be here.

"This is gonna take a lot longer than a bathroom break. I hope you know that," I say. He huffs and moves to the sink, running his hands through the water, then through his hair.

"Better not. Hurry up," he grumbles.

The urge to rush him and tackle his ass against the wall and sink and nasty floor is definitely simmering in my legs. It wouldn't take much.

Drawing in a calming breath through my nose, I say the only thing I believe will work, that will get him to actually stop and listen.

"I love you."

He shakes his head like a cartoon mouse getting smacked with a broom. His mouth hangs open, unprepared to deliver a reaction. Those are not the words he was expecting, and that's why they needed to be said.

"Thanks, I guess," he finally says, stretching his lips out over his teeth and awkwardly mashing them together. He's uncomfortable, which is weird because we're brothers—it shouldn't be hard to say those words to each other. But after Abby's party I struggled to remember the last time he and I had. I couldn't think of it, which means it's been too long.

I step into him, and he flinches a little when I raise my hands. Placing my palms on either shoulder, I look him in the eyes and let the uncomfortable quiet strangle us as we're forced to look at ourselves, at our own faces on someone else. It takes several seconds for him to return to character, for a softness to shine through this hardened armor on his face, but it happens. Slowly, it happens.

"I love you," I repeat.

He swallows at hearing it the second time. His eyes shift to the side then back to me.

"I love you too, man."

We both breathe out hard, our chests in sync with every in and out movement our lungs make. Once I think he's ready for more, I tell him the part that's even harder for me to say.

"I'm sorry." My mouth waters delivering the words because while I truly am for many things, I'm not sorry one bit for others. That doesn't matter, though. I realized last night that forgiveness doesn't get put on a scale.

It's going to take my brother some time to work through hearing these words, and I don't expect to hear them back, though it sure would be nice. He folds his arms over his chest, closing himself off as he steps back until he can lean against the wall.

I maintain eye contact with him the entire time, even when he can't hold it on his end, looking down often and rubbing his finger in the corner of his eye. Ready, he finally snaps his gaze up to mine and tilts his head to one side.

"Abby?" I hate that he starts here. It's not the place to begin.

With tight lips, I shake my head and look down.

"It's nothing," I lie. I don't swallow the painful rock lodged in my throat for fear he'll see it. It's my one big tell. I lift my chin and lean my head to the side to match his.

He smirks and puffs out a short laugh, moving his hands to his pockets and relaxing a little more.

"Guess she ruined both of us, huh?"

I shrug in response.

"Something like that," I say.

He studies me, looking for the cracks in my answer, the way to really get to the core. I'm not yet ready for core sharing when it comes to her. I'm giving her up for him, and it's going to take me a long time to not be truly bitter about it.

"I have to ask you something, and . . . it's . . . " I pause, rubbing my hand over my mouth while I fight through the wave of anger that still courses through my body over the things I've discovered in the last few days. "This is hard for me to talk about. Hard to wrap my mind around, but Hayden . . . I found the Olsen Academy letter, man."

His eyes widen fast. His mouth remains a straight line, though. He's been practicing for this moment, probably for years. Still, the unexpected timing was too much to prepare for now that I confront him about it in our gross-ass high school bathroom.

"Don't give me the story. I want the truth. I can take the truth, okay? It's this awful resentment we've both fostered that I can't handle. Tell me. Tell it to me straight." I brace myself for his response, which takes him several seconds to form.

"It was a really shitty thing to do, Tor. I'm sorry," he says. I wasn't expecting him to start so humble. It makes it easier to hear, somehow. His ability to admit that he did take something precious from me somehow makes the wound sting less. It stings all the same.

I nod and slowly spin where I stand, rocking on my feet. My head falls back and I look up at the ceiling tiles, marred with dangling pencils and gum.

"It was in fact a pretty shitty thing to do, Hayd. I'll give you that. You nailed the description spot on." I suck in my lips hard, making a near impenetrable straight line that holds in the other things I'm tempted to say.

Hayden groans, lowering his chin to his chest and letting his head fall into his open hands. His fingers scratch at his scalp, and it takes me a few seconds to realize that he's . . . he's crying. When he raises his head, I'm met with red eyes and a sour face.

"Tory, I messed up. I messed up, and it messed up everything, and I don't know how to make it right." His confession churns my stomach.

"Messed up how?" I question.

Another deep breath for both of us. Hayden brings his fist to his mouth, holding it to his bottom lip while he blinks at me, trying to get the words out. My fingers itch to grab his wrist and yank his fist away, but he needs it right now. He needs to hide a little, as silly as that seems.

"I saw mom and Mr. Fuller," he admits.

My brow pulls in so tight I can feel the fold above the bridge of my nose.

"Like, at our house?" I question.

"Freshman year, at football camp. When they first—" He can't finish that statement and nobody wants him to. It's an awful image.

"Hayd." I shift to lean against the sink. I press my palms into my eyes, dizzy from this information. I pull one hand away and lift a brow as I look at my brother. "You knew? You knew all this time?"

He shakes his head.

"I wasn't sure. I thought it was only that first time and maybe that was it, but then this summer—"

"Oh, my God, summer. They kept it going over summer," I groan. I flip around and grip the sink, taking in my own sick expression in the scratched-up mirror.

"When your letter came, I thought if you and Dad left, I'd be there alone with Mom, and then . . . " His shoulders rise up to his ears as he shakes his head. "I deleted the email, but then the letter came and I wanted to throw it away, but also, I knew it was important to you. I've thought about throwing that thing away every day for nearly four years."

"Why didn't you?" I mumble, once again dropping my chin to my chest as I lean over the sink. "God, Hayd. I wish I'd never known. It would have been better than this."

I can't help but play through the what ifs of my life, a thing I have been doing constantly since I found out Hayden sabotaged my shot. Yeah, Mom and Dad probably would have split up a long time ago, and Hayden and I probably would have lived apart, but I'd be at Olsen and on my way to D1 somewhere big, maybe more. But I wouldn't have had Abby. Probably not ever.

My hands grip the porcelain and I shake it a few times, knowing if I want I could probably rip the sink from the wall. I stand straight and let my hands fall to my sides while I just breathe.

"It all got away from me, and then it seemed for so long like things were just . . . fine." Everything about the look in his eyes is the opposite of fine. My brother made some self-ish, stupid choices, but they've taken a toll on him. This is why he's struggling so much. While I can get mad and let anger rule me for a little while, he's still trying to tuck everything that's wrong into this little box to keep it safe, keep our family whole.

"I love you." I say it with my gaze toward the floor. The same words I started this with, and maybe I'm saying them because I need to remind myself a bit, too.

"I swear to God, brother, if you're about to hug me," he says, trying out my brand of humor, a default mode I prefer over emotional moments. I laugh at the attempt. *Not bad.*

"I'm gonna hug you," I say, moving in closer. He recoils, but only for show.

"It's coming, big man. Might as well let it happen. Feel the love," I ramble on, getting close enough that we can touch.

We stare at one another with limp bodies and tired hearts, for once truly the same in almost every single way. We embrace mutually, and I hug him with as much force as he hugs me. My hand grips his shirt over his shoulder, and we rock a little because that keeps us from crying. After simultaneously slapping each other's back, the secret bro way of signaling it's time to stop hugging, we pull apart and back away from one another.

"You should probably get back to study hall. She'll red card you for the game because she's mean like that," I say to him.

He nods with a short sniff, toughening up his posture to enter the same way he left.

"No more shit on the court, okay?" I hold out my hand for him to take, and he does so without hesitation.

"Nothing but the good kind of trouble." He shoots me a brief crooked smile. That's what Coach refers to us as when we're on the court together. We're trouble for the other team. Too much to guard, too fast to catch.

I wait for Hayden to leave first, sticking around in the bathroom until the period ends and I can head to the gym and dress out for the game. I'm going to have to talk to Abby first, if I can get her alone. I have to make her world right while also making things right with Hayden, but I'm not sure I'm strong enough to do what needs to be done. She makes me forget the line.

20

ABBY

I'm leaving.

Wednesday.

The moment school breaks for the long holiday, my mom and I are locking up the house and driving up to Toronto for what will be months. I'm leaving, just when things are happening. Just when things feel right.

I'm leaving.

I got the call this morning, and there's not a way to say no when producers who took a chance on you for their big budget movie say they need you a month earlier than expected. Leaving will give us space from my dad, too. He's renting a house about four miles away and about four times the size of ours. He's doing it to show off, and it's gross. It's also an irresponsible thing to do with his money, which does not bode well for him being involved in my finances at all.

Now that I'm eighteen, I'm allowed to file suits of my own, and I intend to break my company into pieces and give him the worthless part while forming a new one with only my mom and me. He doesn't know it's coming, and he'll be really ugly about it, but I'll be in Toronto, with my mom. And he doesn't have a passport.

This all leads back to this moment. The one I'm about to have.

I'm leaving, and I have to tell Tory.

He texted me to wait outside the locker room at four. It's about five minutes past and I feel a bit foolish, and a bit like a predator who hangs around boys locker rooms to catch peeks of their asses. I've seen two so far, and I will never be able to erase those visual assaults from my eyes.

I'm about to text him to catch me later, a little thankful that maybe I can put this talk off a little longer, when the door pops open again. I look up briefly, trying to avoid seeing something I don't want to see, but it's Tory jogging up the steps and out to me.

He scans the area around us before bending forward, leaning his palms on the concrete bench I'm sitting on, and holding my lips with a soft kiss. I tilt up as he hovers above me for a few seconds, his mouth lingering, sucking in my top lip just a little then letting go. He leans back to sit next to me, kicking one leg over the bench to straddle it while I sit in front of him.

"You sticking around for our game?" His eyes crinkle, a hopeful expression.

"Wouldn't miss it," I say.

"Good, good." He nods, his tight-lipped grin pushing into his cheeks.

I'm leaving. I am leaving.

He looks down at the concrete between us, tapping his

fingertips manically while he chews at the inside of his cheek.

"What's going on?" I reach up and touch his cheek, and he lifts his eyes, giving me a half smile that doesn't stick around long. He keeps his gaze on me, though, all kinds of worries and thoughts rushing behind it.

Tory reaches up and cups my face, pulling me in for another kiss, once again chaste, the same fated feelings attached. His hands fall back to the bench, gripping the sides as he sits up tall and holds on as if he has to hold himself to this spot on the earth.

"It's Hayden," he says.

My heart rushes with so many chemically induced and heart-wrenching emotions that for a moment I think I might overdose on feelings.

"Did he find out about . . . us?" I keep playing our night together over and over in my head, thinking about how close Hayden's room was to us, how he could have come home at any moment, how guilty my face must have seemed when he came to my party. He's sharper and more intuitive than we give him credit for.

"No, at least, I don't think so. He knows how I feel, but I know how he feels so I guess it's a wash." He shrugs, despondent and lifeless. He squints from the sun as he brings his gaze back to me, his words suddenly stalled. I have the power to save him from having to say any more.

"So . . . I'm leaving Wednesday."

His brows lift and his breath halts for a beat.

"Yeah, I know," I say, looking down to where his hand is still curved around the edge of the concrete. I place mine on top of it, threading my fingers with his until his grip loosens and he rolls his palm over to completely give me his hand. I play with his fingers, wishing I had the time to really study them, to learn how they look with mine, how they look on me, around my waist and near me while I sleep.

"I got the call last night. Something about budget, and getting my shots early before Jordan has to film something else. The good news is it means I'll be back for prom and graduation." I dip my head to catch his eyes again and grin at the word *prom*. It doesn't seem to do much for him, though.

"So you're leaving, for like . . . a while." He draws in a deep breath and leans back.

"Probably four months. I'll have a tutor."

I should be excited about this, but I dread every moment. My big break feels like a crash and burn, and it's making me rethink my dreams and goals. I'm giving up one of the most important times in my life. I'm giving up this feeling—*love*. I'm falling in love with Tory, and walking away before it has a chance to take hold.

"Maybe it's for the best . . . with Hayden and all," he says, his eyes meeting mine in fits. They're glassy, but he masks it, coughing and hazing them as he purposely looks back toward the sun.

"Maybe," I choke out.

"Another time, maybe. Or life. Or maybe our future selves. I don't know," he rambles, squeezing the bridge of his nose and holding his breath. He averts his eyes as he stands, and I stand with him, feeling the need to wrap him in my arms and hold him here, to me.

"We're in warm-ups, and I just slipped out. But you'll

be at the game, right? You'll stay?" His arm swings out and his fingers latch on to mine, like fragile hooks holding together too much weight.

"I'll stay," I promise. I will, and it will hurt. Because I am leaving.

Tory leans in and presses his lips to my cheek this time, pausing there long enough to graze his nose along my jaw and plant one more kiss on the bare skin peeking out from the large neck of my sweatshirt.

"See you after, then."

Our fingers slip apart and he walks away backward for the first several steps. He turns around to jog, disappearing down the steps to the locker room door, slipping inside and never once looking back.

I talked June into coming to the game. She was the second person I told that I was leaving early, so she hardly even grumbles about having to sit on these bleachers with me. Of all the things I'm going to miss out on for months, time with her ranks as one of the highest.

"One thing I do like about basketball over football is it's inside, even if it's crowded," she says.

"It's because our basketball team is a million times better than football," I gloat.

"You're biased," she retorts.

We take our seats at center court but in the very top of the bleachers. I learned last time that it's nice to have a wall to rest your back against. Plus, I kinda like keeping everyone else in my line of sight. You never know where the haters are gonna come from.

I haven't filled June in on Hayden yet. That's the other reason I want her and I to have this time together.

"I'm more impartial than biased now, by the way," I say, leaning into her. She pulls her water bottle from her mouth and it makes a pop. Her mouth hangs on to the O shape.

"You broke up?" I can't tell if she's really shocked or just playing the part.

"Come on, you know you were shocked to see us together in the first place. And yeah, it just wasn't right, and with me leaving and all . . . " *And with me being in love with his brother.* That part stays in my head.

"Yeah, I guess I can see that. Are things good between you, though? I mean, when did this happen? At your party?" She studies me for a second, reading the truth in my wincing face.

"Oh, shit. Before?"

I nod and sigh.

"Oh, that must have been hard or weird or . . . hard *and* weird?" She turns her attention back to the court where both teams are lining up for the tip-off.

"Hard and weird pretty much sums it up." I chuckle. The whistle blows and Tory sails over the St. Agnes player, pushing the ball through the air to his brother who rushes it down the court for a fast two points. June and I both stand and shout.

"Okay, I can get into this basketball game thing," she says. Tory steals the ball the moment she finishes her statement, this time taking it all the way himself but stopping at the three-point line and putting up a shot that floats through the air in perfect silence. When he sinks it, we stand again, a roar erupting.

"Yes! Go Tory! Go Hayden! Go Eagles!" June is red-faced, screaming, and I tug her arm to drag her back down to sit with me.

"Slow down there, mama Eagle," I tease.

"It's just . . . this is so exciting. Things happen so fast, and there's not all these timeouts and measurements and—"

We stand again for another steal, this one by someone other than one of the twins. Another layup, and our team is up seven to zero with less than a minute burned.

We're giggling from the excitement, and it injects much needed joy into my body. For a little while, I'm able to forget that I'm leaving something new and special, and that I hurt someone kind and soft, and that I'm going to miss my best friend. For the next hour, I simply exist in this bubble, in a world where the boy I love and the boy I admire absolutely put on a show together on the court, and I'm lucky enough to watch it unfold. Hayden and Tory bond before my eyes. They celebrate each other, and they work as this singular unit that positively cannot function without the other half.

And then it hits me. Maybe they can't.

"In another life," I mutter, not realizing my thoughts spill out loud.

"Hmm?" June leans in.

I shake her off, claiming to be talking about the other team, but the way she continues to look at the side of my face makes me believe she knows better. She also knows not to push.

The game ends with us on top by twenty-seven points. It was basically a blow-out, led by the D'Angelo boys. A reporter from the local paper asks them to stick around for a short interview and a picture, so June and I move down to the bottom row to listen in. The questions are pretty typical, but the D'Angelo answers are not. They goof with each other, poking fun in a way that also praises, and whenever the reporter tries to bring the spotlight to Tory, he instantly shifts it, giving credit to Hayden. Before they get up, one of their teammates rushes by with a cup of ice water and splashes it across the backs of their necks, and they take off after him into the locker room.

"I guess we can just hang around outside," June says.

I follow her out the doors and glance to my car. I can't wait around and see them both. Whatever balance they have happening between them, it's necessary. It's how they'll get through the next few weeks and months. It's how they're going to navigate their lives. They don't need me to stick around to tell them both nice game.

"Actually," I begin. June's head falls to the side, a frown tackling her lips. "I know, I know, it's just that I have so much to do. I have to pack!"

"You haven't packed?" She's shocked. I actually have, but there are still a few things I could work on before leaving. I won't be at school tomorrow or Wednesday either, so in many ways, this really is good-bye.

"I know, and you know how I am with shoes," I joke, reaching around her shoulders to hug her tight. She squeezes me.

"They have a weight limit for the plane, you know."

"Good thing we're driving."

"Ha, well . . . tires can only hold so much, too."

My lips pucker a smile that turns into laughter, the kind that settles between two friends who would rather part like this than through tears.

I back away, wanting to run before the boys come out.

"I'll call you before we go. We'll talk. And we'll talk every day, okay?" She's the one promise I know I can keep. I need her too much.

"You better. And I want coordinated video chats that just happen to have Jordan in the background," she says.

I pull my phone from my pocket to wave it, catching her in one last photo before I go.

"Unbelievable," she retorts.

I grin, turning to walk the rest of the way to my car, and I cradle the phone in my lap once inside and look at the cross-eyed, open-mouthed face my friend is making. I save this one as my backdrop, and pledge to let it help me get through four months apart.

As I pull out, the team files out through the locker room doors, a certain two walking out last. I pause at the parking lot exit, my blinker on, ready to turn. It would be so easy to turn around, and I almost do.

But I don't.

21

TORY

I should have gone to say good-bye. Hayden did. He even bought Abby a gift –a keychain with one of those little director's clapper boards on the end. He wrote her name on it. It was thoughtful. I'm not very good at thoughtful right now. I'm nice and settled in on pathetic.

It just seemed better to let things end where we left them. Nothing definitive, just an air of possibility. No painful tears. No explanations to Hayden or our friends —*ourselves.*

She hit the road yesterday. Hayden called out of school to see her off. I went to class, and not because I love being one of the handful who shows up on half days before holiday break to watch various versions of *The Grinch*, but because school was a damn good place to hide for the day.

There's no hiding from Thursdays, though. It seems a month since I stormed out of Dr. Majestic's office. In one week, I've managed to unearth four years of secrets my brother has been keeping, bought a car, moved some of my shit to my dad's place, and fallen in love. Oh, and I hit rock bottom in terms of ever wanting to fall in love again.

All in all, a pretty well-rounded week leading up to therapy.

In a show of faith, or maybe in an act of naiveté, I drove Hayden to therapy tonight. He wanted to have the full cop experience. I think he was a little disappointed when I didn't actually have a siren and the flashy lights. They rip that shit out before auction. I do have a spotlight, though. That'll come in handy the next time I take this thing off-road out on McCaffey's land.

The drive in was good. I only hope we survive the drive home, because the longer the four of us sit in this waiting room just . . . *waiting,* the more palpable the tension becomes. Right now, it's thick enough to melt the paint off the walls.

"D'Angelos. Welcome," Dr. Majestic says.

"Wouldn't it be great if she wore a wizard hat for one of these?" Hayden whispers behind my back. Dad and I both snicker.

"Tory!" My mom hushes me with her finger to her lips, and in a sign of normality, my father and brother straighten their posture and pretend they don't know me.

"Unbelievable," I mumble, elbowing my brother in the ribs. He grunts but laughs through it, proud he can still say things and blame them on me. This has been happening since we learned to talk.

We take the same seats as last time, only the doctor planned ahead and pre-moved the recliner for me. I give her a nod and flop into my seat, toying with the handle on the side to kick my feet up. My brother and dad chuckle but I stop when my mom gives me side eyes.

"Fine," I grumble. I'm trying to keep it light on purpose —because I still don't want to be here. Maybe I can will this time to fly by and be painless.

"Let's pick up where we left off," Dr. Majestic begins, and there goes any hope that this will go easy.

"Tory, we didn't get to work through some of your speed bumps before you left."

"Speed bumps?" I question.

"She calls our conflicts speed bumps. She says it makes them easier to acknowledge," Hayden says, one brow raised.

I lock eyes with him.

"Ah. Speed bumps. Okay, well, no speed bumps for me. Smooth sailing, or driving rather. I'm a racetrack." I show my hands and lift my shoulders, playing the part of an easy-going man, though I really have no idea what one of those looks like.

"I see," she says, crossing her legs, clicking her pen open, and leaning forward, wrists crossed atop her knees. She has this way of drawing her breath in through her nose that makes her mouth look like it's about to unleash a barrage of new questions. But all that happens is more silence, and more studying of my silence.

"Yep," I finally say.

She nods, but still no words.

My head swivels to face my brother, who simply blinks back at me. *No help at all.* My dad is growing uncomfortable watching me under scrutiny and shifts his posture on his end of the couch.

"Honey, it's fine. This is a safe space." My mom finally gives.

The match to my lighter fluid.

"Safe space?" My voice is loud. I have no in-between.

"Yes, you are safe to be honest here," she says, which sets off a fit of laughter in my brother's belly. It brews slowly. Coming out through his tight lips, it spits until he finally has to cough it out.

"Are you all right?" My mom turns to him, coddling like she normally does, only this time my brother shirks off her attention.

"Oh, I'm totally fine. Race car ready just like Tory," he says, and I smirk at his quick response and comradery.

"Me, too. More of a pace car, but smooth ride," my dad adds in.

Unable to handle being ganged up on, my mom throws up her hands and covers her face. It's a move we've seen her do often, crumbling in the face of confrontation to get everyone to stop. Thing is, that visual got my brother to tuck away the things he saw and knew. It forced him to be afraid of setting off a massive landslide of dominoes. And that . . . *that* is one hell of a speed bump.

"Natalia, do you want to share how this is making you feel?"

My mom milks the moment, her breath quivering with overdone emotion, until she waits too long and my brother takes over for her.

"It makes her nervous because she can't control any of it. She can't mess up and just make things go away," he says.

"That's not it at all, Hayden."

"Oh, it is. And it's more than that," my brother unleashes. "Mom, I knew. I saw you and Mr. Fuller. I saw you at camp, and I saw the signs that it was still happening when we got home, and I saw the signs again months ago when I figured *surely, they've ended things by now.* But no, you just kept living double lives, throwing everything we are in the garbage because it wasn't enough, and I spent four years pretending it was normal because I didn't want our little bubble to burst."

"Unbelievable," my dad says under his breath, closing himself off more. He's flawed too, just differently.

"Are you saying you didn't know?" My brother lashes into him now, and while my instinct is to defend my dad, I think maybe that is *my* flaw. I pick sides without hearing the full story.

"Yes, Hayden. I just wrote it all off, figured she could go have her fun and I'd do all the work." My dad waves his hand dismissively. He's making a bad joke of all of this, out of us in a way, and his words only make my brother grow bolder.

"First of all, you're lying. She didn't hide it well, and there's no way you weren't suspicious. Hell, Dad, I had a girlfriend for like, six weeks, and I knew Tory was with her behind my back."

My mouth widens and my lungs deflate with the sucker punch. It's fair, but it's also not the topic. And it's over with Abby, because I chose Hayden.

"Tory," my mom comes to life again in time to scold me.

I stand up and cup my ears as I glare at her.

"Oh, no. You do not get to judge me," I say, only to have Hayden take over my point.

"Handle your own problems, Mom. Handle this—*us*! This is your mess. You and Dad, you're in a marriage. Tory and I are fucking eighteen and dating and figuring out who we are. You should have gotten all of your mistakes out of your system by now."

"Yeah," I agree, pausing at the word *mistake*. I lower myself to my seat and fade into the background, letting the chaos move forward without me. I glance over to the doctor while my family's shouting silences in my own head. She's listening, but she isn't writing down a damn word. It's the expression buried underneath the professional façade that really piques my interest. She's getting us to do just what she wants, what we *need* to do more of. She's getting us to talk. To listen.

For an hour, we yell over one another, Hayden doing most of the talking to the point that his voice is ragged by the time our session is done. My parents leave in their separate cars, my dad driving back to the city and my mom to our home. I still feel confident my dad's albums will leave the house soon. I'm pretty sure there isn't a resolution to their marriage in any of this, but maybe there's one for us as a family. Maybe there will be a way for things to be civil, and for Hayden and I to quit carrying the weight.

Hayden and I leave the office after my parents are gone, walking quietly to my car. I turn it on and maneuver the aux cord while my brother buckles up so I can shuffle to his personal playlist for the ride back. One of his favorite Motown songs comes on and he turns to face me with a suspicious line on his mouth.

"You pick this on purpose?" he asks.

I hold up my phone and show him the playlist labeled HAYDEN'S SHIT. He laughs, taking my phone and scrolling through the songs.

"You're missing some good ones," he says.

I grab my phone back and smirk.

"I've got like fifty. Let me learn to like all of these first and then we'll talk about you adding some."

I shift into reverse and check my mirrors.

"Maybe you make me a playlist of your shit," he says.

"Can do, only my stuff isn't shit. Just your stuff," I tease.

"Ahhh, you like my shit and you know it. I've seen you singing Wilson Pickett." He crosses his arms, confident that he's right.

"*June* likes Wilson Pickett, and she made me listen to it," I reply.

I pull us out onto the main road and we get a mile or so down the road before I finally throw him a bone.

"All right, fine. The Wilson Pickett stuff is pretty good."

"See? I knew it!" He rocks in his seat, mouthing the words to whatever song this is now. Something about loving somebody's baby. I'm sure after a month of driving back and forth from Dad's with this playlist, I'll know the words, too.

"You know, Dad's cool with you coming out, too. We could go the same weekend sometimes, or . . . separate. If you want some one-on-one time, I get it." I glance at him while I drive, gauging his reaction. The best I can gather is that it's thoughtful, his tight lips not frowning but not quite smiling, either.

"Maybe," he finally answers.

"I hope so," I say, and I mean it.

We make it the rest of the way with nothing but HAYDEN'S SHIT serenading us, and the more songs that play, the more I soften to his favorite sounds. We pull in the driveway and sit with my car running just so the current song can finish out. I kill the engine just as it ends, and we let the mood we've built embrace us for a little while longer.

"Why her?" I finally ask. I think that's my speed bump. It's definitely the question I've been asking myself when I can't sleep at night, when I shower, when I drive, when I should be learning in class. I think, given Dr. Majestic's definition, that equates to an emotional speed bump. It's too high for me to get over on my own.

Hayden's silence makes my chest tighten.

"She just . . . *listened,*" he finally says.

My eyes drop, along with my heart. I can't fault him for falling for her for that. Abby does listen. It might be what forced me to finally see her through different eyes. Through *possible* eyes. While Hayden was opening up to her about the things happening in our family, I was shutting down, but it doesn't mean I wasn't talking to her. I talked, just in my own way. While we bonded over Lucas and June, I made snide jokes about love being a farce and she made them right along with me. But she was always sure to leave me with a glimmer of hope before we parted. Like when Lucas and June finally got together and she leaned into me and said, "See, some people get their happy endings." She's not as cynical as she pretends.

"Did you love her, at least?" I wasn't sure about asking this question tonight. It feels like an overreach, a step maybe neither of us is ready for. But now that I'm in the moment, my belly hungry to be settled, my heart anxious to be soothed, I have to ask.

"I thought I did," Hayden admits, sinking down in his seat and leaning his head against the window to look up at the stars. I do the same. The sky's lit up again, like it was the night Abby came over.

"You still think so?" I ask.

"Nah," he responds quickly. I'm a little surprised to hear his answer, and I roll my head against the glass to look at him through the corner of my eyes.

"No?" I echo.

He shakes his head.

"I think I needed her, and that's not quite the same," he says, rolling his head to look at me.

"How about you?" I figured this question would come. I've been ready to answer it for a while.

"Yeah. I did. I do." I shift to look at him more head on. I can tell my admission catches him off guard as he sits up and pulls in his brow.

"You love her?" He makes it sound so impossible.

"I love her. I was about to ask her out the day you showed up holding hands," I confess.

"Fuuu—" His mouth hangs open as it hits him. "The flowers."

"The flowers." I nod. "The motherfucking flowers."

We both lean back into our windows and stare up at

the stars. My window is fogged from my breath, so I pull my sleeve down over my wrist and rub it clear.

"I'm really sorry, Tor. If I had known—"

"It's all right. I never said," I cut in. I hold my fist out in the space between us without looking to him, and he reaches over to pound mine just by feel. We're back in step. I don't know how long we were out of it, but in a strange way, it was Abby who put us back together.

22

ABBY

Christmas in Toronto is unreal. I've seen snow lots but never like this. It's more like someone came through at night and replaced everything in the city with frozen blocks of ice. It's beautiful, but it's painful.

I've slipped twice so far. Not bad falls, but enough to leave a bruise on my hip. Mom wasn't so lucky. She fell and cracked her wrist on a curb. I guess if you're going to be stuck in a cast for four to six weeks, it might as well be in the cold.

Mom and I promised each other no holiday gifts, but I did get her this pack of cast wraps so she could bling out her plaster arm. She seems to have taken to the rainbow peace symbols for her first week of wear.

She broke the rules and got me a gift, too. Hers was a package too, but a major step above some pack of fun acrylic sticker. She gave me a settlement package. In my favor. She'd hired a private investigator the moment I confessed about the nude photo bribe. It took the guy a while to earn his fee, but he finally came through in spades. Seems Jake from the party got a payday a week or two before he met me—a wired deposit from my dad. The chips fall into place easily when you're willing to really look at them, but even as my mom was telling me, I didn't want to see things clearly. It was too ugly. Regardless, it was true.

My dad paid Jake to dupe me into those pics—to the tune of twenty grand. The hundred grand never went anywhere; it was all for show. Oh, and since I was seventeen at the time, and Jake was nineteen? Well, leverage. Zero prison time traded for never, ever seeing us again. It's going to take me a while to be able to open up about all of the betrayal. I've been able to tell June, but even with her, I can't get through the details without shutting down.

On a positive note, though, my company is now mine, and mine alone. My mom is setting up the structure, but she insists on being listed as an employee. She keeps saying being fireable is the one thing that ensures good parents don't go bad, but I'm pretty sure that's more of a soul-and-ethics sorta thing. If I ever make it truly big, the first thing I'm going to do is pay off the debt on her house. She'll sleep easy knowing that the walls my abuelo put up are hers forever. I want to secure that legacy for her.

With the break in shoots, Mom and I decide to make a short trip home for New Year's. June's mom is throwing a party, and apparently June went and invited a lot of people. I'm gone a week and a half and my friend becomes a party animal. Hayden says it's because she liked throwing my birthday party so much. She and her mom are good at catering and planning and decorating and, well, all of the things I'm *not* good at.

My mom's been sleeping so little that she finally conks out on the couch. I don't dare move her. She's getting too skinny, a thought that makes me sound like my abuela in my head. I drag the comforter from her bed over her and hit the mute button on the TV. The light will comfort her if she wakes in a strange location. With my phone, wallet, and key from the nearby table, I tiptoe out of the apartment. The busy sidewalk is freshly covered with a sparkling dusting of snow. It's nice to see before the morning traffic makes things so dirty.

It may be freezing here, but one thing my mom and I are suckers for is ice cream. We found this unique little place called Sweet Jesus on our first day in town. It's housed in an old church, and the ice cream is the best calorie gain I've ever experienced. Our goal is to have one of everything on the menu before we quit filming in March, but at this rate, I'll be through the list by the middle of January. I can always double up, I suppose.

The sidewalks are busy and the city is bright with holiday lights. The line for ice cream, even in the snow, is out the door. I take my spot and huddle against the building to stay warm in my fuzzy coat.

I palm my phone, hiding my face deep in the fur of my hood and scroll through pictures on my friends' feeds. It's hard to find photos of Tory, but it doesn't stop me from constantly searching. He usually fights it like he is in this one I stopped on. It's a selfie Hayden took, and Tory is hiding most of his face with his palm, his tongue sticking out far enough to touch his chin. It's enough to see his lips.

Excited to share my news about coming home, I flip to my contacts and stop on Hayden's name. We didn't talk for a few days after I left, but he texted out of the blue one night saying he needed someone to listen. It made me smile, and it's made me less lonely to have him only a text away. He gives me little updates about his brother, but I don't ask about him much. It seems they're in a good place, and I don't want to stir up anything that's better left put to rest. My feelings and hurt and scars over Tory aren't for Hayden to hear. Besides, I like just listening.

I press the call button by his name and bring the phone to my ear. I hate when people walk around on video chat, talking to one another in crowds for everyone to hear. I refuse to be that, even though *everyone* I work with—including Jordan Shotwell—is one of those people. I caught my mom doing it the other day and duly chastised her.

After four rings, I'm close to giving up, but Hayden picks up, sounding winded.

"Hey! One sec," he says, the phone muffling with his movement.

"Hey, I'll be right back!" he shouts to someone there with him.

I hear a door shut and the background noise disappears.

"Sorry, we were ballin'. I needed a break. Good timing!" He's panting a little, and I hear his water bottle filling up in the distance. I picture their fridge, the kitchen counter I sat at with Tory when I first practiced the part I'm playing now. I'm glad he rehearsed with me. If I hadn't started early I never would have been prepared for the schedule change.

"Just you and Tory?" I ask, wondering if his brother came inside, too.

"Us, and"—he stops while he takes a drink—"Cannon, his cousin Zack, and Chaz."

"I thought you hated Chaz?" I protest.

"I thought you hated Cannon," he fires back.

"I do!" I realize I'm being loud so I duck my head back between my shoulders and pull the zipper up on my coat, holding my phone inside the insulated cubby I've made for one.

Hayden laughs and says something about needing a fourth or whatever. Their tournament is next week. It starts the day I leave, so I won't be able to catch any games, which bums me out.

"How's Mr. Shotwell?" He asks this every time. My friends are more star-struck than I am, but maybe that's because I have to maintain a level of cool. I wouldn't be able to produce tears in front of the man if I stopped to realize how mega-huge his fame really was.

"I didn't get to see him when we wrapped. I think he's back in New Zealand until we start back up again in two weeks."

"Wow, New Zealand. He invite you to his posh palace to yacht and dine and all that stuff?" Hayden teases.

"Yes, we're besties." I roll my eyes.

"Two weeks off, huh? What are you going to do?"

"Well . . ." I lead. "Guess who gets on a plane tomorrow?"

"Jordan Shotwell," he answers, purposely being wrong.

"You're an ass," I throw back at him.

"I'm kidding. You. You're getting on a plane. When do you get in?"

"Not until like four. And we have to do some legal things before the weekend, but I hope maybe I'll get to see you guys by Saturday?" I say *we* in a generic sense, but I'm pretty sure Hayden gets the implication.

"That can probably be arranged. You know June has a shift, but she gets off at two. Maybe . . . we bowl?" He throws that idea out there because after my first showing, I swore to him I was retiring, knowing I would never best my big honkin' forty-one.

"I don't know. I'm officially on the Champion's Tour, and my sponsors don't like me falling back to amateur status."

"You know the Champion's Tour is for seniors, right? Like fifty-five-plus?"

"You're kidding!" I protest.

I've moved through the door of the parlor, so I tuck myself into a corner to finish our conversation before it's my turn to order the Unicorn Dust Sundae, my flavor choice of the day.

"All right, bowling it is," I relent, actually a little excited about my sophomore attempt at the game.

"It's on. I better get back before they try and take on Cannon without me. Dude's six-foot-three and absolute trash at basketball," Hayden says.

"Okay. Tell everyone I say hi."

He ends the call with a quick, "I will," and I wonder if he means it.

T

I get to Eight Lanes early. I texted Hayden after our call a few days ago and told him to keep my arrival a surprise for everyone else. To make it work, I have to slip in while June's on break. It's been easy to hide from her in lane one because every other lane is full of league bowlers. I've spent the last thirty minutes watching them from afar to pick up tips.

The secret is in the swag. I need one of those wrist-guard thingies, and this lotion that goes on your thumb. And some of them have balls that actually glow. I want a ball that glows.

I'm mesmerized by a man next to me. Bud Fox. I know that because it says so on his ball. And on the front pocket of his bowling shirt. And on his ball bag. I bet his name is tattooed on his wife. I'd say she could do better but really, in terms of bowlers, I don't think she can. Bud Fox is epic. I wonder if he's on the tour.

"Hey, sorry I'm late," Hayden says, slipping into the seat next to me. I startle, then shift instantly into a breathy squeal. It's good to see him.

I wrap my arms around his midsection and hug him tight, my head falling against his chest. Nothing about our embrace is weird, and I don't give it a second thought until minutes later when I realize it happened and we both acted natural.

"Okay, so June will probably wander over first. I don't know how you want to play this, but if you'd like to surprise them all at once, you can always hide behind the ball rack, I guess?" He points over his shoulder to the curved wall filled with colored spheres.

"Yeah, that works," I say, getting to my feet and stretching. I feel as though I've been on the go since I first left home. Two weeks of flights and filming and freezing temps has left me a little achy. I might be ready for that Champion's Tour after all.

"She's coming," Hayden whispers.

I crouch down and waddle my way behind the rack, sitting on my knees when I'm well out of sight. I hear June's voice a few seconds later and my legs twitch with the desire to spring up and see my friend. I hold tight instead and listen.

"Lucas is almost here. He said Tory was dragging ass. I think the whole driving back and forth thing is getting to him," she says.

I lower my head. He's still keeping up with the splitting time thing between his parents. Hayden hasn't mentioned it. He decided to stay at his mom's; I don't know why I figured Tory did, too.

"I know. I think he's just trying to make sure my dad isn't alone. He's got a few work trips coming up in January, so Tory should be home for a solid block then."

"You want me to get the names up?" June asks.

"I got it. Let me know when you see the guys," Hayden says. I lean forward to catch his eyes and he's doing the same from his seat. When we connect he gives me a thumbs up. I can't believe I'm really going to pull this off. I can't believe I'm going to see Tory. I haven't seen him since he sat with me on that concrete bench and told me he couldn't hurt his brother.

"I see them," June says. My pulse explodes into a splatter of beats. My mouth waters as if I'm about to be sick, and I feel faint. I'm not sure I can really see this through. I move from my knees to my ass so I can bend my head down and breathe. I completely fill my lungs once . . . twice . . . and the ringing in my ears stops.

"Hey, man. How was the drive?" I recognize Hayden, so I hold my breath, waiting for the voice I've been craving.

"Brutal. I think it's the soundtrack," Tory says. I smile automatically. It's good to hear him and his brother joke. It's good to hear *him*.

"You're just being stubborn," Hayden says.

There's a bit of chatter while everyone shuttles around getting balls and swapping out shoes. I can't quite tell if it's a good time to just pop out, so I lean forward again, hoping to catch Hayden in his seat. I lurch out from around the corner just as Tory leans down to pick out his ball, and our eyes stall on one another for almost a full second before I scream and fall back.

With my hand over my thundering chest, I blow up at my hair, looking at the only great kiss I've ever had. The dent on his forehead tells me he's not quite sure what to make of this situation, but the longer it's there, the more I realize he isn't happy to see me. I don't think he's sad.

I don't think he's anything.

"Abby?" June leans over the wall, her hair flopping down in braids on either side of her face.

"Surprise!" I whimper, waving my hands in the air.

Tory puts his ball down and steps toward me, reaching out a hand. I stare at his palm for a beat before taking it. The moment we touch will be a sign of where things stand. His hand completely wraps around mine as he yanks me to my feet. He steadies me with his other hand, resting it on my shoulder, but while that hand drifts away once I'm upright, the one pressed against my palm still holds on tight. His eyes haven't left mine, either.

"I'm home . . . Yay!" I celebrate in a quiet, playful voice, my cheeks burning from all the attention I've gotten myself. I really blundered this.

"Abby!" June rushes me, ripping my hand from Tory's so she can somehow lift me and twirl me around. I've got twenty pounds on her, so I'm not sure where her strength comes from, but it's nice to feel so loved.

"Hey, Cortez," Lucas says, waiting his turn. June holds my hand while I hug Lucas, and she keeps a hold on me while Hayden adds my name to the scoring screen.

"You knew about this?" Tory asks his brother.

A wave of nausea knocks me into a seat. June comes with me, glancing at me with concern. I play it off by kicking off my shoes and swapping them out for bowling ones.

"Yeah, she wanted to surprise you guys," Hayden answers, not even looking at his brother as he readies the screen.

I look up as Tory's eyes shift to me, and the hurt in them is undeniable.

"You talk a lot?" He's asking me, but Hayden doesn't realize this. He answers without giving it much thought.

"Sometimes. Just when we have time. Hey, you're up first." He shifts in his seat so his legs are out to the side and nods to his brother.

Tory walks back to the rack where he left the ball after I ruined my surprise entrance. He picks it up as though it's made of Styrofoam, then takes long strides toward our lane.

Without taking aim, he hoists the ball at the pins but sends it flying through the air a good ten feet before it thumps down on the alley.

"Ooops," he says, laughing in that menacing style of his, the one he uses when he means to push buttons. He claps his hands together, like a gymnast dusting off chalk, and then pivots when he's under the screen to look up at his score. The ball took out one pin, so he plays this up just to be an ass.

"This was a bad idea," I mutter. June is the only one close enough to hear, but she doesn't react other than sliding her foot over to rest against mine.

Tory finishes his turn and moves to the stools behind our seating area, propping himself on his elbows. I stare at him until it's my turn, willing him to look back at me, but he doesn't. Not once.

I manage to knock six pins down my first time, and seven my second. Lucas turns into my biggest champion, rooting for me like an obnoxious wrestling fan every time I take the ball in hand. When the game is halfway through, Tory finally leaves the shelter he's hiding in and joins the rest of us.

Things finally find a natural ease, and I'm sure to everyone else, everything feels normal. But if any of them stopped to pay attention, they'd realize that amid our banter and celebration, Tory and I haven't exchanged a glance, a word, or a touch, not once since the game began.

It's my final turn of the first game, and after a series of single pin frames, I'm four pins away from beating my whopping forty-one record. I take a deep breath, the rumbling echo of Lucas pounding the floor like football fans do on the bleachers as my backdrop. My pal Bud Fox hushes him more than once, but Lucas doesn't listen, continuing his homemade thunder.

I glance over my shoulder on a whim, just to see if Tory is watching, but he's looking down at his phone. Dejected, I line up the ball, using his advice and aligning myself with the middle arrows. I shuffle forward and release, my thumb getting stuck and sending the ball in a sidespin down the right side of the lane.

"Come on, baby. Come on, baby," Lucas hums behind me. I think he's genuinely invested in my outcome. I'm only sad that Tory isn't watching.

I take slow steps backward, stopping right in front of Lucas, who is down on one knee as if he somehow has the power to steer my ball down the lane in spite of my poor toss. My ball hits two pins in the front, and a third behind them, but not with enough force to fully knock it down. My hips roll along with the movement as the pin rolls on its base, finally falling to the side at the perfect angle and taking its neighbor down with it.

"Yeah!" Lucas rushes up behind me and lifts me from under my arms. My feet kick wildly as I laugh.

"I have never seen anyone so excited over a forty-two," June jokes, waiting to high five me the minute Lucas puts me down.

I get another high five from Hayden, and I move to the back seats where Tory is sitting, hoping he'll have some sort of reaction. He's on his phone, the device pressed to his ear. His eyes flit up, never fully meeting mine, and he holds up a finger as he stands and walks around the counter to the stools he was hiding on for half the game.

"You guys wanna go again?" Hayden stands with one knee on the seat at the computer. I glance to June who nods.

"I'm in," Lucas says.

We all turn our focus to Tory, waiting while he finishes his call. He holds his phone in his palm for a second, staring at the blank screen before acknowledging us.

"Hey, sorry guys. I'm out. Cannon is coming by to get me, but we'll catch up more. Yeah?" His gaze swings to me, his eyes finally reaching mine.

"Sure," I rasp.

A polite smile barely makes a dent in his face and he holds up a hand, moving on to our other friends, who all seem as dismissed and offended as I am.

Tory swaps out his footwear and carries the bowling shoes to the counter before heading out the exit. My friends hold their tongues until he leaves, doling out theories over why he might be upset as soon as he's gone.

None of them are right, and I know they're not, but I listen with feigned concern and continue to indulge their theories throughout our next game. Lucas and June leave after we enjoy a round of wings, on the house because Morty, the alley's manager, says I'm the biggest star to ever come out of Allensville. Not quite ready to go home, I wander over to the pool tables and lift a cue in challenge to Hayden. Truth be told, for once I might need *him* to listen.

"I'm pretty bad at pool," he says, taking the stick and helping me rack the balls.

"I'm not that great, either. It should be a real duel," I say.

He simpers at me and takes the cue ball in his palm,

setting it on the felt and offering for me to break. I bend, looking the part, and run the stick through my fingers like a violinist uses a bow. My results aren't nearly as impressive as I don't hit the ball squarely, sending it immediately off to the side and into a corner pocket.

"Mulligan?" I arch a brow.

Hayden laughs, pulling the ball out and rolling it to me.

"Sure."

My second attempt is a little better, scattering the balls around the table but not sinking a single one. Hayden walks around, eyeing different angles, but before he lines up what I think is his best shot, he stands up tall and sets his stick down flat, his palms on the table's edge.

"Tory's in love with you."

I blink, frozen by his words. I'm not even sure I heard them right. And I can't tell by his expression whether he's guessing or saying something backed by fact.

"I'm sorry, what?" I shake my head and squint my eyes.

"He told me. Right after you left, after the awesome therapy session I told you about that first time we talked when you were in Toronto."

"Tory . . . said he's in love with me." I repeat the words, still not believing them. Not that I think it's impossible, I just know what Tory said before I left. How deeply he cares about his relationship with Hayden. And also, how little credit he gives the idea of love. About as much as I do.

Hayden takes one of the balls in his hand and rolls it against the felt, ricocheting it off the bumper and back into his hand. Our game is done. That's fine; it was only an excuse anyhow.

"Look, Abby . . ." He rolls the ball again, but I cut it off before it makes it to his hand this time, catching it in my own. His gaze lifts to meet mine and he exhales. "Tory is in love with you. He told me, and I know he's not going to do anything about it. I can't let that happen. Me and him . . . we're in a good place."

I blink away the threat of tears.

"Why doesn't he tell me?" I ask.

Hayden levels me with a sideways look, his mouth a flat line. He doesn't have to say the words. Tory won't hurt Hayden.

"What do I do with this? What . . ." My words run out.

Hayden leaves his cue and rounds the table, stepping directly in front of me and lifting my chin so he can look in my eyes.

"You tell him you love him, too."

A sloppy laugh falls from my lips, part nerves and part sob. I nod to him and he pulls me into a hug. Hayden and I were always better friends. Tory was right the first time he said it—he and I, we would always be more.

23

TORY

My dad left yesterday for a business trip to Canada. Playing bachelor was fun for exactly twelve hours. I drank one of his beers but the novelty wore off before I went in for another. I walked around in my boxers for a while, but ultimately, I just ended up cleaning the apartment. Being alone is turning me into Hayden.

A buzz from my phone wakes me from a near nap, my third of the day, so I tap the screen awake to read the text.

HAYDEN: *June says if you don't come to her New Year's party she is never talking to you again.*

I blink twice at the message and decide to call his bluff.

ME: *That's a lie. She'd never cut me out.*

When it takes him a few minutes to respond, I sit up. I don't really believe she would, but I don't like the idea of disappointing her. I'm sure she understands that I don't want to see Abby. I know Hayden must. Why does it feel like he's pushing so hard?

My phone buzzes with a photo attachment from him, and I open it to see a picture of June flipping me off. I shake with a short laugh.

ME: *Fine. I'm coming.*

I toss my phone into the center of the bed and pace the empty guest room. Hayden has been here once, and only to see it. It's not very homey, but that's not really in my dad's skill set. It seems a waste for him to buy us a bunch of shit here anyhow, since who knows where we'll be next fall. I should find out about my offers soon. Hayden's picking between Colorado and Nevada. I could go with him. Both coaches expressed interest in me, too, but I think it might be good to have our own college experiences. I'm more interested in staying in the Midwest. Who knows, maybe we'll play each other in the Big Dance.

It's after ten, so I better hit the road before drunks start to spill out onto the backroads I take on my way into Allensville. Tossing a few staples into my duffle, I rush through a shower and land on my gray sweater that buttons at the neck and a pair of dark blue jeans. I look dressed up enough to pass for New Year's formal, I think. Besides, I know there's no way June will get Lucas in anything fancier than this.

It takes me more than an hour to get into town, the highway dotted with patrol cars waiting to pull people over. I keep to the speed limit exactly. When I turn onto June's street, almost every space along the road is blocked. I cruise by her and Lucas's driveways, and they're full of cars as well.

"Damn, this is a real party," I say to myself.

It takes me two passes to find an open space that I can

wedge my car into. It's not the best parking job, but it will do. I plan on leaving early anyhow. I just need to make my friends happy and show some face time. I reach into my bag and grab my cologne, giving my neck a quick spray before getting out of the car. I like to let the scent linger in there; it masks whatever that strange smell is that's been there since I bought the thing.

The music is thumping loud enough to be heard four houses down. I hope the Mabees invited all the neighbors, otherwise they're going to get a noise complaint. People can be real assholes about partying on New Year's. I mean, the entire premise of the holiday is to stay up until midnight.

I'm halfway up the driveway when my palms start to sweat. I know what it is: it's seeing Abby's car. I've been avoiding her. She messaged me twice after bowling and I put her off, making excuses. It's the reason I ran to Indy to stay at my Dad's. Seeing her—and knowing she's stayed in touch with Hayden—cut something open inside of me—fresh wounds over old ones. My jealousy reared its head, and I don't like the monster that emotion turned me into.

I'm nearly to the door when someone tugs on my arm and pulls me into the hedges that line June's house. My fists clench, ready to fend off some drunk asshole, but before I take a swing I realize it's my brother.

"Dude, it's wet over here. What the hell?" I brush droplets from my pants and sleeves, then lift my foot to check my shoes for mud.

"I told Abby," he says. I look up at him and wonder if that's supposed to make sense.

"That it's wet out here and she shouldn't romp around

in the bushes? Yeah, man. Good call. You really saved her."
I look back down to the clump of mud on my Nikes. These
things were pristine.

"Jackass. I told her you love her," he says. My eyes
shoot up again, and my fists reform.

"What the fuck, dude?" My body is overrun with the
falling sensation, the same one I got in that creepy elevator
ride at the amusement park that drops you several stories at
a time over and over just for fun. I don't like the ride, and I
don't like this feeling now.

Hayden grabs my shoulders and his fingers dig in
enough that I'm forced to give him my attention. I'm also a
breath away from starting a lawn brawl with him.

"She loves you, too. You know she does. Hell, I know
she does. And I'm truly, one-hundred percent happy about
that."

I stare at him, at a loss for words. The elevator in my
gut pauses for a moment while I register everything, but it
yo-yos again when my mind processes what comes next in
the chain of events.

"No, I went down that road, and it was . . ."

"It wasn't the right time," he fills in.

It's not what I was going to say, but his point is more
valid. Chasing Abby Cortez was a rush. Tasting her was a
dream, and loving her was an epiphany. The only thing
that made it not possible was the damage it created
between me and the man squeezing my arms out of their
sockets.

"You would be okay with this?" I turn my head in
skepticism.

"Tor, you have June. And you know what? *I* have

Abby." I happen to glance over his shoulder through the window as he says those words, spying inside just as June rushes through the main room with a stack of plates in her hand, playing hostess.

"She has to regret the idea of throwing this party," I say, changing the subject.

Hayden turns to see what I'm seeing, then laughs.

"She does, especially since her mom is totally lit. The adults are all drinking and the rule was that the seniors should stick to soda," he says.

"That didn't happen," I predict. He shakes his head in response as we take in the scene inside.

I could find more ways to stall, and I think my brother would let me because he knows how very little I enjoy being vulnerable. But Abby cuts across the room we're studying, dressed in a dark gray sweater almost exactly like mine and leggings that hug her curves. The sight of her makes my fingers flex, imagining the path they could take from her knee up to her breasts. Her hair is down in waves, and her lips sport her favorite shade of pink. She flips her hair over one shoulder with a laugh, and for a moment my breath stops, her eyes looking right at me.

"It's too bright in there. She can't see out," Hayden assures me.

My shoulders relax, but my muscles tense again almost immediately because I know I'm about to do something about what my brother said.

"You're sure?" I ask again, needing the extra push.

"Tory . . . go," he says in a low voice, pushing me forward.

I leave the brush and stomp the mud from my shoes,

waiting while my brother does the same. Taking away my choice, he opens the door, pushing it wide enough that people see me trailing behind him. If I turned and ran now, Abby would hear about it. She'd look for me, wondering where I went.

I follow Hayden inside and close the door behind me, surveying the room for familiar faces. June spots me first, rushing up to me in her frenzied state. I'm a little proud when I smell a hint of beer on her breath. She's always been such a straight-laced partier.

"Lucas is out back. There's a fire pit. But it's almost midnight so he better get his ass inside," she says, her mouth near my ear so I can hear over the pounding club-style music. It's an assault on the ears.

"She's upstairs," Hayden says, glancing up and encouraging me to follow his eyes. I look in that direction and see Abby leaning her back against the railing. She's surrounded by people, probably waiting in line to go to the bathroom or something. I'm not sure I should be so public about this just yet.

"Two minutes," my brother says, cupping his mouth so I can hear him. I scan the room for a clock and verify the time. It's actually only around a minute now.

The music dies, and someone switches on a television, the volume cranked to announce the countdown for everyone in the house. My gaze again moves up the stairs in search of Abby, and this time, she's looking down at the people gathered around me. I will her to find me, and she almost does a few times, but her gaze never completely settles on mine.

Without time to spare, I push through the crowd gathered in the living room to see the big screen mounted on June's wall. The count is at twenty by the time I get to the steps, and I slice through people on my way up, evading a few shoves along the way.

The count hits fifteen when I'm about four steps below Abby, fourteen when she finally turns and sees me. Twelve when she weaves through the crowd, heading deeper into the dark hallway toward June's room. It's seven by the time I catch her, and five when my hand finds her slender wrist. By three, we've stumbled into June's room, her door closed by two.

One.

"I love you," I say, not waiting a second longer to get the words out of my heart and into her ears. It's midnight on New Year's Eve and I should pull her into me and kiss her senseless. But saying those words was far more important.

Her arms remain stiff at her sides, her brow pinched, and her lips quivering—trembling the way they did the first time I felt them against mine.

"It's okay if you don't feel the same. It's okay if you want me to leave. I will. I'll leave right now, and I'll be fine with that because I got to tell you I love you. But if there's a chance you feel the same way, if there's the remotest chance that your heart kicks a little when you see me, that your breath maybe dropped when I said those words, then I swear to God, Abby Cortez, you better kiss me in this new year. If I love you and you love me, I want to start this right."

Her eyes dip to my chest, then flicker back up to my face. She's nervous, and I'm not sure whether she's weighing her options or looking for an easy way out. "Auld Lang Syne" blares from downstairs, and most of the party is either kissing or shouting *Happy New Year* while repeatedly blowing those dumb paper horns. My confidence wavers with every second that passes, though I couldn't possibly give her a better speech than the one I somehow just delivered. My gaze dips down to the floor and I move to step to the side so she can leave.

"I love you, too," she utters, her voice meek and shaky.

I raise my chin.

"I love you," she says again, this time the wavering gone.

"I love you," I say to her again, enjoying this volley of words. I take a step toward her and she does the same.

"I love you."

"I love you."

We repeat in rapid succession as we erase the distance between us until she leaps into my arms and I catch her as her legs wrap around my waist, our mouths finding their homes against one another's. We are a perfect fit. Our kiss is natural and explosive. Every time is like this, a rush and a comfort, a death and a birth.

"I love you," I utter against her, my mouth suddenly unable to stop speaking these three small words. The way her mouth feels when it smiles against me is as potent as her kiss.

She kisses along my jaw as I hold her against my body and walk us toward June's bed. Her mouth finds my ear and her arms encase my head as she mouths those three words to me again. She straddles my lap as I sit us down, and my hands glide up her sweater, pulling it off in one swift move. She pulls mine off next, and her bra is not far behind.

"June is going to kill you," I say, chuckling against her mouth as she tugs on the button of my jeans.

My thumbs are already hooked in the waist of her leggings, lowering them over her hips and over her ass as she pushes me down to lay flat on my back. She flips her hair up and her hungry eyes meet mine.

"Let her try," she hums, a devilish curve accented in her favorite color. Dropping her lips to my chest, she kisses her way down my stomach until she reaches my open pants. My eyes roll back at the sensation of her hand on my hard cock, and when her tongue runs along the tip I nearly pass out.

"What do you want, Tory D'Angelo?" She's a vixen, her mouth poised over me, tempting me with my own biggest weakness—every man's thinnest defense.

Knowing the only thing that will truly satisfy me is satisfying her, I sit up and trail my hands to her ass, grabbing the bare skin with a firm grip that makes her gasp.

"I want to be inside you." I lift her and trade positions, her back now on the bed and her body under my control. She wriggles out of her leggings and panties while I kick off my jeans and search for my wallet to pull out a condom. I tear it open and work it down my length while her knees part, and her trust makes me pause and gaze at her naked flesh. I love how absolutely bold she is with her body.

There is no shame in anything she does with me, nor should there be.

She brings her finger to her mouth, biting on it in such an unbelievably seductive way, and I accept the invitation. Lowering myself until our bodies align, I hold my weight up on my elbows so my hands are free to draw gentle lines along her face.

"Goddamn, are you beautiful," I say, drawing another pale pink smile from her lips. I bite the plump bottom of her mouth teasingly, holding it hostage in my teeth until my own smile makes me lose my grip.

"You're covered in my lipstick." She giggles, drawing lines of her own along my shoulders and neck until her palms stop at my jaw.

"Then I'm wearing your favorite color," I say. Her eyes blink to mine and she stares into them, wordless for several seconds.

"You see me," she says.

"I do," I agree, my hands gathering up the soft waves of her hair at the side of her face. I lower my head until it rests on hers, and her eyes close as she hums.

"I love you, Tory D'Angelo." Her next sound is a sigh of pleasure as I push into her with a slow, deep stroke.

The minutes tick by, and we let them, milking every moment for what it offers. I taste each whimper she makes, kissing her lips raw and tangling her hair in knots around my hands. The party rages on below, the thumping music picking up again to carry on until someone down the road complains. Here, in my best friend's room, I fall in love for a second time with the same girl I did the first. I fall in love with every touch, with every word, and with each gasp for air we share until our bodies are limp and wrung of energy.

By two in the morning, Abby is fast asleep against my chest, our naked bodies fused together from hunger and passion played out for hours. By three I fall asleep and dream about her. And by four, she's waking me up to do it all again.

EPILOGUE
ABBY

Keeping us a secret wasn't easy. I didn't want to lose a minute of time with Tory before I had to board the plane again, but I also didn't want to ruin something so fragile and new by throwing it under the microscope of our group of friends. Hayden is the only one who knew, and he promised to keep our relationship to himself until we were ready to welcome more opinions. He believed in us, and that was enough.

We decided prom would be our big coming out. Only now that I'm standing on the top step of Lucas's winding staircase, June's mom's studio lights casting me in a glow powerful enough to spawn angels, announcing that I've been in a loving relationship with Tory, Hayden's brother, for more than three months, seems terrifying.

"Why is your mom so obsessed with taking photos of us walking down stairs in high heels?" I ask my friend. She laughs from just over my shoulder.

"Just a little longer," she promises. She said that thirty minutes ago.

We've been lined up in this same position for about twenty minutes, taking turns standing in different spots. When we started, the guys were all paired with us, and Tory kept pinching my ass. He's making me regret picking the short black dress. I know I look good in it, though. It works with my curves, and I tested to make sure it wouldn't ride up while I danced. I intend to put these shoes and this dress to work. Tory has promised me he'll salsa. We'll see how long before he bows out.

"Okay, now just one more for each couple," June's mom begs. Collectively we groan, but none of us really mind making Kristen Mabee happy. June and Lucas go first, so I take a break from smiling and duck into Lucas's room.

Most of our parents are here in the house, and June's mom has been patient letting my mom art direct some of my shots. It's a habit for her, having been on set with me for so many test shots.

The D'Angelos both came, and Natalia even helped me with my dress. Their divorce is almost final, but oddly their relationship has never been better. Tory said his dad comes to the house every Sunday for dinner, and they usually end up sitting around the table as a family for two hours just talking after the food is gone. Some people are just meant to be friends.

My dad moved back to Miami, and I filed a restraining order and an injunction, extra protection on top of what he pledged in our settlement. With some luck and a lot of legal maneuvers, he should never bother me or my mom again. I had to do something for peace of mind while I was away at college. I don't worry about my dad hurting her, but I do worry about the harassment. I think his DNA is just woven to make him cruel.

"We're up," Tory says with a soft knock on the door.

I suck in one last, deep breath and work the nervous energy out through my fingertips.

"Show time?" I say to him.

"Now or never," he responds. We pause at the door, and when our eyes meet, we laugh. The idea of never coming clean about us has crossed both of our minds. Keeping secrets is hard, especially one like this that deserves so much public display of affection.

"Ready," he declares, running his hand down my arm, his fingers finding mine and weaving through all the empty spaces. I turn into him and straighten his tie, flitting my gaze up to find him smirking.

"Now we're ready," I say. We squeeze each other's palms and step through the door, making our way to the landing, then down a few steps.

"Great. Okay . . . Tory?" June's mom immediately begins directing.

"Yeah?" my boyfriend responds.

"Maybe come down a step so you're lower; it will balance out your height," she explains.

"Oh, yeah, sure," he says, taking a step and turning to face me with a wiggle of his brow.

"Oh, but first? I want to tell you all one thing."

All eyes jet to us, including those couples I don't know well. Our group has blossomed while I've been gone. Life has rolled on. Hayden is dating Lola. Naomi met a girl.

Cannon apparently has a soul and possibly decent taste in women. And Tory—he's still head over heels in love with me. And he's about to show the world.

In one smooth movement, Tory tugs me into his arms and leans me back into a daring dip, the fingers of one hand splayed on my bare back, the other griping my thigh. He holds my leg up against him and kisses me in front of every person we care about in Allensville, Indiana.

"Holy fucking shit!" Lucas's words are the first to ring in my ears, and I laugh against Tory's lips.

"Wooooo!" June shouts. Her mom whistles with her fingers.

There's actual applause, which seems like overkill, but the adulations only make me want to kiss him more.

I'm dizzy by the time he tips me upright, and he holds my body close to his while the stars circle my head. We spend the next several minutes basically being interviewed by our friends, and there are actual *awes* when Tory gives Hayden full credit for us ever happening. It's credit due, though, because without his gentle pushes, I'm not sure either of us would have ever given in.

The party bus finally honks outside, saving us from more prying questions, like the one I fear June is about to ask. She put two and two together, and I'm judging by the distance her brow travels up her forehead, she realizes that Tory and I totally had sex on her bed.

The D'Angelos paid for the enormous Hummer to drive us all to the prom. Even though the distance to the ballroom is short, we still manage to test out every gadget and feature. By the time we roll up to the dance, we have the disco ball spinning and the neon lights changing colors.

I think the guys would be happy with their dates for hours in this small, intimate space, but I for one have plans to dance until my feet cave in.

Answering my prayers, Jennifer Lopez's "Let's Get Loud" is kicking as we make our way in, and before Tory can plant his ass in a chair, I wrap his tie around my hand and lead him out onto the dance floor.

"Not gonna lie. You intimidate me a little, Cortez," he says, tugging his tie loose when I let go. He unbuttons the top button of his dress shirt and stretches his arms like he's getting ready to compete in a triathlon.

"Your arms aren't as important as your hips," I say, shouting over the music. His eyes slant, playfully frightened. "Here."

I put my hands on his hips and stand about a foot away so he can follow my movement. It's basically a figure eight, only it isn't just two dimensional, it's three. When I roll my hips, Tory's head falls back in a fit of laughter.

"What?" I ask.

He points to my body, drawing his finger up and down.

"There is no way I can do that," he says.

I look at him sideways, knowing he can. He just needs the right encouragement.

Taking his hands in mine, I place them on my hips and look him in the eyes as I proceed to move again. After a few beats, his feet are moving with mine, and by the time the song is really in its groove, he's gotten it down, at least enough to hold me close and let our bodies grind. I knew he would like this. I can teach him the fancier stuff later.

The DJ carries right into another salsa song, so we stay on the dance floor, our bodies damp from both the exertion and the sexiness that comes with being this close to one another and moving like this while clothed. I catch June attempting to follow my steps while dancing with Lucas, so I pause with Tory and give an impromptu lesson. By the third song, I've managed to teach four couples to do a basic step, and the vibe is singing to my heart as we all sway to the rhythm.

The tempo finally slows, and I'm grateful to have a moment to hold Tory to me and barely move. It also gives me time to prepare for the second big reveal Tory and I planned for tonight—this one for each other.

"Do you want to do it now?" I ask, knowing he'll get what I mean.

"Hmmm, I'm not sure. What if—"

"We're different?" I finish for him.

He peels back enough to look me in the eyes, his mouth set with worry.

After we'd been dating for two months, the college talk started to take on realistic consequences. With our past, and with the mistakes we've seen our parents make, we didn't want to fall into the trap of having one of us give up a dream to follow the other person to theirs. We came to the decision that we would narrow down our schools and share our decisions with one another at the same time —tonight.

"There is no wrong decision. And I will love you no matter what coast you're on," I say, moving into him and pressing a soft kiss to his lips.

He hugs me tightly against his chest and spins us around.

"I don't know . . . ugh," he grumbles playfully. I can tell

there are sincere nerves under the surface of his jokes.

To assuage them, I cup his cheek and stand on the tips of my toes, touching his nose to mine.

"I love you, no matter what." I repeat the core of our pledge. I'm not sure when we started saying it to each other, but it's become habit. It's become a promise. It's our future.

No matter what.

"Okay, on the count of three," he says, his chest rising with a deep breath. I follow suit and fill my own lungs.

"One," I say.

"Two," he follows.

We pause; there's no turning back. A promise to each other means no cheating. We said we would share at the same time, and if we make it to three, we must. We don't hang each other out to dry.

Our eyes lock, and I wait until certainty passes through the hazel oceans of his irises. His mouth turns up, and his cheeks lift. He's ready.

"Three," I say, immediately followed by the word, "Chicago."

"Northwestern."

Our nerves have vanished.

Two schools, twenty miles apart. A train ride.

There were endless combinations that could have been. He didn't know my final five, and I didn't know his. Maybe fate whispered to us in our dreams. Or maybe sometimes, friends are also meant to be in love forever.

THE END

PREVIEW OF BOOK 3 IN THE
VARSITY SERIES

By Ginger Scott

PREORDER THE E-BOOK NOW:
https://amzn.to/3bgh7pN

Hollis Taylor is allowed to break the rules. She's coach's little girl. And she's good. If that means she gets to bump one of the guys for the starting catcher's job on the Public High baseball team, then the others on the squad better suck it up and deal.

Breaking rules has taken Cannon Jennings far in life. One of the nation's top pitching prospects, he came here to throw to his cousin and show college recruiters everything he could do on the mound. Taking his signs from a girl was not part of his blueprint, especially one that screwed over his favorite relative and best friend.

Too bad he broke the biggest rule of all before he knew exactly who she was.

It was just a New Year's kiss. Totally forgettable. Especially under the circumstances.

So why can't he stop thinking about it?

Cannon Jennings

I'm perfectly content ringing in the new year with a sparkler and the leftover pizza. Unfortunately, my cousin Zack is an extrovert. He *needs* to feed off the energy of others. I prefer to cut out distractions.

"It's one party, Can. You need to pull the stick out of your ass and enjoy one night. One party will not derail your future."

Zack has been on my ass about loosening up for weeks. Deep down, I know he's probably right...to an extent. If I keep grinding like this through my entire senior year, I'll burn out before I even land at summer camp wherever I get signed. But when you've dreamed of pitching for Vandy since you were six years old and it's legit within your reach, it's hard to let up off the gas, even just a little.

"Come on, man. It's New Year's Eve." Zack's head falls to one side and his lip juts out.

"Are you gonna fuckin' cry?" I toss my glove to the corner of the sofa and get to my feet. Zack rubs his hands together while shuffling his feet in this weird-ass jig.

"I'm not going if you're going to do that," I say, pointing at his lower half. He freezes and instantly stands tall, rolling his shoulders and clearing his throat.

"Sorry. Must have been overcome with shock that Cannon Jennings is actually going to do something social," he says.

"*Pfft*," I huff at him. I grab my keys and my lucky hat and we both head out to my car.

Zack is overexaggerating. I've been social. I went to a party a week ago, and I've made some decent friends. I've done pretty well for being the new guy at school. I moved in with my cousin over the summer as part of the grand plan my dad and my uncle, Zack's dad, devised to maximize the attention we both could get for offers to play college ball. Zack has caught for as long as I have pitched, and we used to play together when we were younger. But Zack's family moved to Indiana for work right after junior high, and it broke up our dream duo. We've both done all right without the other, but we've got one more year to really show our stuff, and Allensville Public High just hired a new coach—one with Division One coaching experience. It means I'm sleeping on the couch at Zack's while my parents sell our place in New Mexico. Once they do, though, we'll move into a rental together—and I'll have a bed that doesn't fold up during the day.

"I don't really know June very well," I mention as we pull up to the Mabee house. We only live two blocks from them, so the drive was easy.

"Yeah, but you know Lucas, so it's all good," Zack reassures.

He gets out of the car with an actual skip in his step,

still cradling the six-pack of micro beers he stole from his dad.

I let myself enjoy the quiet of the car for one more breath. He's right. I've gotten to know Lucas pretty well. And the D'Angelo twins. They're all pretty decent athletes, and it's nice to mess around and do things with a group of guys who aren't all about baseball. I gel with Tory D'Angelo the most. He's got plans to play basketball in college, so he gets my constant focus. I swear, as much as my cousin Zack *says* he wants to play college ball, he doesn't seem to have the obsessive passion that I think it takes.

My cousin raps on the window, tired of waiting on me, so I get out and put on my best *happy-to-be-here* face.

It's a strange collection of people inside. Someone who clearly is someone's father opens the door for us, and he eyes the beer in Zack's hand as we enter.

"Maybe we shouldn't have brought beer," I whisper to my cousin, but he ignores me, weaving through the house and into the garage, where an extra refrigerator is stuffed with drinks. He pulls a beer out and hands it to me, taking one for himself, too. I arch a brow, not sure this is allowed.

"It's fine. June said as long as we don't make it obvious around the adults, we're good to go." Zack pops the cap off and takes a swig, gesturing for me to do the same. I do, but only because I think drinking half of this beer might settle the knots in my chest. Maybe I'm not so great at social things.

We weave through the house to the back yard where I find more faces I recognize. My shoulders relax a little when I spot Lucas sitting near the fire pit with space next to him. I nod toward him, letting Zack know where he can find me, and head toward the flames. I'm beat to the open seat by two seconds when Lucas's girlfriend, June, slips in. I'm about to bail when an absolute goddess steps into the space behind them.

I don't know a lot of people in town or at school, but how I've missed this face, I have no idea. She's tall, maybe only an inch or two shorter than my six-foot-three, and her long blonde hair looks like molten gold as she stands near the fire. I can't tell if her eyes are gray or blue, but I need to get closer to settle the debate in my head. She's supermodel hot, but playing it down in a pair of baggy jeans and an old baseball jersey worn over a hoodie to keep her warm. I bet her dressed-down look keeps her under the radar. Most of the fucking douchebags at this school only want to keep score and see who can date the hot girl first. Lucky for me, though, she's shown up here tonight dressed for the part of *exactly my type.*

"Jeter fan, huh?" I say, stepping up next to her and tugging on her jersey sleeve.

A short laugh puffs from her naturally pink lips while she takes a small sip from her cup. I think she's actually drinking soda, so I casually set my beer on the small patio table behind me.

"Yankee's fan. Jeter's all right," she says, a wry smile on her mouth. I hold her stare for a full breath, partly to challenge her and also so I can get a good handle on the color of her eyes. Blue, and maybe a little green too.

I match her smirk with one of my own, letting it crawl up into my cheeks before glancing down at the small patch emblazoned on the right sleeve of the jersey. This thing came from a game.

"Bullshit," I say, nodding toward it.

She twists her head to the side and tucks her chin, noting the authentication patch with a slight breath and a smile.

"You got me," she says, her eyes flitting up to mine. I hold them for a long second again, this time because I like the way it feels when I challenge her to hold my stare right back. She's a worthy opponent, and I'm the first to break.

"You a fan?" she asks.

"Of the Yankees? Fuck no. But Jeter's special—he's like a level above the Yankees. He's folklore," I say.

Our baseball banter must annoy Lucas and June because they make a lame excuse to leave us alone. We take over their seats, propping our feet on the lip of the firepit and settling in so we can face one another to the side.

"I have another one of these . . . signed," she says, pulling down the front of the jersey to even out the Yankees logo.

I lift my brows, impressed. Also, I catch a hint of her accent, which I'm pretty sure is from the heart of New York.

"Super fan, I take it?"

She wobbles her head side to side, playfully, and her eyes dance with this proud kind of joy that you only get when you have a childhood full of memories at the ballpark. I know because I've got them, too. Between spring nights at New Mexico State and spring breaks spent in Arizona hunting autographs from my favorite MLB stars at training camps, I've got a pretty full childhood of baseball fairytales of my own. I can't wait to write my name into those stories.

"I'm Cannon. I'm new here," I say, holding out my hand.

She blinks at it, her lips parted for a few seconds before speaking. She finally takes my palm in hers, her grip impressive.

"I'm Hollis, and I'm new here too."

Definitely from New York.

"Long Island?" I question.

She quirks a brow and blows out from her lips.

"Heck no. Staten Island, baby." She's teasing me, and it's cute as hell. I should have known—Long Islanders are Mets fans.

"Ah, right. Well . . . nice to meet you, Hollis. I'm from New Mexico. Not nearly as exciting as your big city," I say with a shrug.

"I don't know," she says, leaning her head back and looking up at the sky. I follow her gaze to the stars and the embers popping in the air above us. "You probably have some pretty epic views where you're from."

She's right. We do. Or, at least . . . we did. I guess these are my views now.

"We're both really from Allensville now, don't you think?" I put that idea out there while we both stare up at the black sky, speckled with salt diamonds and masked by smoke.

She sighs.

"Yeah, I guess we are." She drops her chin to her chest

and I do the same. "We came from both ends and met in the middle."

She has a way of letting this faint smile linger on her lips after she finishes talking, and I am having a hard time looking away from it every time it appears. I'm doing it now, and normally, I'd be embarrassed by my overt infatuation with a girl. I'm really shitty at flirting. But Hollis—she makes this pretty easy.

"So, what brought you here? To the middle?" I ask.

Her brow pulls in with thought, but that faint smile is still there. She's calculating something. Maybe it's how much to tell a guy she just met.

"Family . . . or work. My dad moved here for work." I sense that she seems conflicted by something, so I don't pry. She probably misses a lot of things from home. I get that. I miss my parents, but at least they'll be here eventually. Can't really move New York to the middle of Indiana.

"We moved here for family too, sorta. I came to play ball with my cousin. He's here, somewhere." I glance over my shoulder only to find that everyone in the back yard has disappeared. We're completely alone out here.

"I'd introduce you, but . . ." I hold out open palms when I look back to her and she giggles. The sound she makes pushes my half smile up high into my cheeks, and I quickly realize I'm grinning like a fool. I don't stop it, though. I let the ache remain on my foolish face because I think maybe I've just met my soulmate in pinstripes.

"We must have missed the memo," she says, looking beyond me and into the house.

It was after eleven when Zack and I left the house, so

I'm guessing the countdown is probably on for the new year.

"You wanna go in?" I ask her, moving my gaze back to her eyes. This time, she dares me, studying my face closely like she's waiting to call my bluff. I don't have one. I'll literally go wherever she tells me to. I'm hoping—

"I don't like crowds. You cool ringing in the new year out here with some girl from Staten Island?"

Foolish grin makes its second appearance on my face, so I lick my lips to tame it just a little.

"Not at all," I say, leaning forward with my feet on the ground and elbows on my knees. "Though, you're an Allensville girl now, aren't you?"

She breathes out a laugh and stands, stretching her arms to the sky. It lifts her jersey and sweatshirt just enough that I get a glimpse of her cream-colored skin and the silver stud in her belly button. I never thought that would be my thing, but it's totally my thing. Maybe it's only my thing on beautiful blondes from Staten Island.

"Let me get used to being an Indiana girl for a while, then we can move on to the local titles, yeah?" She sounds so tough when she talks, and the contrast with her angelic face would be almost comical if it weren't so goddamned mesmerizing.

I stand so I can match her height, and maybe get a better read on whether it's okay to kiss a girl you just met at a party you didn't really want to go to. I kinda think maybe it is, but only because she didn't really want to be here either. And because she's wearing a Jeter jersey. And because I'm pretty sure her eyes have put a spell on me.

With a foot of space between us, I measure how close

we come in height while she glances around me to the house filled with people who have started counting down from ten. I was right to guess we're only two or three inches apart. She licks the corner of her lips and smiles, her cheeks suddenly red, and not from the heat of the fire.

"Happy New Year, Hollis from Indiana," I say, my lips in a closed-lip smile to stem off the hungry vibrations urging my body to lunge at her and taste her tongue with mine.

"Happy New Year, Cannon from Indiana," she says back, biting her lower lip but only briefly. She's trying to keep up the act that she's tougher than I am. Maybe she is.

I step toward her, my movement slow and cautious while I read her body language. She doesn't move away, and her hands aren't nervously fidgeting at her sides. They're tucked in the pocket of her hoodie, the front of the jersey lifted so she can slip them inside the warmth underneath. She's so calm I'd almost think she's sleeping with her eyes open, but I know she's not. She's staring at me with a dare—a welcoming dare.

I take another small step, lifting my hand to her chin and touching the pad of my thumb to the soft skin just below her pouting lip. I brush away her hair and bring my other hand up to cup her face.

"Happy New Year," I whisper one last time, mostly to test the waters and see if she flinches. She merely breathes the words back and closes the remaining inches between our mouths until we're locked in an electrifying kiss that feels like fucking home. I lift her chin, coaxing her mouth open just enough for me to slip my tongue inside to taste her sweet mouth. Her lips move with me, and her hands come up to grab at the front of my own hoodie, tugging on the strings as she slips away slowly with a giggle.

My face is numb in the wake of our kiss. It was ten seconds of my life, but quickly rockets up on my top-five moments list.

"Thanks for the New Year's kiss, Cannon. I have to get home, but . . . maybe we can hang out sometime?" She lets go of the strings, her finger drawing a line down the center of my chest as she backs away.

"Most definitely," I say, a bit stupefied that I've been so quickly whipped by a girl I barely know. Maybe it's the haze of New Year's Eve, or maybe I really have been over-working myself and I'm exhausted. Whatever it is, I'm grinning like an idiot again and it doesn't go away for the rest of the night.

***

I've never had a coach want to hold a meeting with his potential players on January second, but that's what makes coming here an even better decision. Coach Taylor has a reputation for being stern, and he sent us all texts on New Year's Day telling us he wanted to get started with workouts before tryouts come up. There was a subtle over-tone that the serious players would be here, so Zack and I got here before anyone else just to prove we're a cut above dedicated.

It's cold as hell outside, so Coach invited us all in to the small clubhouse behind the dugout. This might be a great program I'm walking into, but the facility is shit. Back home, we had brand new everything. My school was barely eight years old, which in terms of a high school lifespan is infant-like. This place was built in fifty-seven. This club-house has a plate on the door that says DEDICATED IN 1965. I'm not sure we aren't breathing in lead and asbestos.

"Gentlemen," Coach says, clearing his throat and getting our attention. There's another cough from the back, but I can't quite see who it's from. From the way it sounded, it came off a little bit snarky, like someone making fun of the new coach's style. Coach seems to have picked up on the same nuance I did because he's staring back there with a scowl on his face.

Bad idea, dude, whoever you are.

"First, thank you all for coming in today. The bad news is this isn't just a meeting. We'll be running two miles, too. I'd like to see you all come in under ten minutes by the time season starts."

The collective groan is comical. Me and Zack, though . . . we keep our mouths shut. Some of the guys showed up in slip-ons, and I have a sneaking suspicion Coach is not going to care. They'll be running in those or barefoot. Zack and I always dress. In fact, we have our gear and cleats in the car just in case.

Coach spends the next few minutes going over basics, like I had to do at my old school. I've already taken care of the things on the list like my physical and the waiver forms. I zone out through most of his talk, but perk up when he mentions competing for roster spots. Zack doesn't flinch, probably because he's been the starting catcher since freshman year. He's solid. I am too. Hell, from what Zack told me, I will probably be the ace this year; but still, it's never good to assume. There's always someone working hard out there. I just have to work harder.

"I'll be pairing you guys for head-to-heads and training. Competition fosters greatness, and I don't believe positions are guaranteed. They are earned. You understand me?"

"Yes, sir," we all say. Funny how we know we're supposed to.

"Okay, so listen for your names to be called. This will be your group until we move into official tryouts in a month and I have our final roster. I'm keeping fifteen, and other than pitchers, some of you might not get to play. If you're okay with that, stick around. If not, well . . . thanks for coming in today."

Nobody leaves, but I can tell a few of the guys sitting in front of Zack and me want to. I glance sideways at Zack and he just lifts his brows.

"This guy isn't fucking around," he says.

I breathe out a laugh and shake my head.

"Jennings," Coach says.

Zack and I both answer.

"Oh, right. I meant Cannon first. Pitcher only, right?" Coach peers at me, his finger pushing up the brim of his hat just enough to bring his eyes out of the shadow. They're crystal blue and a bit like lasers, wrinkled at the corners from squinting in the sun for years, I imagine.

"Yes, sir," I respond.

He nods and makes a note on his clipboard.

"Jennings, Zack," he says, reading my cousin's name as it's probably written. "You'll be working with Hollis."

Hollis? I casually glance around the room, not seeing the girl of my dreams. Maybe I didn't hear it right.

The first thing I notice on Zack is the way his forehead creases, a dent between his brows like it's been hit with a marble. His mouth is parked in an O shape, so I slide my right foot into his to jostle him from this sudden state.

"Hollis . . . uhm, okay. Sure . . . " He heard the same name I did. He also did not say *yes, sir,* and given the way Coach narrowed his eyes on him, it was not the right move.

Coach holds his clipboard against his chest, folding his arms over it and leaning his head to the side. I think if he could give Zack a detention for that answer, he would.

"Is there a problem with that?" Coach's brows are lifted in expectation. I tap my foot against Zack again, willing him to respond.

"No, sir. No," he sputters out.

"Good," Coach says. "You might learn a thing or two from her."

From her. Oh . . . fuck.

"You mind working out with a girl, Jennings?" Her voice is as rich with her Staten Island roots as it was when I kissed her two nights ago. Puzzle pieces fly together, her accent . . . Coach's accent. His eyes and her eyes. New to town—her dad moved for work.

I turn just enough to catch her pulling her catcher's helmet and mask from her head, her blonde hair tied up in a knot at the base of her neck.

"Gear's a little tight, but it should do," she says, handing it to her dad.

Fuck me, that's her dad.

"Thanks for taking it for a ride," he says, nodding to his daughter.

Fuck me, that's his daughter.

"Sure, but next time . . . remember it's *ladies* and gentlemen when you're talking to us, 'kay?" she says, reaching forward and punching his arm playfully. Guess I know where the laugh came from when he started his speech. Pretty sure he's not going to punish her for it, either, on account of her being right and all. Oh, and being his freaking spawn.

"Hey, Cannon from Indiana," she says, the same mischievous bend to her lips that made me feel absolutely drunk on her mouth forty-eight hours ago.

I don't dare respond with the same flirtatious tone I used last time, instead opting to nod as she backs away with a wink. I think I just got played.

"Your partner is leaving without you, son," Coach says to Zack. My cousin is still a bit stiff from the shock of having to fight for his position . . . against his new coach's daughter. Talk about delicate.

"Oh, yeah . . . thank you. I'll catch up," Zack says, his words all jumbled and hesitant. His confidence literally just crawled away and sank through the cracks of the clubhouse's concrete floor.

Not wanting the same fate, I grab my bag from under the bench so I can escape without taking more blows to my ego. I'm nearly out, too, when Coach stops me by hollering my name. I turn with my back flat on the door, my mouth suddenly dry with the unknown of what's next.

"I see you know my daughter."

There's a pregnant pause that's thick enough to choke

our football team's offensive line. I keep expecting him to say more, to ask a question or shoot me some warning to stay away from her, which of course I will absolutely obey. He doesn't. Just that one statement, along with his laser stare from his weathered death eyes.

"A little. We just met," I say, finally, my delayed response clearly exposing my nerves.

"Hmm," he says with a nod.

I pull my lips in tight, mostly to keep from saying anything else.

"Go on," he says, after another painful pause.

Yes, sir. I only think it this time.

I round the clubhouse and look out on the track, where Hollis is literally about to lap someone. Zack hasn't even finished tying his laces. My cousin is in trouble, but not as much as I am. If I want to make it to Vandy, or anywhere *like* Vandy, I need to be at the top of my game. One midnight kiss, though, and my season is cursed. So help me if that vixen ends up calling my pitches.

PREORDER NOW!
Cannon and Hollis's story continues in Varsity Rulebreaker,
releasing Oct. 8, 2020.
Now available for preorder here:
https://amzn.to/3bgh7pN

ACKNOWLEDGMENTS

I fell in love with Tory D'Angelo somewhere around the first 30 pages of Varsity Heartbreaker. To keep this smart-ass boy at bay while I finished writing his best friend's story (well, *both* best friends, since June is also his best friend) was no easy task. He was persuasive and insistent in my head, talking to me when I was trying to sleep at night with his cute little "oh, and I'm gonna be funny, right? And unpredictably thoughtful? And you'll write me hot, right? Like, abs and all that shit but also perfect hair, and...I like nice clothes. Give me good style."

Tory got his way. And I hope you guys did too. I hope you enjoyed his angsty ride through his senior year, his ups and downs, and the way love and life played out. I was just the chick at the keyboard for this one. That story is all him. And of course, Cannon is already talking.

As always, full credit goes to my team that holds me up. This starts with my rock, my sweet Autumn. Bless you for having the same F'd up sleeping schedule I do, my friend. And thank you for every single thing you do for me. It's far beyond the PA and publicist job title. It's really more of a confidence whisperer/life coach/guide. My betas, Jen, Shelley, TeriLyn—I love you and am so glad you tolerate the pieced-together way I send you things. One day you'll get the whole thing at once (probably not, but it felt good to put that in writing). Brenda Letendre and Tina Scott, your edits help me find my best foot and put it forward. Lost without you.

If you enjoyed this book, I would be SO VERY GRATEFUL if you could leave a review. The book market is a lot like swimming through mud sometimes, and getting the word out in this increasingly noisy world is becoming so hard. I am incredibly thankful to my readers and supporters for every boost they give. It's those viral shares, the recommendations to friends, that help get my stories seen, and I don't for one minute take any of that for granted. I get to do this because you give me your time and your passion—you tell others to give my books a try. My stories are for you and you alone. Well, maybe a little for me, too, but without you all, there's really no heart. You are the heart—my heart. Thank you for letting it beat so wildly!

ALSO BY GINGER SCOTT

The Varsity Series

Varsity Heartbreaker

Varsity Tiebreaker

Varsity Rulebreaker (October 2020)

The Waiting Series

Waiting on the Sidelines

Going Long

The Hail Mary

Like Us Duet

A Boy Like You

A Girl Like Me

The Falling Series

This Is Falling

You And Everything After

The Girl I Was Before

In Your Dreams

The Harper Boys

Wild Reckless

Wicked Restless

Standalone Reads

Cowboy Villain Damsel Duel

Drummer Girl

BRED

Cry Baby

The Hard Count

Memphis

Hold My Breath

Blindness

How We Deal With Gravity

ABOUT THE AUTHOR

Ginger Scott is an Amazon-bestselling and Goodreads Choice and Rita Award-nominated author from Peoria, Arizona. She is the author of several young and new adult romances, including bestsellers Cry Baby, The Hard Count, A Boy Like You, This Is Falling and Wild Reckless.

A sucker for a good romance, Ginger's other passion is sports, and she often blends the two in her stories. When she's not writing, the odds are high that she's somewhere near a baseball diamond, either watching her son swing for the fences or cheering on her favorite baseball team, the Arizona Diamondbacks. Ginger lives in Arizona and is married to her college sweetheart whom she met at ASU (fork 'em, Devils).

FIND GINGER ONLINE: www.littlemisswrite.com

facebook.com/GingerScottAuthor

twitter.com/TheGingerScott

instagram.com/authorgingerscott

www.ingramcontent.com/pod-product-compliance
Lightning Source LLC
Chambersburg PA
CBHW020401260626
47156CB00007B/2192